The Soft Whisper of Dreams

The Soft Whisper of Dreams

Christina Courtenay

Sequel to The Secret Kiss of Darkness

Published 2015 by Choc Lit Limited
Penrose House, Crawley Drive, Camberley, Surrey GU15 2AB, UK
www.choc-lit.com

A CIP catalogue record for this book is available
from the British Library

ISBN 978-1-78189-223-7

Printed and bound by CPI Group (UK) Ltd, Croydon, CR0 4YY

To the Choc Lit team and my fellow ChocLiteers

Acknowledgements

Thank you as always to the Choc Lit Tasting panel who gave this novel their approval. Special thanks to Sarah C, Sonya B, Linda S, Dorothy, Caroline, Liz W and Betty.

Chapter One

'Now then girls, as you've probably guessed, your parents' will doesn't contain any surprises, except for ... What I mean to say is that you will, of course, share their assets equally. There's no question about that.'

Mr Parker, the family solicitor, was perched on the edge of the sofa, his papers spread out before him on the coffee table in neat little piles. Madeline Browne and her younger sister Olivia occupied the two armchairs facing him, and they waited in silence for him to continue.

'Yes, and ...?' Olivia, impatient as always, prompted when he didn't immediately go on.

'Well, there is one small detail which I am obliged to disclose to you,' he said finally, 'although it won't make any difference to the will itself.' He looked extremely uncomfortable and cleared his throat twice.

A fly buzzed at the window, attempting to escape to the freedom outside and Maddie wished she could do the same. She swallowed down the tears that threatened to spill over once again. *This is beyond awful.*

'Your parents added a codicil to the effect that, uhm, I have to tell you ... er, in short, they thought you ought to know that you're not sisters by blood.' He managed to spit it out at last, and added, 'Maddie, you were adopted.'

Maddie drew in a sharp breath and stared at the solicitor. *'Adopted?'*

'Yes, that's right.' Mr Parker nodded for extra emphasis and shuffled a pile of papers which were already perfectly aligned.

'But what ...? Why, I mean ...' Maddie couldn't believe

she was hearing this and had trouble making her brain process the information. There was a strange sensation in the pit of her stomach, as if she had swallowed an ice bag and her entire middle had gone numb. She'd known the reading of the will would be painful, but this was totally unexpected. *How could Mum and Dad have kept that a secret for so long?* And why on earth hadn't they told her? She was twenty-seven, not a child any more.

As if he'd heard her thoughts, Mr Parker said, 'I'm afraid I don't know why they didn't want to tell you before now. Perhaps they thought it was for the best?' He shrugged. 'They didn't confide in me about that matter.'

There was another silence, this one distinctly more uncomfortable. Mr Parker shifted nervously on the sofa and leaned forward to re-shuffle his papers yet again. Maddie sat transfixed, unable to move a muscle, but her sister's next words broke her trance.

'If Maddie's not my real sister, why should she have half my parents' money?'

'Olivia!' The solicitor's eyes opened wide in scandalised surprise at this blunt and callous question, but Maddie herself didn't bat an eyelid. In fact, she almost smiled for the first time since receiving the news of her parents' car crash. The question was entirely in character with the way Olivia's devious and selfish mind worked. No one knew that better than Maddie.

'As your parents' adopted daughter, Maddie has just as much legal right to inherit their assets as you do, Olivia. The paperwork is all in order.' The solicitor's mouth had settled into a thin, uncompromising line and his brows drew together into a formidable frown of disapproval, but Olivia wasn't fazed. Her thinly plucked eyebrows rose over heavily made-up eyes, attempting a look of injured innocence.

'But if she's no blood relation, shouldn't I at least have the larger portion?' Olivia's face was cold under the thick layer of foundation, her expression one of clinical detachment. There was no grief for their parents' passing. No sign of guilt at wanting to deprive her sister of her inheritance. Nothing to indicate that she even understood the cruelty of what she was saying. Mr Parker's mouth fell open in disbelief.

'Really, Olivia, this is beyond anything!' He turned to Maddie with an apologetic gesture, clearly floundering in the face of this unexpected turn of events. He began to fidget with an elegant silver fountain pen, capping and uncapping it. 'I'm at a loss for words,' he added unnecessarily.

Maddie decided it was time to come to his rescue. While listening to Olivia's questions, a quiet fury had begun to build up inside her. It wasn't something which had come on suddenly, she realised. The anger had been increasing steadily over the years, but she had always reined it in out of respect for their parents. Now there was no longer any reason why she shouldn't let it out and the rage gave her the strength to deal with this now, once and for all.

'Don't worry, Mr Parker.' Maddie leaned forward to lay a soothing hand on his sleeve. 'This has all come as a huge shock to me, as you probably guess, but it's made me see one thing clearly – Olivia is not, and never has been, a sister to me. No matter what I did the two of us couldn't get on. I've always wondered why, because I wanted us to be close, but today you've given me the answer. Thank you.'

'Always playing the saint,' Olivia sneered under her breath. 'Nothing ever changes.'

Maddie didn't rise to the bait. She'd had years of

practice at ignoring her sister's barbs for the sake of a peaceful existence and in order to spare her parents grief, as they had hated confrontations of any kind. Besides, there was no point in retaliating. Olivia had skin thicker than an armadillo, and somehow, in the end, she always had her way.

'Your parents adopted you because they didn't think they could have any children,' the solicitor interjected. 'I have known them for years and they loved you as if you were truly theirs. That fact didn't change when they were blessed,' here he hesitated slightly and cast a doubtful glance at Olivia, 'with a natural child.'

'I know, Mr Parker.' Maddie held up her hand to stop him. This was all too new, her emotions were still very raw, and she would rather not discuss it. All she wanted was to escape from this room, this house and Olivia's presence. 'I agree, I couldn't have had a better mum or dad. They gave me what I needed most when they were alive – their love. I don't want anything else from them now. Let Olivia have it all. It doesn't matter.'

'But Maddie, of course it matters. We're talking about a substantial sum here.' The stunned expression had returned to the man's face.

'No, I'm serious. I know her better than anyone.' It was Maddie's turn to glare at Olivia. 'And I can see that she'll stop at nothing until she has her way.'

Olivia turned away to study her immaculately painted talons, as if the discussion had nothing whatsoever to do with her and she hadn't been the one to set the cat among the pigeons in the first place. Maddie clenched her teeth together hard.

'There is nothing Olivia can do,' Mr Parker protested. 'It's all legal.'

'I don't care. I don't ever want to see or hear from her again, so if you would be so kind as to help me remove a few personal items and keepsakes, she can have the rest. You'll take care of the paperwork, right?' Maddie was seething and she could feel the red-hot lava of emotions bubbling up inside her, waiting to erupt, but she was determined not to give way. She could cry later, when she was alone. For now, she'd leave this place in a dignified manner and never look back. Never come back. It was the only way.

Olivia, who had been listening to this exchange with a small smirk of satisfaction playing about her mouth, suddenly frowned and looked at Maddie suspiciously. 'What are you taking? You're not having Mum's best—'

'Olivia!' Mr Parker barked out the name this time in a voice which reminded Maddie of a headmaster speaking to a naughty child. If only Olivia's real parents had tried that approach occasionally, she thought, they wouldn't be having this conversation now. 'I suggest you count your blessings,' the solicitor continued with a withering look at Olivia, 'and let Maddie choose whichever items she wants. If not, I have a good mind to force her to accept your parents' bequest. Don't believe for a moment that I couldn't do it. Or even, if need be, retain it in trust for her children. Do I make myself understood?' He looked sufficiently fierce for his words to have the desired effect and Olivia nodded in simmering silence.

'Don't worry, Olivia,' Maddie gave a brittle little laugh, 'we've never had the same taste so I'm not likely to want any of the things you like.' She stood up and headed for the door.

'We'll see,' Olivia muttered as she followed her former sister out of the room, arms crossed belligerently over her chest.

Mr Parker brought up the rear, anger and disbelief still written all over his face. As he caught up with the sisters, Maddie saw his confusion and whispered, 'Really, this is the best way. Now I can be free of her for the rest of my life. Trust me, it'll be worth it.'

Mr Parker would have to take her word for it.

Chapter Two

'Kayla! It's so good to see you, and thank you again for having me to stay at such short notice.'

Maddie hugged her friend Kayla Marcombe and tried to hold back the tears that were threatening to overflow. Here, at last, was one place where she felt welcome. That thought almost opened the floodgates, but somehow she kept them closed for the time being.

'Oh, Maddie, you know we love to have you here any time. It's only natural you should want to get away from London after the last few weeks.' Kayla put an arm round Maddie's shoulders, despite the fact that her friend was almost a head taller, and pulled her towards the huge curved staircase. 'Was it really awful?'

'You have no idea.' Maddie shuddered at the memories and followed her tiny friend up the stairs, hardly noticing the grandeur of her surroundings. Kayla was married to a baronet and lived in palatial style at seventeenth century Marcombe Hall in Devon, but Maddie had visited them frequently and the magnificent house had ceased to impress her. To her, it was simply Kayla's home now.

'Come and tell me all about it,' Kayla invited, leading the way into one of the many guest rooms. This particular one was decorated in shades of primrose and lilac, but Maddie wouldn't have cared if it was neon orange. As far as she was concerned, a spartan cell in a nunnery would have been preferable to her London flat at the moment. She'd desperately needed to escape.

Annie, the Marcombe's housekeeper, clattered into the room with a laden tea tray. 'Welcome to Devon again,

Maddie,' she beamed. Maddie felt as if she had come home, and the kindness of the old woman compared to that of her own so-called sister was almost too much for her composure. The threatening tears hovered on her lashes.

'Thank you, Annie. It's good to be here.'

Annie tactfully left the two friends together, and Maddie curled her long, slender legs into a deep chair with a sigh. Kayla poured them both a cup of tea, added lots of sugar to Maddie's and passed her both the tea and a plate of biscuits.

'This is heavenly, just what I needed. Why does it taste so much better here in the country?'

Kayla laughed. 'The water perhaps? It might be marginally cleaner here.' She sank into a chair opposite Maddie's. 'So come on, let's hear it. You weren't very coherent on the phone. All I could understand was that your life is a disaster.'

Maddie smiled ruefully. 'That's the understatement of the year. Sorry, Kayla, but I've had a terrible time of it. First it was the shock of my parents' accident. Being woken up at midnight and having to rush off to hospital, only to find it was too late ... well, you can imagine how I felt.' She closed her eyes, reliving the horrible events of that night. They were etched onto her brain, a nightmare vision.

Kayla nodded sympathetically, but didn't interrupt.

'Then there were all the arrangements for the funeral to be made,' Maddie continued, taking a sip of the scalding hot tea. 'Olivia was no help at all as usual. I lost count of the number of times she changed her mind or pretended she'd never said something when she had. And the funeral itself ...' Maddie shivered violently at the memory.

Standing at not just one parent's graveside, but two at once. It was so unexpected, so shocking, and had brought the reality of their deaths home to Maddie as nothing else could have done. 'It was so final, Kayla. The end of a part of my life.'

'I can imagine,' Kayla murmured soothingly.

'On top of everything else, Olivia and I had to see the solicitor that same afternoon. He insisted, and since he's a family friend we couldn't refuse. And then he dropped his bombshell – he told us I was adopted. That was the final nail in the coffin.' She smiled feebly at her own bad joke, but at the same time tears welled out of her eyes and ran down her cheeks. She swiped at them ineffectually. 'For God's sake, Kayla, why didn't they tell me?'

The anguished question was one which she had asked herself repeatedly since leaving her parents' house. 'I wouldn't have loved them less and it would have explained so much.' She shook her head. 'I always knew I was different somehow. I mean, for a start, none of my family looked anything like me. Olivia must have sensed it too, although that might have been wishful thinking on her part. But I thought it was my fault, some fundamental flaw in me. All along it was just the fact that I was adopted.'

'They never even hinted at it?'

'No, never. I was treated exactly the same as Olivia. I honestly don't think they ever wanted me to know.'

'Perhaps they were afraid you would leave them, want to find your real parents?'

'Why would I want to do that? My birth parents obviously didn't want me, so why should I want them?'

'Curiosity, maybe? Most adopted children want to find out about their natural parents.'

'Well, not me. I've had my fill of rejection for a while. I have to take stock of my life now and seriously consider where I'm going. I need a complete change of scenery. A fresh start.'

'Take your time. You only just got here. We don't want to lose you too soon, so stay as long as you like. It's lucky you were just temping at the moment and not in a permanent job.'

'Yes. And I have some money put by for a rainy day. Somehow I think it has arrived. In fact, it seems to be pouring at the moment.'

'No, no, that's defeatist thinking. There must be some positive things happening in your life too. Didn't you tell me you'd met this gorgeous man recently? What was his name again?'

'David. And I didn't mention him because he's no longer in the picture.' Maddie clenched her fists. 'He was a bastard.'

'What? But I thought ...' Kayla looked bewildered. 'You were so in love, last time I talked to you. Surely that was only a couple of weeks ago?'

'That was before I found out he'd been hitting on my flat mate Jessie when I was out. Thank God for true friends! If she hadn't told me, I might have made an even bigger arse of myself.'

'Oh, poor Maddie, I guess you're right. It really is pouring on you at the moment. Never mind, let's go and find Wes and the kids and let the future take care of itself for a while. You'll soon figure everything out. In the meantime, you can have a vacation. How does swimming down in the cove sound?'

Maddie dried her tears and managed a watery smile. 'Absolutely fantastic. I'd rather swim in saltwater than produce buckets of it, which is all I seem to be capable of at the moment.'

Maddie woke early the next morning, drenched in perspiration and with all the bedding twisted round her legs. She lay in the semi-darkness of dawn, breathing heavily while her heart thumped against her ribcage. The dream had returned. Maddie groaned. 'Not again, please,' she whispered, but she knew that no one would be listening to her plea.

It was a dream which had plagued her as a child, and later as a teenager, playing out the same scenario night after night. It was always incredibly clear and always followed the same pattern. Afterwards she remembered every minute detail even though she didn't want to.

Each time, she was in a sunny garden surrounded by rose bushes, bearing flowers of every hue. There was a swing hanging from the stout branch of an old apple tree, and somehow she knew it was hers. Whenever she looked at it she felt a sense of ownership and pride. Possessiveness even. The dream always began with her rushing towards it.

She was small. She knew that because she could never climb onto the swing unaided. Sometimes a pair of strong arms lifted her up and pushed her to dizzying heights, making her squeal with laughter. More often, though, she just hung on top of it, face down, and twirled round and round endlessly until the vertigo forced her to pause for a while.

If she stopped she could see the house. White, with windows that were pointed at the top – Gothic architecture, she assumed – and it was almost completely covered in wisteria, honeysuckle and various other climbing plants.

It was a happy place, at least that was the impression she had. But in the dreams she never went inside. She always stayed in the garden.

Sometimes a giant with red hair and a beard came out of the house and walked towards her, smiling broadly. Then she would run to him, arms outstretched, and he would lift her sky-high, dancing around with her aloft. She laughed out loud, bubbling over with happiness.

That was where the dream ended most of the time, and she would wake up feeling bereft as if she had lost something infinitely precious. She had no idea what it was, but more often than not she cried, unable to halt the flow of tears.

Occasionally the dream ended differently, however. In her mind, she called it the dark version. The one that absolutely terrified her. The red-haired man would come out as before and she would run towards him, but soon after he would turn away and go back into the house. Then she was grabbed from behind by a pair of dark, hairy arms. A hand clamped down over her mouth, causing her to struggle in panic, fighting for breath. Twisting, turning, arms flailing, legs kicking frantically, she tried to catch a glimpse of her assailant, but there was only a fleeting impression of dark hair and eyes, a black beard and anger. Hatred even.

At that point she always woke herself up with a strangled scream for help, and she knew that was what had happened this morning. She had dreamed the dark version and the images were particularly vivid, leaving a bitter taste of menace in her mouth. It took her ages to still the frantic beating of her heart.

The dream hadn't recurred since she'd moved to London several years previously, but it would seem she'd been wrong about thinking she'd grown out of it. Perhaps it had been brought on by the recent pressure she'd been under? Maddie sighed.

It seemed so real. Could it mean something? 'Stop being an idiot,' she told herself sternly and headed for the shower. The mind was a wonderful thing, but it could also behave irrationally. Dreams were only that, dreams, and she'd do best to try to forget it and hope it didn't happen again.

Chapter Three

Alexander Marcombe stared out through the bars on the window and thought longingly of the sea. The day was hot and muggy, and he could feel little rivulets of perspiration pouring down his back. A refreshing swim in the Atlantic would have been perfect, but he would happily have settled for just a breeze. He sighed. The tiny cell was unbelievably stuffy.

Prison was definitely not a bed of roses, but then it wasn't supposed to be, he thought ruefully. Despite everything, in some strange way Alex was thankful for his lengthy stay as Her Majesty's guest. It had finally made him grow up, and on reflection – and he'd had a lot of time for that during the past three years – he thought it was the best thing that could have happened to him. Making his cellmate understand this concept, however, was a different matter.

'You're a weird son-of-a-bitch, Marcombe.' Foster, a huge brawny man in his mid-twenties, shook his head in total incomprehension. 'How the hell can you say you've enjoyed it here? You must be off your rocker.' He scratched his head. His shock of dark hair had been given a crew-cut a month previously, and now it resembled the back of a hedgehog.

'Quite possibly, but I didn't say "enjoyed" exactly. I said it had made me mature, made me see life in a new light. I've learned some very valuable lessons during my time here and I don't intend to forget them in a hurry. And I certainly wouldn't want to return. Ever.' Alex's mouth tightened. There had been tough times when he'd wanted only to lie down and die, but something had made him carry on. Pride perhaps? Or just sheer bloody-mindedness.

'Yeah, yeah, that's what they all say. When you go back outside though, and no one wants to give you a job in case you steal something, you'll soon go back to doing what you've always done. What else is there? And before you know it, you're back in here.'

'I suppose you have a point there, but that won't be the case with me.' Alex knew Foster had already spent roughly half his life in one institution or another and tended towards a cynical view of the whole system. It was difficult to persuade him otherwise and he did seem to be stuck in a Catch 22 situation.

'Oh, I forgot. You toffs stick together, don't you? I 'spect you'll find a job just like that.' Foster snapped his fingers loudly to emphasise his point.

'Not quite, although I daresay it might be true for some people. No, I don't think any of my former friends would employ me, but I'm lucky enough to have an older brother with more tolerance than I deserve. He's been incredibly patient with me over the years, and now he's promised to give me a home until I can stand on my own feet again.'

'He ain't a criminal?' Foster asked suspiciously.

Alex laughed. 'I don't think he could be further from it if he tried. No, he's a lawyer and I can't see him ever doing anything that wasn't right and proper.'

'Sounds like a dead bore to me,' Foster commented grumpily.

'Now there you're wrong. Conscientious and hardworking maybe, but he has a great sense of humour and you'd have a hard time finding a better sailor or sportsman. And there's a mischievous side to him as well.'

'Hmph.' Foster lay down on his bunk and turned his

face towards the wall. Then he added in a slightly wistful tone of voice, 'The only thing my older brother ever did for me was talk me into joining him in a bank robbery that went wrong, and I found myself back in here faster than lightning. Rob's a bastard.'

'Yes, so you've told me.' Alex didn't know what to add to that so he stared out of the window again. 'I can't wait to get out tomorrow,' he said finally.

'Well, good luck to you. No offence, but I hope I don't see you again.' Foster turned around to face him, and Alex was pleased to see he was back to his normal, laid-back self, smiling again.

'No chance, not in here anyway.' He grinned confidently. 'But why don't you come and see me when you get out, instead of that brother of yours? Maybe I can help you find the straight and narrow.' Alex noticed Foster raise his eyebrows in scepticism. 'Only if that's what you really want, of course.'

'And how would you do that?'

'Well, I'll find you a job.'

'Hah! Fat chance, mate.'

'No, I'm serious. Or do you really want to keep visiting institutions like this at regular intervals for the rest of your life?'

'I can think of better places.'

'Well there you are. You'll be free in a couple of weeks, right? By then I should have adjusted to life outside and I might be able to help you.'

'I don't think so.' Foster shook his head. 'Why would you want to help me? We're different.'

'So what? At least think about it – there's not much else to do in this hell-hole.'

'You're right there. Okay, I will.'

'Good. You know where to find me, right? Marcombe Hall, not far from Kingsbridge.' Foster nodded and Alex lay down on his own bunk with his hands behind his head feeling pleased. If he could save at least one person from this kind of life, then perhaps that would go some way towards atoning for his past sins. *And God knows, I want to atone for them.*

With the sun warming his face and the breeze ruffling his long hair, Alex took a deep, sweet breath of freedom as he stepped out of the prison doors the next morning. His gaze took in every tiny detail of his surroundings and revelled in them. The outside world at last. He spread his arms wide and laughed out loud.

'Hey, Alex, over here!' His brother Wes had come to pick him up as promised, and when Wes gave him a bear hug Alex felt as if he was already home. Although he was the taller of the two, Alex felt safe and protected, like a small child and not like the twenty-eight year old man he really was.

'Congratulations.' Wes slapped him on the back and led the way to the familiar moss-green Range Rover. 'I never thought you'd come through this so well, but you did it. I'm proud of you Alex.'

Alex knew what his brother meant, but the emotion clogging his throat prevented him from expressing his feelings. Instead he joked, 'That's a strange thing to say to a brother who's just spent three years in prison for drug smuggling.'

'You were just young and stupid.' Despite his profession, Wes dismissed these serious charges with a flick of the hand.

'Thanks, mate.' Alex smiled to show that he hadn't taken offence.

'No, seriously, you were led astray and I doubt you'd even thought it through properly. You were never cut out for a life of crime, Alex. For one thing, you're a lousy liar.'

Alex laughed. 'You'd be surprised what you learn in prison. I've improved on my lying techniques no end, and a few other things besides.'

Wes glanced at his brother's muscular frame and raised his eyebrows. 'Pumping iron or fighting?'

'A bit of both perhaps.' Alex grinned.

'Hmm. You were always good at fighting. As I recall, you gave me a bloody nose and black eye on more than one occasion.'

'You deserved it. Pompous older brother and all that.'

'Hah, that's what you thought. I should have had a damned medal for putting up with you. Little brothers are a pain in the arse.'

Alex playfully punched Wes on the arm. 'Come on, we had fun most of the time.'

'Yes, until I had to grow up a bit too fast.' They both spared a brief thought for the dark times when their mother had gone off with another man and left their father heartbroken, unable to cope. Wes shook his head and changed the subject. 'Well, whatever you've learned, it's done you nothing but good. It's strange, but for the first time since then I feel like I can talk to you as an equal again. I don't have to do the "stern father" routine anymore.'

'Thank God for that!'

'Well, at least not with you.' Wes smiled.

'I'm sure that's a relief. You probably have your hands full with three kids around the place.' Besides an eleven-year old daughter from a previous marriage, Wes had two sons, aged two years and six months respectively with his second wife Kayla. Although he'd never met the younger two, Alex knew they kept his brother on his toes and Wes had been telling him all about them during his weekly visits to the prison. 'Are you sure you don't mind me cluttering up the place as well?'

'Hell, I could use some help. Kayla lets them get away with murder and now she's got her friend Maddie visiting, so the two of them gang up on me. Having you around will even things out a bit.'

'I'll do my best, but don't expect too much. If I remember correctly, Nell only has to smile at me and I'm putty in her hands.'

'Great.' Wes made a face and sighed. 'And here I thought I had finally found an ally. Never mind, they'll soon drive you round the bend as well. Then you'll see what I mean.'

The playroom at Marcombe Hall had been created out of three adjoining rooms on the second floor and was big enough to house the contents of an entire toy shop. To Alex, who had never seen it before, it seemed that was precisely what it did contain, but Wes assured him they didn't spoil their children.

'Oh, not much you don't,' Alex muttered, staring at the play-tent, miniature slide, masses of cars and boxes overflowing with soft toys, not to mention puzzles and books of every description and size.

'This is only a fraction of what's available. You wouldn't believe the things you can buy these days.'

'If you say so,' Alex said doubtfully. 'Looks to me like you could start a nursery school in here.'

His sister-in-law came towards him with a welcoming smile on her face and six-month old Edmund comfortably ensconced on her hip. The little boy buried his face in his mother's shoulder and stuck his thumb into his mouth at the sight of the big dark man. He didn't look at all convinced that he wanted to meet his uncle. Kayla seemed to have no such qualms, however, and gave Alex as big a hug as she could manage with only one arm.

'Welcome home, Alex. I hope Wes has prepared you for mayhem, which is what we usually have in this house these days.'

'Believe me, it will make a welcome change.' Alex suddenly found it hard to swallow past the lump which had formed in his throat. Kayla was acting as if the past three years had never happened, nor the terrible things which had gone before, and it was more than he deserved. But he was grateful. Somehow, he would make it up to them all.

'Alex, come and meet Maddie and Jago.' Wes jolted him out of this uncharacteristically emotional state and Alex looked across the room to where a tall red-haired woman was crawling on all fours with his older nephew on her back. Alex knew the boy had been named after an ancestor, so didn't comment on his unusual name.

'Maddie my horse,' Jago explained happily and grabbed two fistfuls of Maddie's wildly curling mane. She grimaced, but didn't complain. Instead she tilted her head up as far as she could under the circumstances and smiled.

'Nice to meet you, Alex,' she managed, before her rider egged her on across the carpet. 'Sorry, I'll have to talk to you later.'

Alex laughed. 'You really should teach your sons to treat women better, Wes,' he joked before getting down on all fours himself. 'Now how would you like to ride a bigger horse, Jago?' he asked the little boy.

'Oh, yes!' Jago hurled himself off Maddie and landed on the carpet in a heap, but this didn't deter him in the slightest. He simply picked himself up, dusted off his knees and ran over to Alex.

'Thanks.' Maddie sent him a grateful look and collapsed onto her back on the floor, trying to straighten her spine. 'Two-year olds weigh a lot more than you think.'

Alex didn't answer. He was too busy watching her unconsciously sensuous movements. As she stretched her arms over her head, her tight T-shirt rode up showing him an expanse of toned, sun-tanned stomach, and his mouth went dry. His gaze strayed further up, and although she couldn't be described as voluptuous, her breasts, which were clearly visible through the thin material, were perfectly shaped and to his mind extremely beautiful. *Damn it, she's not wearing a bra!* Swiftly, he looked away. Three years was a long time without a woman, but he didn't think that was what caused his body's instinctive reaction. There was definitely something special about her.

When he looked up again she happened to be staring in his direction. He noticed that she had green eyes, slightly slanted like those of a cat, and they widened as if she could read his thoughts clearly. A blush spread over her features and she stood up abruptly.

'What time is lunch, Kayla? I'm starving.'

Alex stared after her until Jago recalled him to his duties. He reflected later that coming home had been both easier and more difficult than he'd imagined, but he would never again take his freedom for granted.

Chapter Four

'Auntie Maddie, it's time to wake up. Stop pretending you're asleep, I can tell you're not really.'

Maddie was rudely awakened from a blessedly dreamless sleep the next morning by Nell, who waltzed into her room without so much as a knock. Maddie buried her head under the covers.

'Go away, your horrible child, it can't possibly be morning yet,' she groaned.

Nell giggled. Like everyone else in the house, she was quite used to the fact that Maddie was most definitely not a morning person.

'Mummy sent me to say that we're going to a fair and you have to get up straight away or we'll go without you.' Nell tugged at the covers from the bottom end of the bed and Maddie hung on for dear life.

'Go ahead. I'm quite comfortable here and I grew out of going to fun fairs years ago.'

'Oh, don't be such a grump, Auntie Maddie, it'll be fun,' Nell insisted, and succeeded in partly uncovering her victim. 'And it's not a fun fair, it's a country fair. We're all going, Uncle Alex too.'

If that had been meant as an inducement, it failed dismally. In fact, it had quite the reverse effect on Maddie. She'd been deeply disturbed by the desire she had seen lurking in Wes's brother's blue eyes the previous day, and even more so by her own reaction to him. When he'd looked at her like that, her body had tingled and she'd felt herself grow hot under his gaze. She could understand why he would react in such a way to a woman he'd never met –

after all he'd been in jail for three whole years – but as for herself there was no excuse. None whatsoever. Especially after the recent David debacle.

'Hmph,' was all she replied now, but Nell was nothing if not tenacious. When all else failed she resorted to jumping on Maddie and tickling her, until there was nothing for it but to capitulate. 'All right, all right, I'll go and have a shower. I'll be down in a while.'

'Okay.' Nell jumped off the bed, obviously satisfied with a job well done. 'You'd better hurry. Annie is making breakfast. It smells really good.'

'Doesn't it always?' One of the greatest perils of visiting Kayla and Wes was the threat to her waistline. Maddie never understood how Kayla could live with Annie and not get incredibly fat.

Nell just giggled again and left, closing the door behind her. Maddie headed for the bathroom. 'Well, I'm up now, so I might as well go,' she muttered. But a little voice inside her insisted that perhaps she was doing it so she could spend more time with Alex and get to know him better. This made her angry with herself, and she turned on the shower with more force than was strictly necessary. *The last thing I need at the moment is a relationship, especially with a former criminal, even if he is handsome as sin!*

The country fair was well attended, despite the continuing heatwave, and the party made their way through the milling throng slowly. Wes carried Edmund in some sort of a backpack contraption, leaving Kayla free to deal with the other children. Jago, however, attached himself like a leech to his newly discovered uncle, whom he seemed to idolise already. Alex obligingly hefted him onto his shoulders, and the little boy squealed with laughter and commented on everything he could see.

'Look, Mummy. Balloon! And doggies. Moo-cow! Lambs! ...' There was an endless stream of fascinating sights, and the others laughed at his exclamations.

'I wish I could get that enthusiastic about all this,' Wes grumbled. 'We would have been much better off having a picnic by the sea.' He wiped his forehead with the bottom edge of his T-shirt.

'We can do that later,' Kayla said, taking his hand. 'Now stop showing off your abs and let's stock up on delicious jams and cakes to take with us. Come on, you know you'll love it.'

Wes grinned. 'Yes, ma'am. I love it when you're bossy.'

He received a light punch on the arm in return, but this was followed by a kiss, so Maddie knew her friend wasn't angry. She envied the couple their closeness and wished she could find a soul mate like that. Not bloody likely. She'd been trying for years, but usually ended up with douchebags like David. She obviously had lousy taste in men.

The booths were many and varied, and Maddie enjoyed herself in spite of her previous reluctance to come. It was peaceful to walk among the noise and bustle of the crowd with nothing better to do than look at all the goods for sale.

'Oh, for heaven's sake!' Wes exclaimed at one point. 'Why would you need a personalised bowl for your dog? They can't read anyway.' The stand full of dog paraphernalia was covered with every weird and wonderful item that could ever possibly be needed by a canine, and more besides.

The others laughed. 'How do you know?' Alex joked. 'They may be smarter than we think.'

'Sure, Dr Dolittle.'

'Oh look, Maddie, a fortune-teller.' Kayla had been scanning the nearby booths to see what else would be of interest, and the purple silk tent with gold tasselling had obviously caught her eye.

'You will meet a tall, dark and handsome man, and marry him and live happily ever after ...' Maddie intoned in a deep voice, then blushed as she realised her description could very well fit Alex. He was all of those things, and more. Fortunately he appeared to be engrossed in a conversation with Nell and didn't hear her.

Kayla cuffed her on the arm. 'Don't be silly, I'm sure she'll be more inventive than that. Go and give it a try.'

'I honestly don't think I want to know what other disasters are going to happen to me. I've had quite enough of them recently,' Maddie replied. 'Didn't you go once before? I seem to recall you were given all sorts of dire predictions and they all came true.'

'That doesn't count. The woman I saw really did have the second sight and she didn't do it for money. I'm sure this one's a fake and will only tell you the good things. She won't want to lose customers. Come on, I'm going to have a go. It'll be fun!'

Wes just shook his head and looked bemused while Kayla dragged Maddie towards the purple tent.

'Men don't understand the fascination of things like this,' Kayla said with a giggle. 'They take everything so seriously. You'd think Wes would be more understanding since he has a gypsy ancestor.'

'Oh, yes, the famous – or should that be infamous? – Jago Kerswell, your little Jago's namesake.'

'Yes. He looked just like Alex, or should that be the other way around? Now that Jago was a tall, dark and handsome man ...' They giggled again, and joined the queue for Madame Romar.

Kayla went first and came out with a smile. 'There, what did I tell you? Just good things.'

'What did she say?'

'I'm going to have another child, a daughter this time – well she would say that, wouldn't she – and I'm going on a journey soon, where I don't know. Anyway, I'll tell you the rest later, it's your turn.' She shooed Maddie towards the opening.

Maddie entered the tent reluctantly, not at all certain she wanted to hear about her future. Although she knew it was all nonsense, a small part of her was superstitious enough to believe there might be a grain of truth in it. Her eyes gradually adjusted to the dim interior after the glare outside, and she went and sat down opposite a dark, elderly lady seated at a table.

'Hello m'dear. Cross my palm with silver and I'll tell your fortune.' The woman was small and birdlike with piercing dark eyes and her hair, although threaded with grey, was still quite black and lustrous. She wore the customary colourful costume with layers of scarves and a multitude of dangling bracelets. Maddie tried to relax. It was all just an act. She took out the required amount of money and handed it over. It disappeared rapidly into a small cash box.

'Right then, young lady, give me your hand please.' Madame Romar took her hand and studied the palm carefully, tracing the various lines with a wrinkled finger and turning it over several times. 'Hmmm.'

Maddie waited in tense silence.

Keeping hold of her hand, the woman then gazed into a small crystal ball on the table in front of her, and Maddie could have sworn she saw a swirling mist start up inside it. She blinked. Madame Romar stared fixedly into the ball for what seemed an eternity and Maddie tried not to fidget on her chair. Finally, when she was about ready to scream, the woman began to speak.

'You are troubled, my child, and it is understandable. You've had a difficult time and it will be a while yet before your troubles are over.'

Maddie frowned. This wasn't what she wanted to hear.

'I see a tall, dark, handsome man,' the woman continued, and Maddie almost snorted. That was just too predictable, but Romar's next words made her sit up and listen again. 'He shares my blood and he will try to help you.'

'Help me? With what?'

'Shhh, do not break my concentration. I see danger. There is another dark man, he is evil, and there is a red-haired man, he is good. You must face them both before you can find happiness. But take care, the danger is strong.'

Maddie stared at the woman. A dark man and a red-haired one, just like in her dream. How could the old gypsy possibly know about that?

'But, how will I find them?'

The gypsy patted her hand, looking sympathetic. 'Perhaps they will find you? But don't worry, there will be happiness in the end, as long as you let yourself believe in it. Remember that, have faith.'

She wouldn't say anything else, and Maddie stumbled out into the bright sunshine in a daze.

'Finally! You've been in there for ages. What on earth did she say to you? You look like you've seen a ghost.' Kayla pulled her towards the ice cream stand, where the others were waiting.

'I, that is ... oh Kayla, it was really weird. She said all sorts of strange things, and she talked about a dream I often have, at least that's what it sounded like. How could she possibly know about that?'

'I don't know. Maybe she is truly psychic, like that other one I saw? That means I really will have a daughter ...' Kayla smiled happily.

Maddie shivered despite the heat. 'I hope she's not. She said I'm in danger, but that I will find happiness eventually.'

Kayla frowned. 'Well, that was a pretty stupid thing to say. She must know she won't get any more customers if she goes around telling people things like that. Forget it, it's probably all a load of rubbish anyway.'

Maddie wished with all her heart she could believe her friend, but now she wasn't convinced any longer.

Alex listened to the exchange between the two women with interest, although he pretended to be doing something else. He knew Madame Romar, as did Wes, although neither of them had let on. She was one of the gypsies who came to camp on Marcombe land once a year and they'd come across her already as children. She'd never told their fortune though, or at least not Alex's. He wasn't sure about Wes, but suspected his brother would have steered clear as well. But perhaps it was time to test the old woman's powers? He didn't like the fear he saw in Maddie's eyes.

'Kayla, would you mind taking Jago for a bit?' He swung the little boy off his shoulders. 'I just need to ... you know.' He nodded in the direction of the Gents, which was nearby. 'I'll be back in a minute,' he added to Jago, who showed signs of starting up a tantrum. 'Then I'll carry you again.'

'Yes, of course. Come on, Jago, let's go and see if they have any nice toys over here.' Kayla and the others moved off and Alex headed for the Gents. As soon as the little group were out of sight, however, he turned and walked back towards Madame Romar's tent instead. Fortunately there was no queue, so he ducked inside.

'Knock, knock?' he said, jokingly.

Romar looked up and a smile spread over her features, crinkling the deep-set eyes. 'Alexander! How lovely to see you. To what do I owe this pleasure?'

He sat down on the small stool opposite her and leaned his elbows on the table, then grinned at her. 'I think you already know the answer to that. Or are you a fraud as my sister-in-law suspected?'

She made a noise of derision. 'Hmph, only to those who don't want to hear the truth.'

'So when Kayla's friend came in just now, you didn't deceive her?'

'The tall red-head? No. She needed a warning, that one, and I might as well tell you as well, since you'll be the one protecting her.'

'She's nothing to do with me,' Alex protested. 'She is just staying with Wes and Kayla at the moment.'

Romar's mouth quirked into an enigmatic smile and she shook her head at him. 'Foolish boy. You think I can't see you like her? And besides, my crystal ball never lies. I saw you.'

'When you told Maddie's fortune?'

'When I looked into her future,' Romar corrected. 'One way or another, you are there, so be careful. Help her. I saw danger, evil stalking her.'

'Of course I'd help her if she needed me to, but ...'

Romar shook her head. 'Just trust me, wait and see

what happens. And be ready for anything. But you must put aside your prejudices. Like that Darcy man on TV.'

'What?' Alex wondered if the old woman was going soft in the head. 'What's he got to do with anything?'

'He was blinkered by stupid ideas. Don't make the same mistake is what I mean.' Her eyes lit up with mischief. 'And he was tall, dark and handsome, just like you. Isn't that what every woman is looking for? This Maddie included.'

'Romar ...' Alex tried to sound cross, but he knew she was just teasing.

She put her hand on his and squeezed. 'Just look after yourself, my boy. You've been through a lot, and so has she, but you're both strong. Make sure good triumphs over evil. It's up to you.'

Alex wasn't sure he knew what she was on about and didn't like having a responsibility like that foisted on him, but he nodded. 'Okay, thank you. See you at Marcombe soon?'

'Yes, we'll be there, as always. It's our summer haven.' She shook her head when he extracted some coins from his pocket. 'No, Marcombes never pay, you know that. You're kin.'

As Alex escaped into the sunshine, he couldn't help but shiver despite the heat. Romar had tried to warn him and he knew she wouldn't do that without cause. He couldn't be sorry if it was something that allowed him to spend more time with Maddie, but what was he supposed to guard against? Apparently only time would tell.

Chapter Five

'So what do you think of Alex then?'

Maddie and Kayla were sitting in the first floor gallery at Marcombe the next morning, looking at the portraits of Wes's ancestors. Directly in front of them were two Gainsborough portraits of his five times great-grandfather and grandmother, Jago and Eliza. Kayla claimed the portrait of Jago was responsible for bringing her and Wes together, and that the man in the painting had actually talked to her. Maddie believed her friend, because she knew Kayla wasn't capable of lying, but it wasn't something they spoke of much now. It was just too weird.

She looked at the picture and saw a marked resemblance between Jago, the bastard son of an earlier baronet and a travelling woman, and his descendants. There was definitely gypsy blood in Wes and his brother. Dark hair, skin that tanned at the slightest touch of the sun's rays, and piercing blue eyes with amazingly long, dark lashes. Not to mention broad shoulders, perfectly defined muscles and smiles that could melt a woman's heart without them even trying ... Maddie tried to control her wayward thoughts.

'What do I think of Alex? Well, if you ask me, he takes after his ancestor Jago in both looks and piratical tendencies. Not to mention womanising, I'm sure,' she replied somewhat tartly. 'Annie was telling me only this morning how he used to bring home a different girl every weekend.'

Kayla giggled. 'Oh, come on, Maddie. He's not that bad and that was a long time ago. He may have inherited Jago's best features, including those incredible blue eyes, but he's definitely grown out of his smuggling days. As for womanising, I'd say Alex has changed a lot since he's been in prison.'

By 'smuggling days', Maddie knew Kayla was referring to the crime Alex had committed. She didn't know much about it, other than that he'd been involved in drugs smuggling, which was very serious. She had no idea why or if he'd been into drugs himself, but hoped not.

'How can you tell he's changed? He's only been free for a few days. The way he was looking me up and down yesterday I'm sure he thinks he's irresistible.'

'Well, isn't he? He's the most gorgeous man I know apart from Wes. Not that I was ever attracted to him, but that was probably because I was already in love with Wes.'

Maddie shook her head. 'I think men like that are nothing but trouble. They know they're handsome and they know they can have any woman they want, so they don't stay with anyone for any length of time. Has he ever had a steady girlfriend?'

'Not that I know of, but ...'

'There you are, then. He's probably not capable of it. And now he's been locked up for three years, he's sure to go berserk with the local female population. I, for one, intend to stay firmly out of the way. I've had enough trouble recently without getting myself mixed up in that sort of situation.'

'You're too cynical, Maddie. I still think Alex has changed. He's grown up a lot since I last saw him and he's much quieter. He hardly said a word last night at dinner.'

'No, but he stared a lot.'

'He probably finds you attractive. What's wrong with that? You should feel flattered.'

'Flattered, my foot. Why would a man like that find me

attractive? A five-foot-ten beanpole with wild red hair and freckles and no figure to speak of? Only for one reason and if he was desperate. I'd say being locked up for three years might make a man desperate.'

'Maddie, you don't do yourself justice. You are very pretty with those gorgeous green eyes, and you're not a beanpole, you have curves. I would love to be tall like you. Everything you wear looks wonderful on you, and what's wrong with freckles anyway?'

'Personally, I'd rather have your figure, but hey, no one's ever satisfied with the way they look, are they?' Maddie sighed. 'And it wasn't me who described myself like that, it was David.'

Kayla gasped. 'No! How could he? The utter, utter bastard!'

'Yep. Told you he was. Didn't exactly make me feel good about myself, I can tell you.'

'Well, all I can say is, not every man is like that.'

'Maybe not.' Maddie smiled. 'Just the handsome ones, huh?'

'No, stop it! Anyway, if you mean Alex, I definitely think you're wrong.'

'Hmm, we'll see.' Maddie decided to change the subject. She didn't want to discuss Kayla's brother-in-law any more. It was best not to think about him at all. 'How about we go and join the others in the pool. It's too hot and stuffy up here.'

'Good idea. I'll go and change.'

On the basement level of Marcombe Hall was a large structure which was partly under the ground floor of the house and partly projecting into the garden in the form of a conservatory. It contained a long, narrow pool with shallow steps at one end and a blue mosaic in the shape of a dolphin at the bottom. At intervals along the walls there were huge tropical plants in blue and white china pots, which added to the hothouse atmosphere. As it was a sweltering day, the large doors leading into the garden had been opened wide to let in the breeze.

The two Marcombe brothers were splashing about in the pool with the children when Maddie and Kayla arrived. Wes was playing with Nell, Alex was throwing Jago high up in the air and little Edmund was paddling, happily floating in the middle of a huge inflatable swan.

'Oh, isn't he sweet,' Maddie exclaimed, pointing to him. 'Can he swim yet?'

'Yes, but he prefers to be in that thing at the moment.'

'I can't believe your children can swim already, they're so tiny.'

'I know. It's thanks to Wes. He threw them in when they were just babies, and as you've probably heard, they do know how to swim then. I refused to let him do it, because I thought they were going to drown, but he tried it when I wasn't looking and it worked, just like with Nell.'

'Amazing.'

'Have you come to relieve us of these tiresome monsters then?' Wes called with a smile.

'No, you're doing a great job,' Kayla replied with a laugh. 'You can keep them.'

'Thanks very much,' Wes said ruefully.

All the same, the two women joined the others in the pool and soon a rather disorganised game of water polo was under way. It progressed with much shrieking and laughter, and Maddie proved very adept at catching the ball. She and Wes teamed up against Kayla and Alex, with a little help now and then from Nell and Jago.

This arrangement unfortunately provided Alex with the opportunity of chasing Maddie, however. As he caught up with her, she felt him wrap one arm around her slim waist to prevent her from escaping, and then he tried to grab the ball with the other, but she held on. Maddie became uncomfortably aware of how close he was holding her, and a shiver went through her.

He chuckled, and the sound of his voice was strangely exciting. The skin of his chest felt smooth and soft against her back, and her breasts tingled when his forearm accidentally came into contact with them. She attempted to break free with one hand, but touching his muscular arm with its fine covering of hair only sent further shivers through her. She could feel a blush begin to spread across her face and down her neck, and for the sake of her sanity she decided to give up the ball.

When Alex swam off with his trophy held high in triumph, she dived under the water to cool her heated face. *This won't do – get a grip, woman!* She knew from experience that it would be madness to become involved with a man like Alex, and she never wanted to go down that road again. Once had been enough with David, the lying, cheating, son-of-a— Maddie stopped that thought. He wasn't worth even thinking about; she'd had her fingers well and truly burned.

But it was tempting. Alex was extremely tempting. 'Irresistible', Kayla had called him. 'We'll just see about that,' Maddie muttered.

'Kayla, I need to go into town tomorrow. Could I borrow a car please?' Maddie was lying on the beach next to her friend in the small secluded cove which belonged to Marcombe Hall, soaking up the sun's rays. There was a fresh breeze from the sea, making it a much more pleasant experience than trudging around hot country fairs.

'I can take you. I have to go to Dartmouth tomorrow anyway.' Alex was sitting on a rock a few yards away, staring at the sea. He had appeared oblivious to their conversation, so his offer took Maddie by surprise.

'Oh. Well, that's very kind, but I was actually thinking of going to Totnes. Besides, you don't want to wait around for me.'

'It's not a problem. And you'll find all the same shops in Dartmouth, I'm sure. Or were you going somewhere in particular?'

'Uhm, no, not really.' She tried to think of some other excuses as to why she shouldn't go with him, but nothing came to mind and it would have been rude to refuse.

'I'm not in a hurry, and we can grab a bite to eat when you've finished shopping.' He looked her straight in the eyes and she stared back, mesmerised. He had the bluest eyes she'd ever seen, even more vivid than those of his brother, which Kayla had enthused about when she first met Wes. Their dark hair made the clear colour of their eyes appear even more intense. In Alex's case, this was highlighted by the fact that his mane was blue-black, whereas his brother's was dark brown.

Almost shoulder-length, Alex's hair fell in layers swept off his forehead and he ran his fingers through it, making Maddie long to do the same. She shook herself mentally. What the hell was wrong with her? She was sure he was only interested in one thing and she had sworn never to sleep with any man again unless he was prepared for commitment. Somehow Alex didn't strike her as the right sort. He looked like the archetypal player and Annie's words the other day had confirmed it.

'Well, thank you then,' she capitulated, unable to come up with any more excuses. 'What time do you want to leave?'

'Would ten be all right?'

'Sure. Ten it is.'

They set off on the dot and Alex commented on her punctuality. 'I thought women were always late,' he joked and she liked the way his eyes twinkled when he smiled.

'Normally I would be,' Maddie replied, 'but I was afraid you'd leave without me, so I got up extra early.'

'No, no, I wouldn't do that. I'm a gentleman, or at least I was brought up to be one.' His face took on a grim expression and Maddie realised it must be difficult for him to adjust to life outside prison again. Against her will, she suddenly felt sorry for him.

'I'm sure you still are,' she said and he quirked an eyebrow at her. 'What I mean is, you must try to forget this business with prison now and put it behind you. You are what you want to be. It's the future that counts.'

He slanted her an enigmatic look. 'That's what I try to tell myself, but I can't help feeling that people look at me in a different way now. Perhaps it's just my imagination, but it's as if there is a huge sign on my chest that says "former criminal, beware". Silly, isn't it?'

She put a hand on his arm and regretted it instantly. A thrill raced through her as she felt his powerful forearm move beneath her fingers and she had to force herself not to jerk away immediately. 'It's all in your mind, Alex. None of us even give it a second thought, I promise.'

'Thanks. I'm doing my best to forget it. At least I don't have to go looking for a job, which is lucky. Any prospective employer would be bound to ask about the three missing years on my CV.'

'What are you going to do then?' Maddie knew she probably shouldn't ask, but she had always been curious about other people and her tongue often ran away with her.

'Didn't Wes tell you? I've bought some holiday cottages which I'm going to do up and rent out. I'll manage them myself and in time I hope to build up quite a little empire.'

'That sounds great, but where did you get the money for that?' She saw his eyes cloud over and realised she'd said the wrong thing. 'I mean, I know you didn't steal it, so did you get a mortgage?'

Slightly mollified he replied, 'No, there was some money in a trust fund for me, but Wes always refused to hand it over before.' He smiled ruefully. 'Sensible guy, my brother. Three years ago I would have squandered every penny on boats, fast cars and … well, things like that. Fortunately he thinks I've changed and can be trusted with it, so that's what I used, plus the money Wes received from the sale of my yacht.'

'You sold your boat? But I thought you loved the sea?' Kayla had told her of his passion for sailing, and she had no trouble whatsoever in imagining him at the helm of a boat, staring into the horizon with narrowed gaze. Now that he had shed the prison pallor and acquired a tan, he resembled his gypsy ancestor even more and Maddie couldn't resist clothing him in pirate's gear in her mind. *Frock coat, tricorne hat, linen shirt with lace at the wrists and slightly open at the neck, showing off his tanned chest …* She felt a slight flush staining her cheeks and turned towards the open window to cool off.

'Oh, I do, but that particular yacht brought back too many bad memories.'

'Well, if I was lucky enough to own one, I wouldn't sell it unless as a very last resort,' Maddie said wistfully.

'You like sailing? I didn't think there was much opportunity for that in London,' he teased.

She raised her eyebrows at him, but didn't rise to the bait. 'Actually, yes I do love sailing and would like to learn how, but I've only ever been a passenger a couple of times.' She shrugged. 'It made me wish I could go more often though. It was heaven.'

'If I want to go sailing Wes has promised to lend me his boat. It's not as big as mine was, but it's not a bad little craft. Perhaps you'd like to come with me some time?'

'Sure. I'd love to.' The words tumbled out before Maddie had time to think about it and she regretted them almost instantly, but it was too late to take them back.

The rest of the journey was spent discussing his plans for the holiday cottages. Alex seemed really interested in her views on decorating, which was gratifying, and Maddie was happy to be of assistance.

'After all,' he said, 'you girls know a lot more about these things than we do, so if you don't mind, I might consult you when I get to that stage.'

'Of course, feel free. As long as I don't actually have to put up wallpaper – I'm rubbish at that.'

The little town of Dartmouth was very picturesque. Maddie had been there before, and therefore the steep hills which surrounded the town came as no surprise, but she was struck again by the pleasant atmosphere. Alex let her out near the city centre where a green oasis gave some respite from the heat.

'Is this okay?' he asked.

'Yes, fine. I know my way around. See you later.'

The shops and pavements were crowded, but Maddie was in no hurry. After she had bought what she'd come for she wandered slowly along the tiny streets, gazing idly into shop windows. Since she had at least another half an hour before she was due to meet Alex at the Three Kings pub for lunch, she walked around the marina, gazing out to sea and studying all the various boats moored there.

The people around her were mostly tourists. The summer months were a busy time of year for this part of the country, especially when the weather was as glorious as it had been for a while now. Maddie played a game with herself trying to guess which of the people were actually locals and which were not. The Devon dialect was of course a dead giveaway, but not everyone living in Dartmouth spoke like that. She thought she could detect the locals by their determination, however. They didn't amble along staring around them; they had a purpose.

It was as she was standing still, eavesdropping on a large group of Americans outside a tea room, that it happened.

Someone bumped into her quite hard and she turned to frown at the person since he or she didn't bother to apologise. Her gaze took in the irritated face of a dark man with a heavy beard, and her body froze as if rooted to the spot. She felt as if she recognised his face, although she was sure she'd never met him, and for some reason he terrified her.

'Look where you're going,' the man snarled at her, before hurrying off muttering, 'Bloody tourists everywhere you go. There's never any peace.'

Maddie stared after him, her mouth hanging open, and a strange feeling of dread began to build up inside her. She had the distinct impression she'd seen that man before, but where? Who was he? She was seized by a sudden urge to find out and set off after him. She followed the man at a discreet distance down the road, as if she was a private eye in an old black and white movie. If she hadn't felt so shaken, she'd have been laughing, it was so ridiculous, but as it was, she walked with grim determination.

The man strode along quite quickly, so she had to hurry to keep up with him, but luckily he didn't go far. Towards the end of the street he turned left, into a small lane leading up a steep hill. It began with some steps and continued as a winding road, leading eventually to a little cul-de sac. At the far end of this stood a chapel of some denomination or other, and the man entered a garden to the left of this building. Without a backward glance, he walked into the house, slamming the door forcefully. Maddie came to a halt some twenty yards down the road.

She was never sure afterwards how long she stood there, but after a while an elderly lady came up and asked her if she was lost.

'Sorry? Oh, no, it's just that … actually, can you tell me who lives in that house over there next to the chapel?' She pointed.

'Why yes, it's Mr Blake-Jones, the minister. Did you want to see him about something? Are you a member of his sect?'

'Sect?'

'Yes, the Saint Paulians they call themselves I think.'

'Er, no, I'm not one of them. Don't worry, it's okay. I'll come back another day.' Maddie looked at her watch. 'I've just remembered I've got to meet someone in five minutes. Thanks for your help.'

She sprinted down the street as if all the demons of hell were on her tail.

Chapter Six

Alex drummed his fingers on the table and checked the time once more. Maddie was late and he was impatient to see her again. He cradled the ice cold soft drink in his hands and tried to calm himself.

He had only known her for less than a week, but it seemed irrelevant. She intrigued him, mesmerised him, and he desperately wanted to become better acquainted with her. *Acquainted?* He almost laughed out loud. *What a stupid word that is.* Hell, he wanted more than that, much more. He wanted to know her in every way, including the biblical sense, no doubt about it. And he didn't have a clue how to achieve this. She had signalled very clearly that he was to stay at arm's length.

It was ironic. Three years ago he could have had any girl he chose. With his looks and self-assurance it had been so easy and he'd never even thought twice about it. Girls were there for the taking. If they happened to say no, it was no big deal, he simply continued on to the next one. But now his self-assurance was gone. And he didn't want just any woman, he wanted Maddie. *Only her.* Why this should be so he didn't know, but he was becoming more convinced about it every day that passed.

This is crazy! She just happened to be the first woman I saw when I got out of jail. But that didn't matter.

In order to test his theory, he passed the time by studying all the females in the pub to see whether any of them would spark his interest. As it was lunchtime, the taproom was fairly full and he could see at least three very pretty young ladies from where he sat. He looked at each one in turn, noting their faces, their figures, the way they smiled and flirted, how they were dressed. Not one of them made him feel even mildly attracted. Unfortunately, the opposite seemed to be the case. The prettiest of the three immediately came sauntering over and Alex could have kicked himself. He shouldn't have shown any interest at all.

'Alex? Alex Marcombe, is that really you? Long time no see!' The girl leaned forward to kiss the air either side of his face, showing him a huge amount of cleavage in the process and enveloping him in a cloud of strong perfume. She giggled flirtatiously. 'I'm Jenna, remember? Olivia's party down on the beach a couple of years back?'

Alex smiled and nodded, although he only had the haziest of memories of that night. 'Of course. Jenna. Good to see you. Sorry, I've, er ... not been around for a while, so I'm having trouble with names.' A lame excuse, but it was all she'd get.

'That's okay, I'm the same. There's, like, so many people around here. Can't remember them all.' She kept her gaze fastened on him and put one hand on his arm. 'So are you around now? We should go out sometime, you know, for old times' sake. I'm always up for a drink.'

'Well, I ...' Alex was out of practice and didn't know how to tell her no without offending her. But just at that moment, Maddie came hurtling through the door, flushed as if she'd just run a mile, and despite her obviously dishevelled state, his pulse started racing. She hadn't even looked at him yet and still his body reacted. Alex cursed silently.

I've got it bad.

Maddie spotted him and came over to join him. 'I'm so sorry I'm late, I forgot the time,' she said, then glanced at Jenna. 'Hope I'm not interrupting?' She pulled out a chair and sat down, picking up the menu and studying it intently. Alex wondered what she'd been up to, but refrained from asking.

'Not at all. Jenna was just leaving,' he said, hoping it was true. Jenna was busy throwing Maddie an icy glare, but his words registered eventually. She turned to give Alex a huge smile and a kiss on the cheek, again bending over much too far.

'I'll call you, sweetie,' she said. 'I know where you live. Marcombe Hall, right?'

'Er, at the moment, yes, but it's—'

Jenna didn't give him a chance to explain that this was a temporary arrangement. 'No worries, I'll find you,' she promised, and Alex was sure she would. She had a steely look of determination in her eyes and for once he felt like the prey instead of the hunter he'd used to be. He didn't like it. 'Byeee,' she cooed and sauntered off with a sassy wiggle.

Damn. Alex could see that Maddie was on edge again now, and just when he'd got her to relax a bit in his company earlier. Typical.

He took a deep breath and tried to sound normal as he asked Maddie, 'Got all your shopping done?'

'What? Oh, yes, thank you.' She indicated the carrier bags she had deposited on the floor. 'I found everything I needed.'

Alex noticed a rather large bag with 'Gillian's Artists' Materials' written on the outside and seized on this topic of conversation. 'Are you an artist?' he asked, curious to find out more about her. Kayla had told him Maddie worked as a legal secretary, just like she herself used to do.

'Well, not exactly. I just sketch for pleasure now and

again. I don't really get much time for it, but now that I'm here on holiday for a while I thought I would have a go. There are so many pretty views around Marcombe.'

'Yes, absolutely. Will you let me see the finished results?'

'I don't know about that.' She looked enchantingly shy all of a sudden. 'I'm really not that good.'

'Please? I promise not to laugh. I can't draw to save my life, in fact, I should think Jago is better at it than I am.' He smiled at her and was pleased to see an answering smile on her face. Good, she was relaxing again. She had a generous, pouting sort of mouth that would be perfect for kissing. Alex almost groaned. *I have to stop this or I'll drive myself mad.*

'Okay, fine, but if you do laugh I'll hit you over the head with my paint box.'

He chuckled. 'Sounds like a horrendous punishment. I promise to behave.' Which was not what he wanted to do around her at all. Quite the opposite. With an inward sigh he picked up the menu.

'Maddie, are you there? Can I come in?'

Kayla knocked, but came into Maddie's room before she received an answer. Maddie didn't mind though. Her friend often popped in for an evening chat after she'd put her children to bed.

'Come on in.' Maddie was sitting by the open window, her chin resting on her arms, and she'd been lost in thought.

Kayla walked over to sit down on the window seat next to her. 'Hey, are you all right?'

'Yes, I think so.' Maddie sighed and stared into the distance once more. *Am I all right?* She wasn't sure.

'Well, you seemed a bit sort of lost during dinner

and now you look almost ... haunted. I couldn't help wondering if something was the matter. Did Alex upset you today? I know he can be quite the charmer, but I thought he had grown out of his old ways and stopped flirting with anything in a skirt.'

'Alex? No, he has nothing to do with this. I'm sorry if I wasn't very good company.'

'That's okay. What's up then?'

'Well ...' Maddie hesitated, then made up her mind. She had to tell someone or she'd go mad. 'Kayla, you know I told you about the strange things that gypsy woman said to me and how they fit in with a recurring dream I have?'

'Yes.'

'Today something happened and I think it might be connected with her prophecy somehow.'

'How do you mean?'

Maddie knew Kayla had experienced strange things herself a few years past, so it didn't surprise her that she didn't question Maddie's feelings. As far as Kayla was concerned, paranormal things happened and she believed in them wholeheartedly.

'It was weird, but a man bumped into me down by the marina in Dartmouth, and when I looked at him I thought I recognised him. At first I wasn't sure why, but I've thought about it and I think he's the man in my dream. The one who grabs me from behind.' She shuddered. 'The one who is evil, as the gypsy said.'

'Did he give any sign that he knew you?'

'No, he was just angry, as if the whole thing had been my fault. Called me a bloody tourist, or something like that. I followed him on impulse and found out he's a minister of some sort called Blake-Jones. Have you heard of him?'

'Oh, yes, actually I have. He's one of those "fire and

46

brimstone" preachers who put the fear of God into their congregations. Leader of some strange sect apparently. A friend of mine told me he has a wife and daughter who creep around like mice, afraid of their own shadows. The man must be a bully.'

'Sounds right. He sure looked like one! Grumpy as hell. Not my idea of a man of God.' Maddie shivered again, recalling that dark visage.

'So what are you going to do about it? Are you going to talk to him?'

'No way, absolutely not! I'd rather not meet him again, thank you very much, but I've come to a decision. I think I need to find out who I really am. You know, who my real parents were, like you said. Perhaps my strange dreams are connected to my past. What do you think?'

'Are you sure they don't just stem from some incident in your childhood? I mean, you would hardly remember anything from before your adoption since you were only a baby. Did you ever ask your parents?'

'I told my mum about the dream when I was little, but she always said it was just my imagination. My parents didn't have any friends or acquaintances with either black or red beards. In fact, none with beards at all. Anyway, if something had happened to me that could result in such nightmares, I'm sure she would have told me.'

'Hmm, well, maybe you're right. You do need to find out more. If I were you, I think I'd be curious anyway. There must have been a good reason why your natural parents couldn't keep you. I mean, having had children myself, I can't imagine ever giving them up, but I suppose there are circumstances that might make it necessary.'

'Yes, that's what I thought.' Maddie had to admit she was curious now. The feeling had been growing ever since she'd found out she was adopted, even though her first reaction had been one of anger and disbelief. Mixed with the curiosity, however, was that fear of rejection which had so far prevented her from making enquiries, but she knew now she couldn't let it stop her. She had no illusions there would be a happy reunion, but even if her birth parents didn't want to acknowledge her, she still needed to find out why they'd given her up. At the moment her background was simply a black void and it needed to be filled with information, whether good or bad. It would help her to come to terms with it all.

'If you don't mind, I'll go back to London for a few days and see what I can find out. Tomorrow I'll call social services to see if I have to make an appointment or anything first.'

'Good idea. I think you have to get this out of your system before you look to the future.'

Maddie nodded. 'Thanks, Kayla.' Her stomach was churning at the thought of what might lie ahead, but there was no alternative. This was something she had to do.

Maddie didn't waste any time and the next morning she made a series of phone calls. When she'd finished she went in search of Kayla, and found her in the kitchen.

'I did it. I found out what to do.'

'Great, so what did they say?'

'Well, the lady I spoke to wouldn't give me any information over the phone, but I've made an appointment to go and see a counsellor next week. It's not a requirement because I was born after 1975 and the law changed then and things became more open, but she said it was a good idea. This is quite a big step to take and I agree with her it would be great to have some guidance.'

'So there's no problem about finding out who your parents were?'

'Not as such. People who had their children adopted before 1975 were told that those children would never be able to trace them, but nowadays they're not given any guarantees. That doesn't mean they want to be found though.'

'I guess not. Tricky, isn't it?'

'Yes, although they have to disclose the information by law, I think they want me to understand the seriousness of what I'm doing. I have to bring proof of identity, and the woman said the counsellor will give me further details at the interview.'

'When are you leaving?'

'I'll go up to London on Tuesday, the interview is on Wednesday.'

'Fine. Hurry back, though, won't you? You only just got here, so we don't want to lose you yet.'

'Don't worry. Wild horses couldn't keep me in London right now.'

London was dirty and noisy compared to Marcombe, and Maddie wrinkled her nose as she stepped off the train. The odours of pollution and humanity hung over everything like a soggy blanket in the humid summer heat, and she felt contaminated by the dust all around her. It was strange, but she had never noticed before, simply taken it for granted as so many other city dwellers did. London was a wonderful place in many ways, and all its inhabitants had learned to live with both the pros and cons. Occasionally, however, it was a relief to escape from the hustle and bustle of the big city. Maddie had an urge to turn around and catch the train back to Devon, never to return, but her determination to find out more about her background won out. She picked up her bag and headed for the exit.

As she made her way by tube to the tiny flat in Fulham which she shared with her friend Jessie, doubts niggled at her. Was she doing the right thing? Was there really anything to gain by digging up the past? Shouldn't she be happy that she had been raised by two wonderful people who had cared for her very much? They had been her family. They'd wanted her, unlike her birth parents. She sighed and wiped perspiration off her brow with the back of her hand. The questions whirled round inside her tired brain, but it all came back to one thing – she needed to know. It was as simple as that.

The flat was a short walk from Fulham Broadway tube station and it wasn't long before she was putting the key in the front door.

'Maddie! What are you doing here? I thought you were on holiday.' Jessie had been sitting on the sofa, engrossed in a book, and looked up as Maddie entered. She smiled broadly and jumped up to give her friend a welcoming hug, her long, auburn hair swinging out behind her. Jessie's violet eyes looked enormous, magnified as they were by a fashionable pair of glasses with lilac frames.

The two girls had met during one of Maddie's temping assignments and had hit it off immediately. Jessie was quiet and bookish and her main hobby was genealogy, which she pursued with never-ending fascination, but she had a quiet sense of humour which appealed to Maddie and the two of them shared many other interests.

'I'm sorry, Jessie, I forgot to call and tell you I was coming. It's only temporary though. Something's come up.'

'Oh? Must be interesting if it made you return to this hell-hole. Honestly, this last week I really thought I was going to die of heatstroke. My office has no air-conditioning and the windows barely open. I've tried to persuade the boss to install some, or at least buy us all fans, but he says it's not worth it for just a few weeks a year. Tight git.' Jessie patted the sofa. 'Come and sit down. I'll pour us a glass of wine and you can tell me what's going on.'

At the end of a catch-up chat, Jessie suddenly remembered something. 'Sorry, I forgot to tell you – your sister rang. Wanted to discuss something with you.'

'Oh? When was this?'

'A couple of days ago. Actually, she's left several messages since then, but I've ignored her.' Jessie smiled. 'I thought I'd let you deal with her.'

'Thanks,' Maddie said, making a face. 'Just what I need. I guess I'd better call her back straight away and get it over with.'

Olivia, as usual, didn't have time for any niceties. 'At last,' she exclaimed, without so much as a 'hello'. 'Where the hell have you been?'

'None of your business.' Maddie was through being conciliatory and she'd hoped never to hear from Olivia again. 'You rang?'

'Yes, I need the silver tea spoons.'

'Excuse me?'

'You heard me – the silver spoons you took. I'm having a little dinner party and I need them back. They belong to the rest of the cutlery set Mum and Dad had and ...'

'No!' Maddie almost shouted, then took a deep breath and started again. 'No, they were given to me by the aunts and uncles on my tenth birthday. There's a card inside the box signed by them all. Mum said they'd decided I was old enough to be given something "useful" instead of toys. So go buy your own tea spoons.'

Olivia went quiet for a second, but soon rallied. 'Fine, whatever. But you'll have to give back Mum's gold bracelet. I don't see why you should have that. Or at the very least, we should sell it and split the money.'

Maddie gritted her teeth so hard her temples hurt. 'Olivia, listen to me. I'm not giving you back a single thing I took from that house. You're getting my entire share of the sale of it so I owe you nothing. Nothing! And for your information, I bought Mum that bracelet, so I bloody well do have a right to it. Now sod off and don't ever call me again, got it?'

She slammed the phone down and fumed silently. If only she'd had a decent sister, how much easier life would have been. But the conversation with Olivia had helped in one respect – she now felt doubly justified in searching for her birth parents. If she found them, she'd have some family other than her adopted sister, and whether they wanted her or not, it had to be better than what she had now.

Chapter Seven

'God, this is worse than going to the dentist,' Maddie grumbled.

She was sitting in the waiting room of a non-descript office building somewhere in Holborn with Jessie, who had come to lend her support. The time for her appointment had come and gone, and she was sure that if it wasn't her turn soon she would return to Devon without any nails whatsoever. She had bitten each and every one down to the quick and they were beginning to ache. Swearing under her breath she sat on her hands.

'Shame we don't have to wear gloves these days,' she muttered. 'I can see why they used to now.' For some reason she was convinced her future happiness depended on the outcome of today's interview, and that terrified her.

'Calm down, I'm sure it will be your turn soon. You know government officials always work at their own pace.' Jessie said reassuringly, and Maddie gave her a grateful look.

'It's lucky I have you and Kayla. I don't know what I would do without you two.'

Jessie smiled. 'Why don't you read a magazine or something? It will take your mind off the waiting.'

'Madeline Browne.' A small woman had appeared at the door and Maddie jumped at the sound of her name. She stood up abruptly, almost overturning the chair in the process.

Jessie whispered, 'Good luck,' before giving her a small push in the right direction. Maddie swallowed hard and followed the counsellor into a maze of corridors.

The woman introduced herself as Bridget Wells, and eventually led Maddie into a small room with a rather dismal view of more office blocks. It was a curiously bare space – no plants, no pictures except for one large print of a particularly ugly Picasso painting and no papers. The desk was uncluttered and even the bin was empty. It gave the impression of being impersonal and cold, even sterile, and was obviously not someone's office, but simply a room used for conducting interviews. A few pigeons were seated on the window ledge outside occupied with grooming themselves, and Maddie tried to focus on them to calm herself. She wasn't very successful though, since she usually found them irritating with their constant cooing and pecking.

'Please have a seat, Ms Browne.'

'Thank you.'

'Right then. Have you brought some form of identification?' Maddie produced the necessary documents. 'Excellent. Now tell me a bit about why you wish to find out about your natural parents, please.'

'Well, my adopted parents were killed recently in a car crash, and it wasn't until the reading of their will that I was informed of the adoption. They had never told me and always treated me as if I was their real daughter. Which, I suppose, to them I was, I mean …'

Ms Wells nodded her understanding as Maddie floundered in her reasoning. She felt confused and once more had to sit on her hands. The temptation to chew her nails was always strongest whenever she was agitated, and it had never been as difficult to resist as today.

She managed to continue, 'Naturally, it made me curious, and although I'm aware that my birth parents may not want me to contact them, I would at least like to try and find out a bit more about my real background. Perhaps to understand why ...' Maddie broke off, suddenly unable to go on because there was a lump forming in her throat. The enormity of the situation had been brought home to her more forcefully by sitting in this bleak, depressing office, talking to a complete stranger, albeit a sympathetic one.

'I see,' said the counsellor. 'Well, your curiosity is understandable, Ms Browne, but it's my duty to prepare you for the fact that you contacting them may cause everyone concerned a lot of emotional stress and anguish. When someone gives up their child for adoption, it can be a very painful process, something they might not want to be reminded of. And although they will not have forgotten, they may not be pleased to hear from you. That, in turn, would affect you badly as well.'

Maddie felt her stomach contract painfully. 'I know,' she whispered.

'It could be that you were adopted because your birth mother wanted to keep her pregnancy a secret, and in her later life she may not want the secret to be discovered. I'm sure you can understand that.'

'Yes, of course I do.'

'I just want you to know the possible effects of your actions before you do anything else. You have to be absolutely sure you are ready to face whatever facts you find. Believe me, you hear a lot of stories about people who find each other after twenty, thirty years and hit it off straight away, but the reality isn't always quite so rosy. In fact, most often it's not.'

Maddie stared out the window, attempting to keep her own emotions in check. This interview was a lot more painful than she had imagined it would be.

'However,' Ms Wells continued, 'on a more positive

note, there is a slight chance your birth mother would have changed her mind by now and is longing for you to contact her. After all, this happened a long time ago, and just as you are curious about her, she might wish to know what has become of you. Her circumstances could have changed as well. You could begin by checking on internet sites where people can reconnect with one another.'

Maddie nodded and fidgeted on her chair, studying her poor mistreated fingernails in minute detail. 'So what happens now?'

'I have here the details of your original name, date and place of birth, et cetera.' Ms Wells pushed an A4 size paper across the desk towards Maddie, who picked it up almost reverently. 'With this information you can apply for a full birth certificate from the Registrar General. That takes about five working days. Once you receive it, you will have to try and trace your birth parents yourself.' A slight frown creased her brow. 'I'm afraid there's been some sort of administrative hiccup though and at the moment we don't have any more information relating to your particular case. There should have been some, but it has most likely been saved in the wrong file or something. We are working on it and we'll soon find it, I'm sure.'

'I see.' Maddie lifted the piece of paper with shaking fingers and read the scant notes. The stark black writing stood out against the pure white of the paper. To begin with, the letters danced in front of her eyes, and she had trouble making sense of them, but she took a deep breath and the words finally settled down into a coherent sentence. *'Madeline Browne, original name Sorcha Kettering, born 19th August 1984, Shepleigh, Wiltshire. Mother's name Ruth Kettering, father unknown.'* The name of the local authority who had authorised the adoption was also stated.

Maddie's chest felt as if it were enclosed in an iron vice, and her stomach refused to settle down.

'Ms Browne?'

Maddie realised Ms Wells was speaking to her. 'What? Sorry, I ...'

'I was just saying that you're welcome to call me at any time if you have any further queries. And I will, of course, be in touch once we find the missing file.'

'Thank you. You've been very kind. I, er ... thanks.' Maddie was about to leave when she noticed something. 'Hang on a minute. The date of adoption – it's three years after my birth. Can that be right?'

Ms Wells nodded. 'Yes, it's not just babies that are adopted. Sometimes single mothers try to cope and later find they can't. But we'll know more about your case when we find that file.'

'Oh, right. Okay. Well, goodbye.'

Blindly, Maddie stumbled out of the little office, down the hall and out into the reception area. *I was three when I was adopted?* So she could have had memories from a time before after all. The dream – was it real?

Jessie was waiting for her. 'There you are! So how did it go?'

Maddie handed her friend the piece of paper and walked towards the exit. 'Let's get out of here, I need air.'

It was heaven to be back at Marcombe, and Maddie told Kayla so the minute she arrived. The peace of the big house wrapped her in a comforting cocoon, and the matter of her natural parents didn't weigh on her mind here quite as much as it had in London.

'It's great to have you back too. Come and tell me what happened.'

Maddie dug the piece of paper out of her bag and showed it to Kayla. 'This is all the information I have at the moment, but I've sent off for a full birth certificate. I doubt if it will have any more details though, but the counsellor said she'll be sending me the rest of my file when she's found it.'

'Found it?'

'Yes, they've been saved in the wrong place or something. Not surprising really, they must have tens of thousands of records to keep track of.'

'All the more reason to keep them in order, I would have thought, but I suppose no one is perfect.'

'Yes, and guess what? Look at the date of my adoption – it shows that I was three when it happened, not a baby, so that dream I told you about could be real memories after all.'

'Wow, how intriguing! But scary too, I suppose ... Well, at least having these details is a step in the right direction.' Kayla scanned the single sheet of paper. 'Hmm, not much to go by, but if you're lucky Shepleigh might be a tiny place and someone will remember. Are you going to go there?'

'I don't know. Perhaps, but first I'll wait for the birth certificate.'

'Good idea. And in the meantime ...?'

'In the meantime, I'm going to have a holiday, like I promised myself when I first arrived here last week. It may be that I never find out anything at all, and for now I think I just want to forget the whole thing for a while. I'm sick and tired of it churning round my brain.'

'Sounds like a good plan to me. How about we go and see what Annie's cooking for lunch?'

A week of glorious weather, outings to the cove and

painting excursions around Marcombe Hall followed. Maddie tried to relax and leave the future to take care of itself. This holiday had been long overdue, and she was determined to enjoy it to the full, putting everything else out of her mind for the moment. She played happily with Kayla's children and had long chats with her friend. From time to time, she also found herself in Alex's company and although his brooding gaze unsettled her, he seemed to be making an effort to get to know her. Maddie wasn't sure she should encourage him as she was determined not to become involved with any more players, but she didn't want to be rude either. He was Kayla's brother-in-law after all, so she couldn't ignore him altogether.

'What are you guys talking about?' Kayla had come to inspect the sand castles Alex and Maddie were constructing for the kids while they chatted about this and that.

'Alternative pop punk.' Alex smiled at her. 'Maddie and I seem to have the same taste in music.'

'Seriously?' Kayla made a face. 'I didn't think anyone else liked that stuff. It's so noisy.'

'You sound like a pensioner,' Maddie teased. 'You like some of the songs I played to you, admit it.'

'Well, all right, but not the screechy ones.'

Alex laughed. 'You and Wes are definitely a match made in heaven. He said the same thing when we were in the car the other day.'

'Then you two must be as well,' Kayla shot back and scooped up Edmund. 'Come on, young man, time to get some of this sand off you.'

Maddie bent her head to hide her burning cheeks. Kayla was right in a way – their taste in music wasn't the only thing she and Alex had in common. They seemed to like the same type of movies, books and TV programmes as well, which was a bit disconcerting. She'd never found anyone whose views were so in tune with her own. It made her wonder if he was just having her on in order to get in her good books.

The truth was she didn't want to have things in common with him. She didn't want to like him, full stop. That way lay danger.

'There's a film on at the local flea pit which you might like,' he told her 'How about we go and see it one evening?'

Maddie shook her head, without looking him in the eye. 'Thanks, but it's too hot to go to the movies. Maybe some other time?' She hoped he'd take the hint and he did.

'Right. Okay.' But when she looked up, his eyes were narrowed, as if he was considering how to persuade her to reconsider. She hurriedly made an excuse and went to wash the sand off her hands.

Damn it all, she didn't want to spend time alone with him. Why didn't he just ask Jenna? For some reason, the thought of him with the willowy blonde made her even more cross, but she told herself to get a grip. If she stayed firm, he'd soon find someone else to go out with.

At the end of the week, the birth certificate arrived at last and Maddie felt as if her holiday was over. She stared at the green sheet of paper for a long time, the icy tentacles gripping her stomach once more. The time for decisions had come.

Kayla, when Maddie finally ran her to ground in Wes's office, appeared distracted but listened to her friend patiently nevertheless.

'You've finally received it? And what does it say?'

'It's almost the same as the information the counsellor

gave me, except for the fact that it gives the name and address of the informant of the birth.'

'And who was that?'

'John Kettering, brother of Ruth. It gives his address as Three Bluehouse Lane, Shepleigh, Wiltshire. I assume it must be where she gave birth to me, or at a nearby hospital.'

'Well, that's good, isn't it? Now you have a starting point. He might even be living there still.'

'Yes.' Maddie sighed and absently twirled a red curl round a finger. 'I just don't know whether I should go on with this or not, Kayla. I'm not sure I can face it.'

'Come on, if you don't I think it will always bother you. Find out about your past and lay it to rest, once and for all. If there's no mystery, you have nothing to worry about. Doesn't it say anything more about your mother?'

'No. The space where it should say her occupation has been left blank. Perhaps she was too young to work?'

'Yes, that's possible. Well, wait and see what the rest of your file says when they find it.' Kayla stood up. 'I'm sorry, but I haven't really got time to chat at the moment. There's been a bit of a crisis.'

'Oh? I thought you looked a bit hassled when I came in. I'm sorry, I should have thought to ask you about it.'

'No, no, it's all right. It's just that my father's been taken to hospital with a suspected heart attack, and my mother wants us to come and stay for a while.'

'Oh, Kayla, you should have said and not allowed me to rabbit on about my insignificant problems.'

'They're important to you, and anyway, my dad is in a stable condition and seems to be over the worst of it, according to Mum, so there's no need to panic. She's a nurse, you remember, and she should know. Still, I can't help but worry and the first thing he said to her was that he wants to see his grandchildren. He dotes on them you know. As for Mum, I think she could do with some company.'

'But what about your sisters and your brother? Can't they help out?'

'Bella is working long hours and can't get time off at the moment, Anthea is only days away from having her first child, and Vic is travelling around India. God only knows where he is! My mother hasn't been able to contact him yet, she has to wait for him to phone. Said he wanted to be away from all the trappings of civilisation or some such rot.' Kayla shrugged and spread her hands as if in defeat. 'That leaves only us.'

'Are you sure you want to bring the children? I can stay here and look after them if you want,' Maddie offered. She could see the worry lurking in her friend's eyes and knew precisely what she was going through. Although her own anguish had only lasted for a short while when she still believed there was hope for her parents' survival, it was the same feeling of helplessness that Kayla must be experiencing now.

'Thanks, but I couldn't go without them. There is one thing, though … would you consider staying for a while to house-sit when we're away?'

'Of course.' Maddie had no hesitation in accepting. The next minute, however, something occurred to her. 'But what about Alex? Shouldn't you ask him first? After all, he is Wes's brother and I'm just a friend.'

'Oh, we already have. You'll be doing it together.'

'What? I mean … oh.' The thought of sharing the house with just Alex was disturbing, despite the size of Marcombe Hall. Maddie had successfully avoided being completely alone with Wes's handsome brother since her return from London, but even his gaze did strange things to her. Without Kayla and Wes as a buffer of sorts, she wasn't sure she could continue to keep her distance.

'You don't mind, do you?' Kayla looked troubled once more. 'I thought you were friends now. Anyway, he's so busy with his cottages, you probably won't see him much.'

'No, um, of course not, we'll be fine. I was just surprised, that's all.' Privately Maddie had her doubts, but she desperately wanted to stay in Devon a bit longer and had been afraid she was overstaying her welcome. Now she didn't need to have any qualms about that. She would just have to remember her resolution about men and treat Alex as a brother.

'You know what? I could sleep in one of the cottages and just check on Maddie from time to time while you're away.'

Ever since Wes had asked him to house-sit together with Kayla's friend, Alex had been trying to think of a way out of it. How the devil was he supposed to share a house with her and keep his hands to himself? It would be agony. No, correction, it would be hell.

'Don't be an idiot. This house is so big, I doubt the two of you will even see each other more than in passing.' Wes was distracted by trying to pack for an unspecified length of time away and didn't even look at Alex.

I wouldn't bet on that. Alex clenched his fists inside his pockets. 'Maddie might feel awkward though. What with me being a former criminal and everything.'

Wes fixed him with a stern 'older brother' gaze. 'Come on, cut it out. It's all in the past and forgotten by everyone, Maddie included. You've got to stop thinking like that.

It's not like it's tattooed on your forehead, you know. You two have been getting along just fine all week so where's the problem? Now please, just do this for me, okay? I'd be happier knowing there was a man about the place. We can't leave Maddie all alone here.'

Annie never stayed in the house at night, except when she was baby-sitting late and Alex knew it. He swallowed a sigh. 'Yes, of course. Don't worry, I'll be here.'

He owed his brother big time and he was determined to make this work.

Chapter Eight

Kayla, Wes and the children left early the following day, and when Maddie came down to breakfast she found Alex sitting at the table, reading the paper. He looked up when she entered and said, 'Good morning,' then quickly returned to his paper.

'Morning.' Maddie looked out of the window. 'Looks like another beautiful day. I can't believe this weather, we've been so lucky this year.'

'Yes, it's glorious, isn't it? Which reminds me, would you like to come sailing with me today? I thought I'd take Wes's boat out. I haven't really had much time recently and the sea is calling to me.' He smiled and Maddie suddenly felt uncomfortably warm. She turned away to make some toast. Should she risk going with him or take the safer option of going to the cove? The thought of bobbing along on the waves with a salty sea breeze cooling her skin was very tempting. *Oh, what the hell ...* She made up her mind, ignoring the voice of reason.

'All right, that would be nice. But what about the house? We're supposed to be looking after it.'

'Annie will be here until we get back. What could happen in broad daylight?'

'Yes, I guess you're right. Okay, what time do we leave?'

'Half an hour?'

'Great.'

In the end it took slightly longer since they decided to bring food with them. Alex helped her to make sandwiches, although she banned him from cutting the bread after the first slice turned out to be a very strange shape.

'Honestly, Alex, haven't you ever learned to slice bread? We don't want to eat doorsteps, you know.' She took the knife from him and proceeded to cut thin, even slices. 'You do the buttering instead.'

'Yes, ma'am.' Laughing, he pretended to salute her. 'I've never had to make perfect sandwiches, you know. Annie's always done it for me, and if I wanted to make my own I didn't care what size they were.'

'Well, it's about time you learned,' Maddie muttered. Alex's privileged childhood, with nannies and housekeepers always at his beck and call, was another thing that stood between them. He may not act the snob, but he was different from her, no doubt about it. She determined yet again to keep her distance although a little voice inside her head muttered something about a lady protesting too much.

'Looks like the sea is fairly calm today,' Alex commented as they headed out of the little harbour where Wes kept his boat moored. 'You don't get seasick, do you?'

'I didn't last time.' Maddie had been pleased to find that she didn't even feel slightly queasy during her previous trips in a boat. She'd been able to enjoy the experiences immensely.

'Good, then you can help me sail her.'

Maddie did her best to follow his instructions, although Alex laughed at her when she kept calling the various parts of the boat 'that thing.'

'Well I don't know one end of a boat from the other,' she said crossly. 'And what's more, I'm not sure I want to know. Maybe I'm perfectly happy just being carried along. It's just a mode of transport.'

'How can you say that?' Alex exclaimed with mock

horror and shook his head. 'Honestly, these city girls, I don't know … Now come on, I need some assistance.'

'With what?'

'You could help me pull on this "thing" here, for instance. I could do it on my own, but it's easier if two people do it.'

Maddie made a face, but helped him all the same.

'Thank you. Now wouldn't you like to try your hand at steering?' Alex indicated the tiller.

'I don't think that would be safe. I'd probably run us aground.'

He laughed. 'No way, there is no "ground" around here. Trust me. Come here and I'll show you how.' Maddie reluctantly joined him by the tiller, and he made her sit between his legs so he could help her steer by guiding her hand from behind. 'Just remember to pull it the opposite direction to the one you want to go, okay? So if you want to turn left, pull the tiller to the right.'

'Got it.'

She tried to concentrate on his instructions, but found it extremely difficult. What she really wanted to do was lean back into his hard chest and let him wrap his arms around her and hold her tight. He was so close, she could smell his aftershave and the tang of the sea all around them. It was heaven, and it was hell.

Finally she couldn't stand it anymore. 'I think I'll leave the steering to you,' she said and stood up abruptly. 'If you don't mind I'll just enjoy the ride.'

They sailed along the coast until they found a secluded cove which appeared to be deserted. Alex steered the boat in and dropped anchor, and they ate their lunch on the little beach. After the meal, Maddie stretched out on her towel and removed her T-shirt and shorts, leaving only a very skimpy bikini. Alex looked away.

'You don't mind if I sunbathe, do you?' Maddie frowned. He had seen her in her bathing suit before, but she felt suddenly shy and turned over onto her stomach.

'No, of course not. I think I'll go for a swim.' He stood up and removed his own shirt, and without giving her another glance he sprinted for the water.

'Wait! You shouldn't swim on a full stomach,' Maddie shouted after him, but he either didn't hear her or ignored her words. 'Oh, never mind then.'

When he returned, quite a while later, she was on her back again and the sun was beating down mercilessly.

'Aren't you cooked yet?' he asked and couldn't resist flicking a few drops of cold water onto her stomach. Maddie shrieked and jumped up. The cool droplets had been almost painful against her heated skin.

'You beast! I'll get you for that.' She bent to pick up a handful of sand and threw it at him, covering his chest and abdomen.

'Why you little ...'

She didn't stay to hear any more, but took off in the direction of the sea. He caught up with her just as the water reached her thighs, and grabbed her from behind, throwing himself down into the waves and taking her with him. They came up spluttering, and spent the next ten minutes or so splashing each other like children and horsing around.

Finally Alex put up his hands to stop her from splashing any further, and shook his hair out of his eyes. 'Enough! This is too exhausting.'

Maddie laughed, then made the mistake of stepping towards him and looking up into his eyes. They both went very still and their smiles faded. The noise of the waves and the seagulls around them melted into the distance, and Maddie felt as if nothing existed except Alex and her.

His next move seemed inevitable somehow and when his arms came up to pull her close they felt warm on her skin. She didn't resist. She wanted to be even closer. As if he'd read her thoughts, he tightened his hold on her. Slowly his mouth came towards hers and she was powerless to break away. She didn't want to anyway.

The salty kiss was soft and gentle at first, as he pressed his mouth against hers with infinite care. Maddie's arms came up, apparently of their own volition, and she splayed her hands against his chest, feeling the powerful beat of his heart. He rained little kisses on her mouth, her nose and her cheeks, and she closed her eyes to savour them. Streaks of molten lava began to snake their way through her body, and she trembled with a desire stronger than anything she'd ever felt before.

This feels so right!

Alex traced the outline of her mouth with his tongue and she opened for him without thought. The kiss deepened and they explored each other for what seemed an eternity. When Maddie put her arms around his neck, he pulled her hard against him and she suddenly felt the whole length of him from knees to shoulders. His sun-warmed skin seared hers and she trembled. It was pretty clear that he wanted her very much, despite standing in ice cold water, and that thought jolted her back to reality. She broke off the kiss and turned her head away.

'No, Alex,' she whispered feebly. 'We mustn't ... I don't want ...'

He drew in a ragged breath, but when she pushed at him he let her go straight away. Maddie's legs wouldn't hold her up and she fell into the water and floated on her back, staring at the sky. Inch by burning inch, her body cooled down.

'Maddie?' Alex took hold of one of her hands, and she put her feet down again. He looked like he was in pain, but in his eyes she saw something else. Misery? Sadness? She wasn't sure. 'I'm sorry, Maddie, I shouldn't have done that. I just got carried away.'

'It's okay. It was the game. Let's just forget about it.' Maddie had a strange urge to take him in her arms and comfort him, as if he were a little boy. But he wasn't; he was very much a man. She pulled herself together and headed for the beach. *I mustn't touch him ever again.* Next time she might not be able to stop.

They continued sailing for the rest of the afternoon and attempted to recapture the easy camaraderie of the morning, but their conversation was strained and they didn't quite manage it. Maddie almost heaved a sigh of relief when the little jetty hove into view and she could retreat to the house. She wanted to run all the way to her sanctuary, afraid of Alex, afraid of the feelings he evoked.

Afraid of her own weakness.

'I need to go to Dartmouth to do my weekly food shopping and pick something up from my sister's and Ben can't drive me today. Have you got time?' Annie asked Maddie the next day. Ben was Annie's husband who worked as gatekeeper and gardener at Marcombe Hall.

'Yes, of course. I can be ready in ten minutes.' Kayla had left Maddie her little Mini to use while she was gone.

'Oh, there's no rush, take your time.'

An hour later Maddie dropped the older woman outside the supermarket.

'Are you sure you don't want any help, Annie?'

'No, no, I'll be fine. You go and buy whatever you need

and come back for me in about an hour or so. Don't hurry on my account.'

'All right then. See you later.'

The centre of town was teeming with people as usual and after she had purchased a few items Maddie bought a huge ice cream and sat down on a bench by the small green. It was another scorching day. Here in the town it was a cloying, humid heat which was almost unbearable compared to the cooling breezes further down the coast at Marcombe. The ice cream was extremely welcome.

Maddie was wearing a big, floppy sunhat, but it made her head feel even hotter so she took it off and put it on the bench next to her. She ate slowly, savouring the chocolatey taste with its tang of coconut, and watched the people ambling past. Behind her, a group of teenage girls were giggling hysterically, while ogling and commenting on any boys that went past. Maddie wondered idly if she'd ever been that silly. She couldn't remember, but she supposed she must have been.

When the ice cream was finished she stood up to find a litter bin in which to throw away the paper napkin and spotted one at the other end of the green. Leaving the hat on the bench, she walked unhurriedly towards the bin, and dropped the piece of paper in. As she turned, a woman bumped into her, and Maddie almost laughed. Was there something about her that made people walk straight into her, or was it this town? Perhaps the inhabitants of Dartmouth were not in the habit of looking where they were going. Her thoughts were cut short by a gasp of horror from the woman, who was staring at her with eyes that seemed enormous in her suddenly pale face.

'Oh, no! Oh, dear God no ...' Before Maddie's astonished gaze the woman crumpled to the ground in a dead faint, and Maddie couldn't react in time to catch her.

Neither could the lady's companion, a young woman in her early twenties, who cried out in alarm. 'Mother!'

Fortunately she'd fallen in the direction of the grass which cushioned her slightly so she didn't hit her head on the gravel path at least. Maddie and the other girl knelt quickly by her side and, grabbing a newspaper the woman had dropped, Maddie began to fan her face with it. Several passers-by stopped to give them assistance.

'Oh dear, what happened?'

'I don't know. She just fainted. The heat I suppose.' Maddie didn't tell them it had been the sight of *her* that seemed to have made the woman pass out. It sounded stupid, even to herself, but the girl threw her a puzzled glance, so she knew she hadn't imagined it. Curious now, she studied the woman. It was difficult to tell her age, but Maddie guessed at mid to late fifties. The lady's white-grey hair had been scraped back into a severe bun, making her seem even older, but the soft skin on her face was only slightly wrinkled. There were deep worry-lines on her forehead and around her mouth, and the bags under her eyes seemed to indicate either that she didn't sleep well or that she cried a lot. Maddie was absolutely certain she'd never met her before.

The woman began to regain consciousness, but as her glazed eyes came to rest on Maddie's face once more, she became agitated again.

'No, go away. Please!'

'Mother, don't be silly, she's only trying to help. You fainted.'

'No! Go away! Oh, why won't anyone ever listen to me?' The wails rose into a crescendo of pitiful crying, and Maddie thought it best to remove herself from the vicinity. If her face was the cause of so much grief, there was no point in trying to be helpful. *Perhaps I remind her of someone she's lost?* She shrugged at the girl, who looked apologetic but relieved at the same time, and stood up. Frowning, she made her way back to the bench and sat down, putting on the sunhat which thankfully was still where she'd left it. Why had the woman taken such exception to her? It didn't make sense.

The wails behind her ceased shortly afterwards and as she risked a peek over her shoulder, Maddie saw the woman being helped to her feet. The passers-by who had stopped to offer assistance disappeared one by one, and finally the lady was alone with her daughter. She looked around furtively, as if searching for something, but Maddie bent her head down so her face was hidden by the brim of her hat and the woman didn't spot her. Apparently satisfied, the lady set off almost at a run towards the nearest street without looking back, pulling the girl with her.

'Mother, what's the matter? Wait!' Maddie heard the girl remonstrating with her mother, but apparently to no avail. The woman didn't slow her pace.

Her curiosity well and truly piqued by now, Maddie decided to follow them.

'I seem to be making a habit of this,' she muttered to herself. 'Maybe I should set up in business as a detective.' This idea was too ludicrous and she smiled to herself while hurrying to catch up.

As she walked behind them, Maddie had a sense of *deja-vu*, and she soon realised why. The two women turned into the exact same street as the dark man had on the previous occasion, and when they hurried into the very same house as the minister, Maddie wasn't surprised. Somehow it had been inevitable.

Stunned, she stood there staring at the door, just like the last time. Thankfully no one came to ask her any questions and she was left alone with her thoughts, which were racing.

If the woman lived in the same house, she must be Mrs Blake-Jones. But why had the sight of Maddie upset her so much? It didn't make sense, unless they had met before. Maddie shook her head. She couldn't make head nor tail of it. Mrs Blake-Jones obviously thought she knew her – and feared her by the look of things – but Maddie didn't recall ever having met her. However, she recognised the woman's husband, who in his turn didn't appear to know who Maddie was. *What the hell is going on here?*

Maddie rubbed her temples. Her head had begun to throb as the endless questions whirled around inside her brain. Nothing made sense anymore. She felt emotionally drained and unable to cope with it all. *It's too much.*

She hesitated, wanting to knock on the door and demand some answers, but somehow she didn't feel she had the right. Judging by the woman's reaction to her, she definitely didn't want to see Maddie. Mrs Blake-Jones had made that abundantly clear. This thought caused Maddie to shake her head once more and turn back towards the car park. She had to get to the bottom of her own mysterious background before she did anything else. Then perhaps she would have some answers. She glanced towards the house one last time, but all was quiet.

Chapter Nine

'Mother, for heaven's sake, would you just calm down and tell me what's going on please? What's the matter with you? Stop pacing around, will you!'

Mrs Blake-Jones came to a halt in the kitchen and sank onto a chair by the table. She slumped forward, burying her head in her hands. 'Nothing, Jane, nothing's the matter. It was just the sun,' she mumbled. 'Just the sun …'

'The sun. Right.' Jane tapped her foot impatiently on the floor. 'Mother, I wasn't born yesterday. You fainted at the sight of that red-haired girl, and then you told her to go away when she was only trying to help. You were very rude, and you are never rude normally. Something strange is going on here.' Jane was utterly baffled by her mother's behaviour, and determined to get to the bottom of it.

Mrs Blake-Jones lifted her face to look at her daughter, and Jane gasped as she took in the sight of her mother's tear-drenched cheeks. She hurried over to put her arm around the slight shoulders, and felt her shudder.

'Mother, please, tell me what's wrong.'

'What's going on in here?' Her mother jumped at the sound of her husband's voice and looked ready to faint for the second time that day. Jane saw all the blood drain out of her face and she appeared to freeze, gazing at her husband with the terrified eyes of a fawn staring into the barrel of a shotgun. Jane frowned.

'Well? Speak to me.' The Reverend Saul Blake-Jones wasn't used to disobedience in his own house, as Jane well knew, and scowled at the two women.

'It's nothing, Father. Mother fainted when we were out,

but I think it was just the sun,' Jane hastened to placate him. The last thing she needed was one of his outbursts. She knew precisely what that would do to her mother.

'I heard you mention a woman with red hair. Who was she?'

'I-I don't know. Her face seemed to upset Mother, but, er, I'm sure it was nothing. Just her imagination.'

The Reverend turned his hard gaze onto his wife and Jane felt her mother tremble violently. She gritted her teeth, wondering for the umpteenth time how she could persuade her mother to leave this house with her. It was as if her father had some hold over his wife and every time Jane tried to make her leave she was met with a blank refusal, even though she knew her mother would dearly like to escape her husband's tyranny.

'Is this true? You saw a red-haired woman?' he asked, keeping his gaze fixed on his wife's pale face.

She nodded.

'Now why would that upset you, I wonder.' He stroked his beard and regarded her thoughtfully, his dark eyes glittering with malice. It was Jane's turn to shiver. For twenty years she had lived with this man who was her father. She knew she was supposed to love and obey him, but she found it impossible. He had bullied them once too often and she didn't think she could stand it another second. She simply had to find a way to escape, but she couldn't leave her mother behind. It would kill her.

'Well, I can think of only one reason for that, my dear,' he was saying now. He put his hands on the table and leaned forward, pinning his wife to her chair with his gaze. 'And we both know what that is, don't we?'

'No, Saul, I must have been imagining things. Lots of people have red hair, you know.' The answer came out in a strangled voice which Jane hardly recognised. She looked from one parent to the other, but they were oblivious to her presence. They saw only each other. *And something else, but what?*

'I don't think so. I knew it was a mistake, I should have taken care of the matter once and for all when I had the chance.' He turned on his heel and marched towards the door.

'No, Saul, please! Don't ...'

He swivelled round and glared at his wife once more. 'This was all your fault so don't you dare say a word. Do you hear me?' he roared, and Jane saw her mother's face crumple as she began to sob loudly. 'I'm not the sinner here and I'll do as I see fit.' And he left without a backward glance.

Her mother's frail body shook with the force of her weeping, and Jane rocked her until the storm passed. When the sobs had turned into small hiccups, Jane finally dared to question her.

'Please, Mother, can't you tell me what this is all about?' she whispered, not wanting to be overheard by her father again.

'No, sweetheart. Please don't ask me to. It's better you don't know.'

With an inward sigh, Jane gave up as the crying began again. She would have to look for answers elsewhere.

'Maddie, there was a phone call for you. A friend of yours, I think.' Alex came out of Wes's office the minute she walked through the front door with Annie. He held out a piece of paper. 'She left a number.'

'Oh, thanks.' Maddie glanced at the note and saw that the caller had been Jessie.

She turned around and found Alex staring at her as if he wanted to say something else, but he must have changed his mind and only nodded at her before heading back into the office. Maddie fled to her room and dialled the London number.

'Jessie? It's me. What's up?'

'I just wanted to see how you were getting on and to let you know that I've checked the marriage records online. Unfortunately there was no marriage for a Ruth Kettering, so I don't know how you're going to trace her. Have you heard any more?'

'The birth certificate arrived the other day and there was a possible lead to be followed. My mother's brother is listed as the informant and there's an address for him in a small village in Wiltshire. But listen, something really strange has happened again ...'

Maddie flopped down onto the bed and proceeded to tell Jessie all about her extraordinary encounter with Mrs Blake-Jones and her daughter. 'Do you think she knew my mother and is trying to keep her secret still? Her reaction was so weird. Although why someone in Dartmouth would know a woman from Wiltshire, I've no idea.'

'I suppose it's possible.' Jessie sounded thoughtful. 'Hold on a minute, I've just thought of something. God, I'm such an idiot!'

'What?'

'I can't tell you now, in case I'm wrong, but I'll call you again soon.'

'But Jessie ...'

'You know what? I think you should go to that village and ask around. People in tiny places have long memories. Your uncle might still be there.'

'I thought of that, but it's a bit awkward. I mean, what do I say? "Excuse me, but do you know of any illegitimate children who were born here twenty-seven years ago?"'

Jessie giggled. 'No, of course not. Just pretend you're the daughter of an old school friend of Ruth's and your mum needs to get in touch with her or something.'

'Oh, Jessie, I don't know, I'm so bad at lying.'

'Come on, you can do it. It's the only way. Anyway, I've got to go now. Talk to you next week. Bye.'

Her friend hung up, and Maddie was left staring at the phone.

She curled herself into the foetal position on the bed. She felt small and vulnerable, and alone. So alone. Of course she had Kayla and her friends, and perhaps one day she would have a family of her own, if she ever found the right man, but it wasn't the same. Kayla didn't know how lucky she was to have parents, a brother and two sisters, not to mention grandmothers, aunts and uncles. Maddie had thought that she had these things too, but now they were gone and even the ones she *had* had weren't really hers. She hadn't spoken to any of her adopted relations since the funeral, and no one had contacted her. She realised with sadness that she'd never really liked any of them anyway, apart from the wonderful couple who had been her parents to all intents and purposes.

She wanted to cry, but she felt paralysed inside, as if her tears were stuck in a block of ice she couldn't melt. Her head still hurt and she rubbed her temples in soothing circles, but it was no use. Someone had crammed an iron helmet onto her scalp and forehead, and if she closed her eyes she could feel it tightening by the minute. It squeezed until she thought she would scream and she debated whether to have an aspirin, but she knew it wouldn't help. The pain was coming from within her and until she could free herself of the feelings of despair it would remain.

'Maddie, can I talk to you for a minute, please?'

'Sorry? Oh, yes of course.' Dinner had been a silent affair and Maddie was so lost in her own misery she'd hardly spoken to Alex at all. Now she followed him into the small, comfortable sitting room at the back of the house, which Kayla and Wes used when they weren't entertaining. The red wallpaper and plush sofas made it a favourite retreat, and in wintertime a fire usually burned in the grate to add to the cosy feel of the room. Maddie normally always relaxed in here, but tonight her nerves were still on edge.

'Maddie, I noticed you were very quiet at dinner,' Alex began, staring out of the window with his hands in his pockets.

'Yes, I'm sorry, I was just a bit preoccupied.' Maddie sank down into a fat armchair and tried to concentrate on her surroundings.

'Well, I just wanted to apologise again for what happened yesterday,' Alex turned to look her in the eye. 'I don't usually rush things like that. I really should have given you more time to get to know me.'

Maddie held up a hand. 'No, please, don't say any more, Alex. I ... it would be better if we just forgot the whole thing. Really, we wouldn't suit. Let's just be friends, okay?'

Alex frowned. 'What makes you say that? I thought that we suited very well.'

Maddie felt a blush spread from top to toe as she realised what he was referring to and she couldn't deny he was right. 'Well, perhaps in that department we would, but I'm not interested in casual relationships with—'

'Ex-criminals? No, I don't suppose you are.' Alex's jaw tightened visibly as if he was reining in his anger with some difficulty. 'I should have known no decent girl would ever want to go out with me. I suppose I'll have to take myself down to the docks and find a whore like all the other criminals,' he sneered and turned towards the door.

'Alex, that's not what I was going to say at all!' Maddie was horrified. She'd only meant to say that he was too handsome, too much of a player, and she didn't think he would ever have a serious relationship with anyone like her. She wasn't exactly a raving beauty. But he had jumped to conclusions.

'Spare me, okay? We can pretend to be friends for Wes and Kayla's sake, just like you said. That's fine with me.' And he slammed out of the room, banging the door so hard the windows rattled.

Maddie started after him, then stopped. She wanted to explain his mistake, but on the other hand he might take that to mean she had changed her mind. Perhaps it was better to let him think the worst? At least then he would leave her alone and that would help her to put a stop to her own foolish feelings for him. Right now, the last thing she needed was the temptation to jump into bed with Alex.

And a temptation it undoubtedly was.

Alex knew he'd probably been a bit overly dramatic, but he was so angry he didn't care. And he was more annoyed with himself than Maddie.

He should have known. Why had he even put himself in this situation? Deep down he'd been aware that women wouldn't look at him the same way as they had before he'd gone to prison. Nice girls didn't date men with his kind of blotted copybooks. Even the über-confident Jenna had stopped flirting once he told her where he'd been for the last three years, although admittedly, when she'd tracked him down as she had promised she would, he had embellished his criminal past a little just to get rid of her. Still, he hadn't heard from her again, nor any of his former friends in the area, so he wasn't too wide off the mark. From now on he had to lower his sights considerably.

Damn it!

Spending the day sailing and relaxing with Maddie had made him forget who he was and he'd made a pass at her. A pass she hadn't repulsed straight away. But then maybe she'd forgotten momentarily as well? The sun did strange things to your brain and made it hard to think rationally. *She came to her senses soon enough though, didn't she ...*

He headed for the garden, knowing the freedom and sweet-smelling flowers and herbs would calm him down.

'I have to look on the bright side,' he muttered. He wasn't locked up any more and if being shunned by decent girls was the price he had to pay, so be it. He'd been an idiot and now he was being punished for it. Would continue to be punished, perhaps for the rest of his life. But at least he wasn't in a locked cell any more.

Face it, Marcombe, Maddie's not for the likes of you.

But who was?

Chapter Ten

It was no good. Maddie was surrounded by temptations and the one she found herself unable to resist the most was another visit to Dartmouth.

Quite what she hoped to achieve, she didn't know, but she had a vague idea that if she went there often enough she might find the answers she was looking for. She'd Googled the Saint Paulians, but hadn't come up with much. Just the address of the chapel in Dartmouth and a short description of their aims – *"To return to the pure Christian doctrines of St Paul the Apostle and follow the laws laid down in the Bible."* That didn't really tell her anything, but she read between the lines and interpreted this as a sect which kept to very traditional interpretations of Christianity. Old-fashioned and opposed to anything modern. Strict and perhaps even dictatorial.

Which seemed to suit the Reverend Blake-Jones from what she'd seen.

Although she was reluctant to approach the man's wife, if that's who she'd been, there might be some way of meeting her by chance. She couldn't stay at home all the time. There must be times when she ventured out of her house for shopping or visiting, and Maddie thought she might be able to make contact. What other option did she have?

Parking the car in the usual place, she sauntered slowly down the street and stopped to buy herself an ice lolly. The day was as sultry as all the previous ones, and even in a skimpy tank top and shorts Maddie was too warm. Sheltering under a tree for a while, she debated what her next step should be. Should she simply wait at the end of the road where the Blake-Jones's lived, or should she wander round the town hoping to meet the woman? It was a small place after all. She sucked the juice out of the lolly, leaving only cool ice which she chewed on while thinking through her options.

In the end she decided to wait at the end of the road and set off in that direction. She hadn't gone far, however, when she heard someone calling out, 'Excuse me? Hello? Could I have a word, please?' There was no one else around, so Maddie assumed the person meant her and turned around.

It was Mrs Blake-Jones's daughter. She must have been walking on the other side of the road, and came hurrying towards Maddie, who stopped.

'You want to talk to me?'

'Yes, please, if you don't mind?' The girl came to a panting halt and attempted to catch her breath. 'I'm sorry, I saw you walking down the road and I had to run to catch up.'

Maddie studied her closely. She had very dark brown hair, tied into a simple ponytail at the back which made her look almost like a schoolgirl. Her eyes were dark too, with long lashes under heavy brows. Maddie thought the girl could have been quite pretty if she'd made the attempt to put on some make-up and perhaps change her hairstyle. But her face was completely bare and almost as pale as that of her mother. She obviously didn't spend much time in the sun.

'Don't worry, take your time. What did you want to talk to me about?' Maddie asked, curiosity getting the better of her.

The girl quickly scanned the area around them, then drew Maddie around and pulled her in the direction she had come from. 'I'm sorry, but could we go somewhere private? It's just … I'd rather no one saw us together. Not here, anyway.'

Maddie raised her eyebrows in surprise. 'Why? I don't even know you.'

'I know. I'll explain later. Please, trust me on this, okay? Is there somewhere we can go?' The girl was pleading with her, dark eyes darting around nervously, and Maddie took pity on her.

'We could go for a ride in my car. Well, my friend's car actually, but still … It's parked just over there.' She pointed to the car park.

'Brilliant, let's go.' And the girl hurried her across the road and before Maddie knew it they were on their way out of town.

As the houses disappeared behind them, the girl relaxed visibly, and she turned to Maddie with a small smile.

'I'm sorry to kidnap you like this, but I have my reasons. I'm Jane Blake-Jones, by the way.'

'I'm Maddie. Maddie Browne.' She turned the car off the road into a small lay-by and brought it to a halt, then switched off the engine. 'There, now we can talk without distractions.'

'Yes. You must think I'm really weird, but the thing is I recognised you from the other day, and I thought you might be able to tell me why my mother reacted in such a strange way. It was as if she was scared of you. I've tried to make her tell me, but she won't, and I really need to know why.'

Maddie smiled ruefully and shrugged. 'Yes, well, join the queue.'

'What do you mean?'

'I mean, I'd like to know the same thing, although I think I might have an idea.'

'Well, that's more than I have. I asked her about it when we got home and she just burst into tears. Then my father came in and when he found out what had happened he was really angry. Why?' Jane looked thoroughly confused.

Maddie sighed and fiddled with the car keys. 'I think it's all to do with my birth. You see, I found out about a month ago that I was adopted and although I don't know who my birth mother was, it would be reasonable to suppose she wanted to keep her pregnancy a secret. I think somehow your parents are in on it. Perhaps she was a friend of your mother's or something? I'm sorry, I don't know if any of this makes any sense and I might be completely wrong.'

'No, I don't think so.' Jane was still thoughtful and regarded Maddie out of serious eyes. 'I've always felt that my father had some kind of hold over my mother and this could be it. He called her a sinner.'

'But why would it matter to him if she kept a secret for a friend?'

'He has very strong views on the sanctity of marriage and illegitimate children. You know, things like that.' Jane blushed. 'Lewd behaviour, he calls it and he would never in a million years condone it, let alone want Mother to be friends with someone who'd done such a thing.'

'I see.' Maddie reflected that life in the Blake-Jones' household was probably not a bed of roses.

'My mother's strange reaction to you proves that she recognised you somehow. I have a feeling she went behind my father's back to keep in touch with your mother. Perhaps that's what made her so afraid?'

'She's scared of your father?'

'Oh yes. I am too sometimes.' Jane shivered.

'Poor you. That must be really tough.'

'Oh, it's not all bad. He's very strict, but as long as we do as we're told, he's fine. He spends most of his time on church matters anyway. The worst thing is that he has a terrible temper and once he makes up his mind about something, nothing will make him change it again. I've been trying for years to get my mother to divorce him, but she won't hear of it. She says it's against her beliefs, but I never bought that for a second. Something's holding her back. I wonder what happened ...'

Maddie stared out of the windscreen and sighed again. 'I don't think we'll ever know unless she chooses to tell us. And I don't feel I have the right to force her.' She chewed on an already abused fingernail. 'Actually, I came to town today with the intention of cornering her somewhere, to see if I could make her at least admit she recognised me.' She shook her head. 'I guess it was a stupid idea.'

'Maybe not. I think I would have done the same.' Jane smiled and Maddie felt an answering smile tugging at the corners of her mouth. In a way, she felt much better now that Jane had confirmed she wasn't imagining things.

'Do you want me to try and talk to my mother again?' Jane asked. 'If I say that I already know part of the story she might tell me the rest.'

'No, don't mention anything yet. I want to try and find some more information first on my own, but if that fails, then I'd be grateful for your help.'

'Okay, I'll wait until I hear from you.'

'How can I contact you?'

'Oh, er, how about if I call you every so often from a payphone, then you can let me know what you find?' Jane looked at her watch. 'Oh, gosh, I must get back.'

Maddie jotted down the phone number for Marcombe Hall and her mobile number on a scrap of paper she found in her pocket and handed it to Jane. 'Here are my numbers. I'm staying with friends at the moment and mobile reception isn't too great there. Normally I live in London.' She put the key in the ignition and started up the engine. 'I'll drive you back now.'

'Thanks. I hope we can get to the bottom of this.'

'Me too.'

Alex splashed a generous amount of paint into the tray and dipped the roller, filling it with sunny primrose yellow. As he began to apply it to the nearest wall, he felt himself relax. He was doing something useful, an honest day's work, and it felt good.

The fact that he was working for himself and not at the beck and call of anyone else, made it even better.

The first cottage he'd bought was a former fisherman's house, one of a long row down by the harbour of the nearest village. It looked tiny from the outside, but appearances were deceptive. Although the front door led straight into a living room, it was fairly spacious and he'd had a local builder knock down the connecting wall, making it open plan with the kitchen behind it. He'd also asked the man to get rid of most of the back wall and build a conservatory, leaving only a small patio garden at the back. That was okay though, Alex thought, as it would save him from having to do gardening on a regular basis. And the transformation inside the house should be stunning.

'Good call,' the builder, Pete, commented as he put the finishing touches to the arch which was now all that separated the kitchen from the living room. 'And it'll be even better once I've done the conservatory. Lots of light.'

The rooms definitely needed light, since the windows at

the front were small, if quaint. Which was why Alex had chosen primrose and white for the downstairs areas. He'd meant to ask Maddie, but after their recent altercation he'd decided to just go with his own gut instinct. Besides, surely you couldn't go wrong with such basic colours?

'Thank you, yes, I think it'll be great.' He grinned at the man, who hadn't once mentioned Alex's past, even though it was probably all over the neighbourhood that the prodigal son had returned. Alex was grateful and hoped to prove to everyone that he was a different man now.

Everyone including Maddie? He quashed that thought.

He looked around, trying to visualise the sort of furniture he'd need to buy, but instead Maddie popped into his mind again. She'd know, he thought. Women had a flair for that sort of thing. One glance and they'd decide what suited a room. *Well, perhaps not all women.* But he had a feeling that Maddie, with her artistic tendencies, would be good at interior decorating. Maybe he'd bring her down here as soon as the building work and painting was all done, despite their differences. They had to stay friends for Wes and Kayla's sake, so this might be a good way of interacting safely.

'So you're going to live here yourself then?' Pete's question brought Alex back to the present.

'What? Oh, no, I'm going to rent it out.'

'Ah.' Pete nodded knowingly. 'Thought so or you'd have had the missus in here sticking her oar in.' He shook his head. 'Mine won't even let me bang in a nail without her permission. Women, eh?'

'Er, I don't have a "missus", but I do have a friend who I might ask.' He grinned. 'Tough if she doesn't like this colour though, it's staying.' He looked at the pretty yellow which made the sunlight seem multiplied.

Pete laughed. 'You tell 'er, mate.'

There was nothing to be gained by procrastinating and Maddie set off the following morning on the long drive to Wiltshire. She'd told Annie she was going to visit a friend of her late mother's and that she would be away all day.

'All right. I'll leave you a cold supper for when you get back in case they don't feed you enough,' was Annie's only comment.

Maddie had laughed. 'I think it would do me good not to eat for a day or two. I must have put on at least five pounds since I arrived here, thanks to your excellent cooking.'

Annie beamed at the compliment. 'Get away with you,' she laughed.

The car radio was turned up and tuned in to one of the local radio stations, and thanks to the regular traffic reports Maddie was able to avoid a huge jam in the vicinity of Exeter. She followed the smaller roads east, rather than the M5, since she found motorways deadly dull. At least on the A-roads there was more to look at and towns and villages to pass through.

She made good time and after stopping at a fast food outlet in Trowbridge for a burger, she finally arrived in Shepleigh just after lunch time. It turned out to consist of more or less just one long street, which also happened to be the main road, with some fairly large houses on either side of it. There were a few little lanes leading off it, but they weren't very substantial. Maddie parked the car and made her way to the village shop, thinking it was as good a place as any to start.

Two elderly ladies were gossiping with the shopkeeper, a cheerful lady in a green apron, and Maddie walked around for a while studying the shelves. She smiled to herself as she heard the broad Wiltshire dialect of the other customers. It had a wonderful ring to it and she found it fascinating. Finally the women took themselves off, however, and Maddie reluctantly approached the lady behind the till.

'Hello there. Haven't seen you in here before,' the woman greeted her with a smile.

'No, I'm just visiting.' Maddie hesitated and gulped in a fortifying breath of air. 'Actually, I was wondering if you could help me. I'm looking for someone.'

'Oh, yes. And who might that be, then?' The woman leaned her elbows on the counter and rested her chin on her hands, gazing at Maddie with interest.

'A man by the name of John Kettering. He was a friend of my father's and the last address we have for him was here in Shepleigh. Then they lost touch.'

'Kettering?' The woman pursed her lips and looked towards the ceiling as if for inspiration. 'Can't say as it rings a bell. What did you want him for?'

'My father would so like to get back in touch with his old friend and I thought I'd surprise him by trying to find him.'

'Oh, what a lovely idea!' The woman beamed.

'Thank you. It would mean a lot to my dad.' Maddie felt bad about lying, but didn't know what else to do. *I can't tell her the truth, after all.*

'Well, the only thing I can suggest is that you talk to the vicar. He's been here forty years at least, so if anyone knows it would be him.'

'That's a brilliant idea. Where will I find him?'

'He'll either be in the church or pottering around his garden which is right next door. Red house with white painted windows, you can't miss it.'

'Thank you very much. You've been very kind.'

'Not at all.'

Maddie left the shop and had to stop and rest for a moment. Her legs were trembling and she closed her eyes to regain control. It had seemed like such a good idea to come, but now she was actually here she found it extremely difficult.

'Don't be so stupid,' she admonished herself. 'No one here would ever guess the real reason for your questions.' With renewed determination she set off in the direction of the Norman church – the square tower clearly visible some fifty yards further down the road.

As luck would have it, she passed the vicarage first and there was an old man in the garden, bending over his roses with a spray can of insecticide. Maddie cleared her throat noisily and he looked up and smiled a greeting.

'Excuse me, but are you the vicar?' she asked.

'Indeed, young lady, I am. Are you in need of my services?' He approached the fence, leaving the can on the grass by the flowers.

'Well, not exactly,' she began, and repeated the story she had told the shopkeeper.

The old man's face clouded over while she spoke and he shook his head.

'I'm terribly sorry, dear, but John Kettering is no longer with us.'

'You mean …?'

'Yes, he died two years ago. He's buried over there.' He nodded towards the cemetery.

'Oh, that's too bad.' The grief Maddie felt was genuine enough, although it wasn't for the reason the vicar would think. 'Dad so wanted to see him again,' she lied, crossing her fingers behind her back in order to somehow make it better.

The old man patted her arm. 'Don't worry, dear, they'll meet again. The good Lord will make sure of it.'

'Yes, I suppose so.' Maddie tried to think rationally. It was really bad luck that the only lead she had should end this way. She decided to try one last thing. 'Didn't Mr Kettering have a sister? I think I heard my dad mention her.'

'Yes, I believe he did, although I've not seen her for years. Didn't even come to her brother's funeral, so she might be dead herself for all I know.'

'You didn't know her?'

'Not very well, no. She came to stay with John just after he moved here. She was pregnant at the time, I believe, but after that she never visited once. I must admit I thought it very odd.'

'I see. Is there anyone here who would know where she lives?'

The vicar shook his head. 'No, I'm sorry, my dear. She kept herself to herself, if you know what I mean. Didn't make friends with anyone. And it was a long time ago, must be thirty years at least.'

Twenty-seven, she longed to shout. *It was twenty-seven years ago and she was my mother.* But of course she couldn't do that. Instead she thanked the old man for his assistance and made her way back to the shop.

'Oh, you're back. Any good?'

Maddie made a little face and smiled sadly. 'Yes, but it turns out Mr Kettering is dead.'

'Oh, dear, how sad. Never mind, you've done your best, haven't you? Can't do no more.'

'Yes, I suppose so.' Feeling depressed and dispirited, Maddie bought several bunches of flowers and returned to the cemetery. She found the grave of her uncle and arranged the bouquet in a vase she found nearby, before sinking down onto the soft grass. She buried her face in her hands and gave in to the sadness and despair which engulfed her. Sadness because she would never know her uncle now, and despair because she had come all this way for nothing.

Finally, with a whispered goodbye to John Kettering, she set off back to Devon with yet another headache and eyes that stung from tears and having to concentrate on the road.

Life was so unfair sometimes.

Chapter Eleven

There was a telephone on the landing outside Maddie's room and its shrill old-fashioned ringing woke her the next morning. When no one answered it, she stumbled out of bed and rushed out to pick up the receiver.

'Hello? Marcombe Hall.' She cleared her throat to stop her voice from sounding like John Wayne with a cold.

'Maddie, it's Jessie. I've got some news for you.' Jessie's cheerful voice grated on Maddie's ears. She had spent most of the night awake, tossing and turning, before finally falling asleep, only to be haunted by the dark nightmare once more. She felt completely exhausted.

'Well, I've got news for you too. I went to that damned village yesterday and all I found was a grave.'

'A grave? Whose grave?'

'John Kettering's. My uncle, remember?'

'Oh, well never mind. It doesn't matter.'

'What do you mean it doesn't matter? It's a bloody disaster, that's what it is!'

'Oh, shut up, Maddie. I'd forgotten what a grump you are in the morning.'

'I'm not a—'

'Listen, I went back online and checked the records for the years before your birth, and guess what I found? Ruth Kettering's marriage. She wasn't a single unmarried mother at all.'

'What? But then why didn't I have a father?'

'I don't know. I sent for the marriage certificate and it just arrived this morning. She was married in 1981 to someone called Saul Blake-Jones.'

Maddie gasped and sank slowly down onto the floor with her back against the wall. Her vision swam and her legs refused to support her. She had to grip the receiver harder as her hands began to tremble violently.

'B-Blake-Jones? That awful man? Oh, my God! No, it can't be true.' On top of her wasted journey of the previous day, it was simply too much. She felt physically sick and swallowed down the bile which threatened to choke her.

'Awful man? You know him?' Jessie sounded perplexed and Maddie told her about some of her strange experiences in Dartmouth.

'Well he might not be your father,' Jessie said. 'Perhaps they had been divorced by the time you were born. I didn't check that, but I will. Why would she put her maiden name otherwise and not name him as the father?'

'Great. This just gets better and better,' Maddie muttered. 'Shit, I've got to talk to Jane.'

'Who's Jane?'

Maddie swallowed hard. 'Blake-Jones's daughter.' She added the details about her meeting with the girl.

'Then you definitely need to talk to her. She might be able to find out more somehow.'

'Yes, you're right. I'll ask her if she knows whether her father has been married more than once and I'll call you when I have more news. And Jessie, thanks for your help. I'm sorry if I was a grouch, but this whole business is getting to me.'

'Don't worry, I understand. Let me know what happens, okay? Bye.'

For fear of missing Jane's phone call, Maddie stayed indoors all day trying to concentrate on a book. When she had read the same page five times without being able to make sense of the words, however, she gave up and went to the kitchen to do some baking.

'What do you want to do baking for in this weather?' Annie asked suspiciously. 'You should be outdoors, so you should.'

'I'm waiting for a phone call and it's very important. Sorry, I don't mean to get in your way, but I need something to do.'

'Oh very well, help yourself to whatever you need.'

Maddie had produced a batch of brownies and a sponge cake by the time the phone finally rang and driven Annie nearly to distraction by being underfoot all day. Fortunately for Annie's sanity it was Jane calling at last.

'Thank God it's you! I've been waiting all day hoping you'd call.' Maddie heaved a sigh of relief.

'Oh? What's up?'

'I need to see you. Can we meet this afternoon?'

'Well, I don't know, it's a bit difficult, but perhaps I can get away for a short while. I'll try to meet you in the car park at half past four, all right?'

'Great. I'll see you there.'

Jane was ten minutes late, and Maddie's fingernails had once again been chewed to within a hair's breadth of their lives by the time the girl slipped into the seat next to her.

'Shall we go outside town like before?' Maddie asked.

'Yes, please. I don't want anyone to see us if we can help it.'

They were both silent on the ride to the little lay-by, but once there Jane started talking in a rush. 'So what did you want to see me about? Have you found something?'

Maddie nodded. 'Tell me something first. Do you know whether your father has been married more than once?'

'No, not that I'm aware of.'

'And what's your mother's name?'

'Ruth. Why?'

Maddie took a deep breath to slow down her heartbeat, which had suddenly escalated to an almost unbearable frenzy. 'And do you know what her maiden name was?'

'Yes, of course. It was Kettering, but why do you want to know?'

Maddie drew in another deep, steadying breath. 'I'm not sure I should be telling you this, but … I think I may be at least your half-sister. Ruth was my mother too.'

Jane's mouth fell open. 'You've got to be kidding, right?'

'Nope. I just found out today that my birth mother, Ruth Kettering, married someone called Saul Blake-Jones. I thought perhaps she'd been his first wife or something. I never dreamed … I guess I should have asked you what your mother's name was last time we met, but it didn't occur to me she could be the same person.'

Jane pulled herself together. 'That explains her reaction, I suppose, and her fear. Do you have any other details?'

Maddie sighed and told Jane of her trip to Wiltshire and Jessie's findings in London. Jane was quiet while Maddie talked, but burst into speech as soon as the story was finished.

'But that's incredible! How could my mother have an illegitimate baby? And when she was already married too. I just can't believe it.'

'I know it seems strange, but unless there's another Ruth Kettering somewhere, it must be true. It's quite an unusual name.'

'Yes, it is. No, I'm sure you're right. That must be why my father called her a "sinner". I thought it was just because she had lied about her friend. But my mother …

good grief, she must have had a secret lover.' Jane shook her head and blinked. 'I'm sorry, this is quite a shock. I guess it must be for you too.' Her eyes were huge in her pale face, but she didn't look unhappy. Suddenly she giggled. 'But it's wonderful too in a way, you know. If we're really sisters I mean. I've always wanted one.'

Maddie smiled back. 'Me too. A nice one, that is, not like Olivia.' She explained to Jane about her adopted sister.

'I promise I would never behave like that,' Jane said. 'I'd love to share things with you. But what should we do now? Do you want me to confront my mother?'

'I don't know. If only we could find out what happened all those years ago without asking her. I don't want to upset her again. Even the sight of me made her cry, although how she recognised me after twenty-four years I don't understand. Unless she's seen me after the adoption? Do you think that's possible?'

'Maybe, I suppose she could have done secretly. Hmm, let me think. There must be some other people who were around at the time. Perhaps one of them would be willing to gossip. Leave it with me, I'll see what I can do. I visit a lot of old ladies on Father's behalf and they do tend to talk a lot. Some of them are pretty senile, but they can remember stuff that happened years ago quite clearly, even though they have no idea what they had for breakfast.'

'Sounds promising.'

'Okay, I'll call you if I hear anything. If not, I'd still like to see you again.' Jane seemed almost shy suddenly, and on impulse Maddie leaned over and hugged her.

'I'd like to see you too and I really hope you are my sister.' She felt a lump in her throat and resolutely swallowed it down.

Jane nodded mutely. Her eyes had become suspiciously

misty as well, and Maddie concentrated on the task of driving back to town. Perhaps she wasn't alone in the world after all. It was a comforting thought.

Although Jane called almost every day after that, she had nothing to report, but told Maddie she was still working on the old ladies.

'I think we'll have to be patient,' she said. 'Their memories are very random, but I'll keep trying and will let you know as soon as I find anything out.'

'And what about your mum and dad – they haven't mentioned it again?'

'No, although come to think of it, Father has been frowning even more than usual and glaring at my mother. That makes her very nervous. And the other day when I came out of the house, he was standing outside the church, whispering something to the organist, Mr Morris. They both stopped talking when they caught sight of me, looking kind of suspicious, if you know what I mean?'

'The organist?'

'Yes, he's my father's right-hand man, always ready to follow his lead. A horrid little man, I can't stand him. Brrr.'

Maddie could almost hear Jane shuddering. 'That bad?'

'Yes. I wonder what they were cooking up between them. Probably some punishment for a member of the congregation who's strayed. They've done that before and I'm pretty sure I heard the words "keep watching" and "accident". As I told you, my Father is very strict and he considers his flock as family, with him as their kind of father or guardian. Some of them have had, uhm, "accidents" in the past.'

'And they accept that?'

'Yes, well, mostly. Anyway, got to go. I'll be in touch.'

Jane hung up abruptly and Maddie got the feeling she was embarrassed by her father's bullying tendencies but was too scared to do anything about it. *If only there was some way I could help her ...* But Maddie didn't have the right to interfere, at least not until they had more information. And that, it seemed, would take time.

Maddie tried to keep occupied while waiting for Jane's calls and Kayla's return. She told herself she was on holiday and had to enjoy it to the full, so that was what she did.

She was just on her way out with a bag full of painting materials when the doorbell rang just after lunch a few days later. As there was no one else about, she opened the front door, and was startled to find a rather unkempt individual outside. He had a shock of hair standing on end which looked as if it hadn't been combed in years, and he was wearing a dirty T-shirt and a pair of extremely faded blue jeans. He was also chewing gum as if it was his main aim in life and looked from side to side furtively. Maddie blinked.

'Can I help you?'

'Mm-hmm, I've come to see Alex,' the man said, shoving his hands into his pockets defensively and gazing over her shoulder, his eyes opened wide in awe at the sight of the grand hall. Despite the fact that he was a very large man, Maddie had the distinct impression he wanted to turn tail and run when he saw the opulence inside.

'Oh, I see. Er, well, come in. I'll get him for you.'

'No need, I'm here.' Alex had come up behind her unnoticed and he stretched out a hand in welcome towards the stranger. 'Foster, nice to see you. So you decided to give it a try, eh?' He smiled at the big man.

'Yeah.' The man nodded. 'Nothing to lose by trying, like you said. You haven't changed your mind?'

'No, not at all. And I promise you won't regret it.' Alex turned to Maddie, who had watched this exchange with mounting curiosity. 'Maddie, this is Foster, one of my *criminal* friends. No doubt you won't want to know him either, so we'll let you be on your way.'

Maddie's mouth fell open, then she snapped it shut in anger. 'Now look here, Alex, I never—'

'Later, Maddie. I have to talk to Foster.' And without another glance, Alex led his friend into the office and shut the door. Maddie was left fuming.

'Ohh, annoying man!' She picked up her bag and stomped to the front door, slamming it shut behind her as she left the house. There was nothing for it, she would have to have a talk with him, otherwise there was no way they could keep up a friendly façade in front of Wes and Kayla when they returned. She kicked a rock out of her way and regretted it instantly as it hurt her toe. 'Damn it all,' she muttered. Why did men always have to be so complicated?

The breathtaking views along the coast soon soothed her ruffled feathers slightly, however, and she determined to put Alex out of her mind for a while. The urge to paint had been strong today and she wouldn't let anything interfere with it. Since arriving at Marcombe Hall, she had sketched continuously, and today she felt ready to tackle watercolour painting. She'd been considered quite good at it when she was at school, but had only ever pursued it as a hobby.

'There's no future in painting, sweetheart,' her father had told her. 'You get yourself a real job and then you can dabble to your heart's content in your spare time, eh?'

It had seemed like sensible advice and Maddie had

followed it without hesitation. Now she wasn't so sure she'd done the right thing. Perhaps with further training she could have made a career out of painting, even if she would never attain the heights of a Picasso or Monet. It would have been infinitely more rewarding than slaving over a keyboard eight hours a day, at the beck and call of a string of different bosses, she was sure.

She set up her easel in a promising spot close to the edge of the cliffs, and arranged her painting materials on the ground next to her. A small folding stool served as a chair, and as always she soon lost herself in the joys of creativity. There was immense satisfaction for her in watching the scene in front of her take shape on her paper and she delighted in choosing the right colour combinations for each particular subject. Time stood still up here on the cliffs, where sounds seemed muted by the wind and the sea.

The painting session was finally brought to a halt by the fading light, late in the afternoon, and Maddie stood up to stretch and relieve the kink in her back. The painting was finished, and she gazed at it with pride. *It may not be the best watercolour ever done, but I like it.* She smiled to herself. It had turned out exactly the way she wanted it to and she was pleased to discover she hadn't lost the knack.

Slowly, she gathered up her belongings and stuffed everything into the bag, ready to take home, but she was reluctant to go back to the Hall just yet and decided to take a longer route back. The path forked not far from where she'd been sitting and she chose the left hand one instead of the usual. This took her up a small hill and into a forested area carpeted with leaves. As she headed in among the trees, the sounds of the wind and sea faded into the background and were replaced by birdsong instead. She took a deep breath and savoured the peace.

Maddie was in no hurry and followed the meandering track deep in thought. She stopped several times to look at flowers that grew along the way, planning further paintings as these would make lovely subjects. She spotted something out of the corner of her eye, but it turned out to be a rabbit scurrying for cover. The sight made her smile.

She looked down and noticed that one of her Roman style sandals was coming undone. As she bent down to retie the fastening, she heard a slight crunching noise behind her and then a whoosh.

Before she had time to turn around, something hit the back of her head very hard and everything turned black.

Maddie woke with a splitting headache and hesitated to open her eyes. She knew the light would be painful, but on the other hand, she needed to know what had happened. Steeling herself, she lifted her eyelids up a fraction, then blinked them open wide. To her surprise, she was in semi-darkness.

'What the ...?' she muttered and tried to sit up. *Is it night time already?*

Her hands gripped the ground around her, expecting the dry leaves of the woodland path, but instead they encountered cold, hard stone. Maddie blinked again and looked more closely at her surroundings. She was surrounded by stone on all sides and when she raised her head she spotted fading daylight high above her head. A hole? *No, a mine shaft!*

She remembered Kayla mentioning that there had once been tin mines nearby but the shafts were now mostly covered up. If that was where she was, this one didn't seem to be. But neither did it have a ladder or any other means of scaling the walls. *How the hell did I get here?*

Taking a deep breath, she managed to get to her feet and searched all around for some kind of footholds, but there was nothing. Her head and one wrist hurt, so had she been thrown into this pit? Or perhaps someone had deliberately put her down here and then removed the ladder or whatever they'd used to get down to the bottom.

Had she been left here to die? The thought made her shudder.

Panic surged through her and for a moment she struggled for breath. *No, this can't be happening.* Trying to get a grip on her emotions, she looked around her one more time. Nothing.

Who would do this to me?

Darting another look upwards, ice cold fingers gripped her stomach and squeezed as her brain grappled with the thought that someone had deliberately done this. Someone who wanted her to die. And that person hadn't even given her a chance to fight back, which she could have done. She'd been doing kick-boxing in London, mostly for fitness reasons, but also with a view to learning some self-defence. When someone just hit you over the head though, what chance did you stand?

'Hey! Is there anyone there? *Hello!*' She tried shouting for a bit, but there was no reply.

Whoever it was had obviously left. And why not? No one would ever find her here. Wherever here was. She sat down and huddled close to the rock wall. A pain shot up her arm, and she lifted her hand to inspect the wrist. It didn't appear to be broken, but she thought it might be sprained. Perhaps she'd landed on it when she was hit on the head? It hurt like hell and she swore out loud, just because it made her feel better. The cursing ended on a sob, and she burst into tears of relief that she was still alive, although for how long? How on earth was she going to get out of here? And even if she did, would it be safe or was someone waiting to finish her off? A violent shudder racked her body.

'Oh my God! What am I going to do?'

Sitting with her back towards the wall, she hugged her knees and tried to think. But there was no answer and she would just have to hope that someone realised she hadn't returned and came looking for her. With a sinking feeling, she knew that might be too late. *No, that's defeatist thinking. Get a grip!* She prayed that Alex would miss her at dinner time, although with his new friend there perhaps he wouldn't notice. He might not even be at home for dinner. Or he might think she was sulking. *Shit!* Her only hope was Annie.

'Oh, please, God, let someone come looking for me. Please?' she prayed.

But she didn't know if He was listening.

Chapter Twelve

Jane looked up as her father came into the dining room. He was twenty minutes late and the two women had been sitting in silence waiting for his arrival while the food rapidly congealed in the serving dishes. Jane had heard him on the phone about an hour earlier and whatever information he was given had made him leave immediately, taking the car and heading off at great speed. She felt uneasy, her nerve endings on full alert. Where had he been?

The Reverend Blake-Jones seated himself at the head of the table as usual, looking pleased with himself, and bent his head to say grace. The others joined in the 'Amen' at the end, before passing him the dishes one by one. He helped himself without a word, and Jane braced herself for the inevitable outburst which was sure to come when he discovered the food had gone cold. Nothing happened.

Jane stared at her father and watched him eat with every sign of enjoyment. She glanced at her mother, but Ruth was too sunk in misery to notice anything around her. For the last few days she had uttered nothing but monosyllables to her daughter and her husband, and appeared to have retreated into a world of her own. Jane had given up trying to communicate with her and had begun to fear for her sanity.

Just as Jane raised the first forkful of food to her mouth, her father's voice boomed out across the table.

'It's over, Ruth. The problem is solved.' Jane jumped and dropped the food back onto her plate. Her mother's eyes turned slowly towards her husband and widened in horror. Then she too dropped her fork and it clattered to the floor. She covered her mouth with her hand to muffle the scream which came out and fled from the table, upsetting her chair in her haste to leave the room. Jane stared after her with a sensation of dread building in the pit of her stomach.

'What did you say, Father?' she ventured finally.

'Nothing you need concern yourself about,' he replied through a mouthful of food. 'Your mother is having one of her fits, that's all. She'll be fine by tomorrow.'

'But—'

He banged his fist on the table with such force that all the china jumped, and Jane gasped. 'Are you questioning my word?' he bawled, fixing her with his dark eyes.

Jane shook her head and picked up her fork. Slowly she started to eat, although the food might as well have been sand. She knew that if she didn't eat, however, he would take exception to that as well, and worse would follow. She'd rather eat dirt.

'Good,' she heard him mutter and prayed that he wouldn't take any further notice of her. As soon as she could, she would flee to the sanctuary of her room.

'Maddie! *Maddiiieee!*'

Maddie woke up with a start and rubbed her eyes with her knuckles. She thought she'd heard her name, but perhaps it had only been a dream.

'*Maddie!*'

No, there it was again. Standing up, she swayed slightly and shivered in the darkness. 'Here! I'm down here!' she hollered for all she was worth. The sound echoed round the mine shaft and she wondered if it could be heard up above. She almost wept with frustration when there was no reply. How was she going to make herself heard?

She shouted again but nothing happened. The other voice seemed to have gone. In despair she slumped down again. Hunger gnawed at her insides, and she was terribly thirsty. Her wrist was throbbing and her head hurt. *This is just hopeless ...*

'Maddie!' The voice startled her and she looked up towards the edge of the shaft. The sky was a lighter patch in the darkness and she saw torchlight flashing above. Soon after, she could just about make out a person leaning over precariously.

'Here,' she yelled. 'I'm down here!'

'Bloody hell! Are you hurt?' It was Alex, and Maddie thought she had never heard anything more wonderful than his voice in her entire life.

'Not much, just a sprained wrist, but I can't get out.'

'Hold on, I'll get help. Will you be okay for just a bit longer? I have to find a rope.'

'Yes. Yes, I'll be fine. Please hurry.'

'I will. Hang in there.'

He disappeared, and the waiting started again. Now, however, she had hope and the time seemed to pass much faster. Before she knew it, Alex's face appeared at the top again, and a rope was lowered down.

'Can you put that around your waist and try to put your feet against the rock?' he shouted. 'We'll pull from up here at the same time.'

'All right.' With shaking fingers she picked up the rope and tied it round her waist, pulling the knot as tight as she could with one hand. Then she braced her feet against the mine shaft wall and grabbed the rope with both hands, wincing as pain sliced through her left arm. 'I'm ready,' she called. The rope tightened, and she felt herself being slowly hauled upwards.

To help her rescuers she walked her feet up the rock face. She stared into the darkness of the stone in front of her, determined not to look up or down. After what felt like eons, she reached the top, where strong hands helped her over the edge. Exhausted, she collapsed onto the ground, trembling uncontrollably.

'Maddie, are you okay?' She was turned over onto her back by Alex, and someone else shone a light over her. She brought up one hand to shield her eyes and saw that the torch was held by Foster, Alex's strange friend.

'Y-yes. I am now,' she stammered through teeth that were chattering with delayed shock.

'We must get you to a doctor. Here, let me carry you.' Alex bent to pick her up, but she held up a hand in protest.

'No, no, you'll break your back. I'm too heavy. Just hang on a minute and I'll be able to walk. My legs feel like jellyfish at the moment, but I'm sure they'll be fine soon.'

Alex grinned at her and put out a hand to stroke her cheek. 'I'm glad you're okay,' he said. 'You had us really worried there for a while. What on earth possessed you to go wandering round these woods? Don't you know it's dangerous? There are mine shafts everywhere and although they're supposed to be signposted, you can't see that in the dark.'

'Of course I know that and I didn't come here on purpose. Plus it wasn't dark at that time.'

'Then how did you fall? Weren't you looking where you were going?'

'Yes, but I was nowhere near this hold. I was walking along the forest track and someone hit me over the head from behind with something. Next thing I knew, I was lying at the bottom of that pit.'

'What?' Alex and Foster exclaimed in unison and stared at her in dawning horror.

'You're not serious? Who?' Alex clenched his fists.

'Yeah, who'd want to go and bash a nice lady like you over the head?' Foster looked completely baffled before scanning the surrounding area as if he expected the attacker to try his luck with him next. 'Did he attack you first, like, you know ...?' He trailed off, obviously embarrassed at the direction of his thoughts.

Maddie shook her head. 'No, no one attacked me. One minute I was bending down to fix my shoe and the next minute everything went black. I didn't even see whoever it was.'

Alex scowled. 'We'll have to tell the police.' It was Foster's turn to shiver, then he appeared to remember that he hadn't done anything wrong and relaxed.

'Oh, yeah,' he said. 'Can't have mad people like that running about the countryside.'

'How did you know where to find me?' Maddie asked. 'Did Annie miss me at dinner?'

Alex looked slightly abashed. 'No, actually, no one missed you. I ... er, was with Foster down the pub and Annie had gone home early. She left us a cold dinner. It must have been a couple of hours later when a friend of yours rang. Someone called Jane.'

'Oh?'

'Yes, she asked if you were at home and when I said I hadn't seen you since lunchtime she got very agitated. She told me to go out and look for you and she wouldn't take no for an answer.'

'I see.' Maddie sat up and brushed some grass off her shorts. 'Did she say why?"

'No, she just said it was urgent. Is she psychic or something?'

Maddie smiled. 'No, I don't think so. I, um, guess she was just concerned about me. I forgot she was going to call tonight.'

Alex gave her a strange look, but said nothing more, and soon after they began the walk home. Maddie leaned on Alex and Foster brought up the rear carrying her belongings.

'We found these over near the edge of the forest.'

'Well, that's not where I left them, but I'm glad my stuff wasn't stolen at least.'

Alex insisted on taking her to the nearest emergency room for a check-up, but there was nothing wrong with her apart from the sprained wrist, which was quickly bandaged, and a lump on the back of her head.

'You should probably rest for a couple of days and if you feel any nausea at all, let us know. It could be you have a slight concussion,' the doctor told them.

'Thanks, I'll take it easy.' The painkillers they gave her helped and Maddie didn't feel sick so she thought a good night's sleep might be enough.

'Can you face dealing with the police tonight, or shall we wait until tomorrow?' Alex asked as they reached the car.

'No, please, let's not say anything, Alex.'

'Why? There's a potential murderer on the loose out there and you don't want to tell the police? Are you crazy?'

'It's complicated, Alex, but I need to speak to Jane first. Please, trust me on this.'

'What's this Jane got to do with anything?'

'I can't tell you right now. Please, Alex, let me handle this my own way.' Maddie felt very strongly that this was all connected to her adoption somehow, and she wanted to get to the bottom of that before she took any action. She knew it was illogical, but she'd feel embarrassed voicing suspicions that might be completely wrong, especially if they involved her new-found sister. And she wanted to know what Jane had to say first. It could be important.

'Very well, but I don't like it. Will you at least tell one of us where you're going if you go out?'

'Yes, I promise.'

The rest of the journey was completed in silence.

Early the next morning Alex went to find Foster, who was temporarily camping out in another of the holiday cottages Alex had bought. He'd asked his friend to help him with the work and Foster had been only too pleased to agree.

'You don't mind painting and decorating?' Alex had asked, and Foster laughed.

'Nah, at least it's honest money, even if it's not the most exciting job in the world.'

This morning, however, he had another job for the young man.

'Foster, I'd like you to follow Maddie around, but without her seeing you. Could you do that, do you think?'

'Sure. Easiest thing in the world. Why? You think that psycho's gonna try and kill her again?'

'I don't know, but I would feel safer if I knew you were keeping an eye on her. I haven't got time to do it myself and besides, she'd be sure to see me and get angry.'

'No problem, you leave it to me.' Foster grinned. 'You like her a lot, huh?'

Alex smiled sheepishly. 'It shows, does it?'

'Yeah, a mile off.'

'Yes, well, unfortunately for me, she doesn't feel the same way.' He shrugged. 'That's life, eh?'

'She probably just wants to play hard to get for a while,' Foster said. 'Women are like that. Weird creatures.'

Alex laughed. If only it were that easy. 'Hard to get' he could overcome. Blatant contempt, no. 'We'll see,' was all he replied. 'Start this morning, would you please?'

'Sure thing.'

'Maddie, are you all right?' Jane sounded tearful on the other end of the phone, and Maddie felt her throat constrict. Someone really cared. *My little sister.*

'Yes, I'm fine. Thanks for making Alex go out looking for me yesterday. If you hadn't told him to, I would still be stuck down a mine shaft.'

'A mine shaft? Oh no ... What happened?'

Maddie told her and when she had finished there was complete silence. 'Jane? Are you still there?'

'Yes, I'm here.' The voice was nothing more than a whisper.

'How did you know I was in trouble?'

'Oh, it was just a hunch.' Jane gave a brittle little laugh. 'Sisterly intuition perhaps?'

'Really? It wasn't something, er ... more concrete?'

'No, no.' Jane sounded suspiciously airy and Maddie could tell she was holding something back.

'Are you sure?'

'Yes, of course. I'm just so glad you're alive. You will be careful from now on, won't you?'

Maddie was even more convinced Jane was covering up for her father and wondered if he'd threatened her too somehow? She'd said he had a hold over her mother – did he have one over Jane as well? Either way, Jane obviously wasn't going to tell Maddie anything else at the moment so she gave up on this line of questioning. 'Don't worry. I'm not going anywhere alone for quite some time, believe me. Have you made any progress with the other thing we discussed?'

'What? Oh that. No, but as a matter of fact I'm going to see someone this afternoon who might be able to help. I'll try to call you this evening if I can.'

'Where are you calling from now? You sound a bit far away.'

'I'm in a phone box in town, but if my father goes out this evening I'll be able to call from home. If not, I'll try tomorrow.'

'Okay. Thanks so much for doing this, Jane. Bye.'

After she had hung up, Maddie went to lie down on top of her bed. She was still a bit shaky and there was a dull ache throbbing in her arm. The doctor had told her she might have nightmares or suffer a delayed reaction to the shock. He'd given her some tranquillisers, but she preferred not to take them. She decided rest would be a better option.

There was a knock on the door and she called, 'Come in.'

Alex popped his head round the door. 'Am I disturbing you?'

'No, not at all. I'm just resting. My wrist is a bit painful. And my head.'

'You were lucky it wasn't broken.' He came into the room and shut the door behind him. Slowly he approached the bed and perched at the end of it.

'Yes. Lucky it was my left one too. At least I can still paint.'

He was silent for a while, staring out the window, then he drew in a deep breath. 'Maddie, have you remembered anything more about your assailant?'

'No. I never saw whoever it was. I just heard a rustling noise, that was all.'

'Have you any idea who it might be? I mean, is there anyone who would wish you harm?'

Maddie looked away. 'Not that I know of. I'm sure it was just some looney who couldn't resist. I must have looked tempting bending over like that and the fact that I was all alone in the woods.' She turned back to Alex and saw him smile and shake his head. 'What?'

'It's just that I could understand it if someone walked past and found you tempting, but not in the sense that they would want to hit you on the head,' he said, then added, 'Sorry, I know you don't want to hear stuff like that from me.' He shrugged.

'Oh.' Maddie could feel the heat of a blush creeping across her cheeks.

'God though, Maddie, women are attacked all the time these days, whenever they're caught anywhere alone, but it doesn't make sense to knock you out and then put you down a mine shaft. It must have taken quite a lot of strength to even get you there, and what would be the point? I mean, he should have tried to … first … oh, hell. Maybe he meant to come back.' He rubbed his forehead with the palm of his hand.

'I know what you mean and I agree. It doesn't make sense, unless it was someone who's deranged. But that is what happened.'

'Are you sure you don't want to tell the police about this?'

'Not yet, no.' She held up her hand. 'And before you ask, I have my reasons, okay? Besides, what good would it do? They wouldn't have anything to go by.'

'Someone might have seen something, or there might be clues on the ground or in that pit. The forensic people do a great job these days.'

'No, I didn't see a single person the whole afternoon. No one goes up that way except us. It's Marcombe land.

Private, isn't it? Leave it, Alex. I'll be careful from now on.'

He stood up and came over to take her hand. 'Make sure you are. Kayla would never forgive me if I lost you while she was gone.' But the look he gave her said something entirely different. It told her he was the one who didn't want to lose her and that confused her no end. Did he really care that much?

She spent the rest of the afternoon pondering this question, but didn't reach any satisfactory conclusion.

Chapter Thirteen

'I'm going to Dartmouth this morning, but I should be back by lunchtime.'

Maddie sent Alex a challenging look across the breakfast table, as if to say 'I can take care of myself.' But could she? He wasn't sure.

Perhaps she'd be safe in the anonymity of a crowd, but if there really was someone stalking her, that person could still follow. And if Maddie was ever alone anywhere, he or she could strike again … It didn't bear thinking of.

God, we're not talking about a prank here! Whoever had hurt Maddie and put her in that pit had surely intended her to die. Or at least to suffer, stuck down there without food or water. There was no way she could have climbed out, even with a wrist that wasn't sprained. It was pure luck that he and Foster had gone that way to look for her. The place they'd found her painting materials had indicated she'd gone the other way and her assailant had obviously put her bag there to mislead them. It was sheer chance that had made Alex take the other way home, just in case.

He bent his head so Maddie wouldn't see the worry that must be clear in his eyes. Damn it. He couldn't lock her up inside, that would just be stupid.

'I saw danger, evil stalking her', Romar had said. Alex suppressed a shiver of foreboding as the gypsy's words suddenly came back to him. Perhaps she'd just meant Maddie being bashed on the head and that was all. But supposing it was just the beginning? Maybe he should go with her? He could come up with some excuse as to

why he needed to go to Dartmouth as well. But she'd see through that, he was sure.

No, he'd just have to tell Foster to pay extra attention so Maddie didn't give him the slip. He trusted his friend. It would have to be enough.

Maddie set off, excitement mingling with dread inside her. Jane had called at last and asked to meet her. They'd arranged for Maddie to pick Jane up on the outskirts of town as before and she couldn't wait to hear what the girl had to say. Had she found the answer at last?

Jane was waiting patiently in a bus shelter by the side of the road, almost completely hidden from view. Maddie stopped the car to let her jump in, and drove off as quickly as possible. Jane scanned the road behind them, but there were no other cars or people in sight and she heaved a sigh of relief.

'Thank God, I don't think anyone saw me. I told Mother I was going to see a friend,' she said. 'Thanks for coming so quickly.'

'Wild horses couldn't have kept me away. You sounded like you'd found something out.'

'I did. At least, I think I did. Try and find somewhere to park and I'll tell you.'

They turned into a small side road and soon found a quiet place to stop. Maddie switched off the engine and turned to Jane with ill-concealed impatience.

'So? What did you find?'

'Well, I went to see Mrs Graham, like I told you. She's in her seventies, and boy can she talk. I think she's the worst gossip in town. Anyway, most of the time she just goes on and on about people I've never heard of and I nod and say "um-hmm" every once in a while. But yesterday I decided to do a little probing and I said to her that there was so much gossip around and most of it was never true anyway. You hear the strangest things, I told her, and said that I'd heard the funniest thing about my mother the other day, which couldn't possibly be right.'

'Go on.'

'I could see Mrs Graham prick up her ears immediately. She's always very interested in any new information. She asked what I'd heard, so I told her a senile old lady had said my mother had had another baby before me. I pretended I thought it was a joke and laughed at the whole thing, but Mrs Graham went very quiet. "What's the matter?" I asked her, and for a moment there I thought she wasn't going to tell me. Then the urge to pass on a really juicy bit of gossip overcame her and she whispered to me that she thought it was true.'

'No, really?'

'Yes. Of course I acted all horrified and that pleased her no end. She likes to be the first with any news and if she manages to shock someone, so much the better. Then she said there'd been a rumour going around that my mother had had an affair with someone and become pregnant. Of course my father had tried to squash any such gossip, but the fact was my mother had gone away for quite a while, apparently to visit her relatives. When she came back she was a changed woman. And my father's sermons grew much more severe, after that. Pure fire and brimstone, she said.'

'And when did all this take place?'

'Mrs Graham said it was twenty-seven years ago. She was dead certain, because that was the year her oldest grandchild was born and he's twenty-seven next month.'

They stared at each other. 'Oh, Jane,' Maddie managed

at last. 'I suppose if we don't have the same father that explains a lot. But why on earth didn't she leave yours and stay with mine?'

'I wondered the same thing and I think I know why.'

'You do?'

'Yes. My father would have killed her rather than let her go.'

Jane's words echoed round Maddie's head on the way back to Dartmouth, and after she'd let Jane off at the bus stop, she continued automatically to the car park. She didn't really need to do any shopping, but she had to do something. Anything to take her mind off the recent happenings and revelations. Window gazing would do in the absence of anything else.

Walking slowly along the row of shops and boutiques, she stopped now and then to finger an item or admire some piece of clothing. An hour later, the intense heat drove her into the newsagents and she bought an ice cold drink. It was heaven.

She drank thirstily, then lowered the bottle and headed for the door. Halfway there she stopped, petrified into immobility by the sight of the Reverend Saul Blake-Jones who looked so much like the dark man in her dreams. He stopped by the door, as frozen as herself for a moment. His face showed surprise, then instant rage, and he fixed her with the most evil glare she had ever received. It was pure hatred and it was definitely directed at her.

The black eyes burned into hers, scorching her very soul, then after one last look of distaste he turned and left without making a purchase. Maddie found that her legs were shaking and she must have turned pale because someone asked if she was all right.

'Yes. Yes, I'm fine, thanks. Just the heat.' She stumbled towards the door and out into the fresh air. Leaning against the wall, she drew in deep gulps of air, trying to stem the rising tide of panic which threatened to overcome her. Snatches of her dream came back to haunt her and she was almost certain it was the same man. The Reverend Blake-Jones. The man who hated her. Had she met him when she was a child? She must have done. There could be no doubt about it. And a look like that would have stayed with any child, she was sure. No wonder he figured in her nightmares.

Maddie rapidly came to the conclusion that old Mrs Graham must have been right and the reason for the man's deep feelings of aversion towards her was his wife's infidelity. As a man of God, he clearly had stronger views on the subject than most people, but were they strong enough for him to want her dead?

Enough to murder me?

She'd been afraid at first that it was Ruth, her mother, who had been her attacker, which was another reason for her reluctance to take the matter to the police initially. But when Alex said whoever it was would have had to be very strong to carry her down into the mine shaft, she'd realised it couldn't be a woman. Now she was sure the perpetrator had been Ruth's husband. It had to be. His surprise at seeing her just then had been genuine and the anger which swiftly followed was understandable if he thought he'd killed her or trapped her in the pit, but found out he had failed.

'Dear God, what do I do now?' she muttered. What could she do? She had no proof, none whatsoever, except for her own intuition. She couldn't even prove that she was Mrs Blake-Jones's daughter since her birth mother seemed terrified of the very sight of her. Although she supposed the police could order a blood test. Did she really want to ruin her birth mother's life though? Because she was sure that if any of this came out into the open, Ruth Blake-Jones would suffer severe consequences. Her husband might divorce her, or worse, just make her life hell. His congregation would shun her as a sinner. And Blake-Jones himself might get off scot free. No doubt he'd claim *he* hadn't done anything wrong.

There was nothing for it. She would just have to be on her guard until Kayla returned and then she had to pack her bags and escape from Devon for good. Perhaps even from England. She couldn't stay. There must be somewhere in the world where she'd be safe from the Reverend Blake-Jones

She intended to find that haven.

The front door to the vicarage slammed shut with a resounding crash which reverberated round all the rooms. Jane and her mother were sitting at the kitchen table, enjoying a cup of tea and they both looked up to stare at each other in dawning horror.

'Oh, no. Please God, no ...' Ruth whispered. Jane could hear her mother's voice trembling and felt the fear build up inside herself. Taking a deep breath, she attempted to remain calm, but only succeeded on the outside. Inside she was terrified.

'Shhh,' she whispered back. 'Stay quiet.'

But it was no use, she knew that. When her father was in one of his black moods, he needed a scapegoat, and it was always one or other of the same two people. He came storming into the kitchen, with a face like an enraged tiger, and hauled the petrified Ruth out of her chair. Before she had time to utter a single word, he began to shake her as if she weighed nothing at all.

'It. Didn't. Work!' he roared. 'The spawn of Satan is still alive!' His eyes glittered strangely and he appeared to be in the grip of insanity.

Jane choked back a gasp and turned her face away. She was sure she knew who he was referring to and it made her both sad and furious that she'd been right in her assumptions. Thank the good Lord her sister was all right.

'Wh-wha-at are y-you t-talk-ing ab-bout?' Ruth managed to ask between rattling teeth. Her husband continued to shake her, then slammed her into the nearest cupboard.

'Your sins, you whore,' he spat at her. 'They have come back to haunt us, as I knew they would. I never should have listened to your begging. It should have ended then and there, as I said. Then none of this would be happening. Jezebel!' He backhanded Ruth across the cheek and with a moan she slid down to the floor. Jane knew it was time to intervene and steeled herself.

I can stand it for Mother's sake. Aloud she said, 'Father, for the love of God …'

He turned on her, as she had known he would. She'd learned that she could always deflect his anger towards herself and thereby spare her mother some of the punishment. 'Do you dare to take the Lord's name in vain in this house?' In two strides he was by her side and it was her turn to be backhanded. Gritting her teeth she glared at him defiantly and turned the other cheek.

On a good day, this trick would sometimes work to remind him of his position as a minister. However, on a bad day it only fuelled his anger further. Today was a bad day. A very bad day.

During the next ten minutes a battle was fought out in the kitchen of the vicarage such as had never been seen there before. At first Jane fought her father alone, gripped by a fury almost equal to that of his.

'I'm not putting up with this any longer, do you hear me,' she hissed. 'This is the last time. I'm going to the police. I'm going to see that you're put in jail or the madhouse where you belong. You bastard! Mother, for God's sake, fight back. Together we can do it,' she shouted.

When her words finally penetrated her mother's stunned brain, Ruth rallied to help her daughter. Jane had often felt sure the two of them together could fight him off if they joined forces, but she had forgotten her mother's frailty. Ruth was knocked out by a couple of well-placed fists and only Jane remained. It was a fight she couldn't possibly win and in the end she had to admit defeat. She feigned a faint in order to stop the beating and slid to the floor at her father's feet, blood streaming from her nose onto the kitchen floor.

He stood for a moment looking down at her, breathing heavily. She stayed motionless in the hope that he would go away, and when she reached the point where she knew she'd scream if he didn't leave soon, he finally left the room with an oath. Jane breathed a ragged sigh of relief when she heard the front door bang once more.

Blessed silence.

She didn't know how long she lay there, but when she noticed that her mother wasn't moving she roused herself enough to call for an ambulance. It arrived quickly and she and her mother were taken to the emergency department of the hospital. Jane was led into a small cubicle, where she was soon joined by a young doctor. He looked her over with grim determination.

'What happened, Miss Blake-Jones? Who did this to you and your mother?'

'My father,' she whispered through broken lips. 'Is-is my mother g-going to be okay?'

'Yes, she'll be fine. I think she has concussion, but there is nothing broken except maybe a tooth or two. Tell me, how long has this been going on?'

'Oh, years.' Jane shrugged. 'I really don't know. Since before I was born, I should think.'

'Good grief! Why have you never said anything? You should have gone to the police or the social services.'

'I couldn't. Mother wouldn't let me. She's afraid he'll kill her.' Jane felt tears start to run down her cheeks. 'I'm not so sure she isn't right.'

The doctor looked grave. 'This sort of thing makes me so angry,' he muttered. 'Let's have a look at you.'

Jane had two broken ribs and a broken finger, as well as innumerable cuts and bruises, but as she lay in her hospital bed later that afternoon she vowed that it was for the last time. Never again would she let this happen to either herself or her mother. It was time to escape.

Chapter Fourteen

Maddie came slowly into the ward the next morning bearing two small bunches of flowers, peering into the various beds to find the right one. She found Jane in the far corner, next to a window, sitting propped up by a mountain of pillows. She drew in a hissing breath and felt tears gather in her eyes.

'Oh Jane, I didn't realise quite how bad ...'

Jane attempted to smile, but it was a rather lopsided effort, and Maddie sat down on the side of the bed and gave her a cautious hug. There seemed to be bandages and bruises everywhere and she was afraid to hurt Jane even further.

Her sister had called earlier that day to tell her what had happened, but she'd only given her the bare bones. Maddie hadn't grasped the full extent of the attack. 'And your mother? Is she the same?'

'No, actually I think she looks marginally better than me. She had the sense to pass out long before I did.' Jane attempted another smile. 'I made the mistake of fighting back you see.'

'Oh, Jane.' The feeble attempt at a joke tore at Maddie's heart. Jane was being very brave and it made Maddie even more furious with the man who had done this to her. She clenched her fists. He had to be punished. 'Have you told the police?'

'Yes. A constable came to take down my statement after I spoke to you. They're going to arrest my father.'

'Thank God for that. At least you'll be safe for a while, but you must get away. You can't stay here.'

'I know. I was hoping you might be able to help us. Do you know anywhere we could stay in London, just until we decide what to do?'

'You can stay at my place. I'm sure my flat mate wouldn't mind. My bedroom is big enough for two. You should be all right there for a while.'

'You're sure that would be okay?'

'Yes, of course. I'm happy to help you any way I can. Do you have any money, though?'

'A little. I've been saving for this for a while. It will last until I can find a job.'

'Good. Don't hesitate to ask if you need any more. I'm not rich, but I have some savings.'

'Thanks, Maddie.'

The two girls embraced once more, then Jane said, 'I think we should visit Mother now. We have to face her together.'

'Are you sure? I mean, she's been through a lot. The shock of seeing us together might be too much for her.' Maddie was unaccountably afraid of coming face to face with the woman who she now knew to be her birth mother. She didn't think she could bear another rejection. 'Remember how she reacted last time.'

Jane squeezed her hand. 'It'll be all right. You'll see. Trust me.'

Maddie closed her eyes and took a deep breath. 'Okay, let's do it before I chicken out.'

She helped Jane out of the bed and they made their way towards a private room further down the corridor. 'The doctor thought it best for her to be alone,' Jane whispered before knocking on the door.

'Come in.' The voice was feeble, but clear.

The two girls entered.

'Hello, Mother.' Jane shuffled in first with an attempted smile and her mother smiled back as far as her swollen cheek would let her. Then the smile faded abruptly as she caught sight of Maddie. She turned to Jane, confusion written all over her face.

'Jane? Wha-what's going on? Who, I mean, why ...'

'Shhh, calm yourself, Mother. This is Maddie, who's come to visit us, and I think you know who she is.' When Ruth simply stared at Maddie and said nothing, Jane prompted her, 'Don't you?'

Ruth put up a hand to cover her mouth and large tears welled out of her eyes. She shook her head and struggled to say something, but no sound emerged. Only sobs.

The disappointment and sadness hit Maddie with the force of an anvil. 'I told you, Jane,' she said. 'I knew it would be too much. I shouldn't have come. I'm so sorry.'

'Yes, you should.' The vehemence in Jane's voice made Ruth jump and she stopped in mid-sob to stare once more from one girl to the other.

'No, I'll leave you now. Call me tomorrow and I'll give you that address.' She fumbled in her purse and fished out a key ring. 'Here are the keys to my flat.' She gave Jane a quick hug and headed for the door. She couldn't stand to stay another second.

'Nooo! No, don't go, please.'

Maddie stopped and glanced over her shoulder and was astonished to see Ruth holding out her hands towards her. As if in a dream, she turned around and retraced her steps.

'You want me to stay?'

Ruth nodded and patted the bed next to her. 'If-if you can bear it.'

'Bear it? What do you mean?' Maddie sank onto the edge of the bed, totally puzzled.

'I let them take you,' Ruth was wracked once more with sobs. 'Ca-can you ever f-forgive me?'

Maddie suddenly understood. Smiling, she took Ruth's hands into her own and squeezed them. 'Yes, I think so, but you're going to have to explain. You really are my mother?' Ruth nodded. 'Well, I'm sure you had a good reason for having me adopted, but ...' Maddie hesitated. Maybe now was not a good time to ask. 'Perhaps you'd like to tell us about it some other time.'

Ruth nodded once more. 'I will, I promise, but it's a long story ... May I hold you? Just once?' she whispered. Maddie went willingly into the open arms, and suddenly she felt whole again. It was a wonderful feeling and she closed her eyes to savour it to the full.

'My own dear little Sorcha,' Ruth sobbed. Maddie remembered that Sorcha was the name she'd been given originally. She felt tears start in her own eyes and when Jane hugged the two of them from the other side of the bed, they all began to cry together. But they were tears of joy. Maddie thought she had never been so happy in her life.

'The police haven't been able to find him.'

The two girls were standing on the railway platform and Jane was holding Maddie's hands. There was a sad expression on her face. 'He must have gone into hiding as soon as he realised that Mother and I had been taken to hospital.' A train thundered by on a different track.

'Yes, I'm sure you're right.' The familiar sensation of dread was lurking at the back of Maddie's mind, but she banished it for now. There would be time enough to think about it later. For the moment she had to say goodbye to her newly discovered mother and sister.

Under police protection, the two women had returned

to their home and packed up their belongings. Anything which couldn't be carried had been sent to temporary storage and everything had been arranged for their journey to London. Ruth agreed to all the girls' suggestions without fuss. It seemed as if she was still in a daze, not quite able to comprehend what was happening to her, and the doctor had told Jane and Maddie that it was probably for the best.

'You will be careful, won't you?' Jane hugged Maddie fiercely and the hug was returned in equal measure.

'Of course. You too. He just might follow you, you know. Don't let M-Mother go anywhere on her own, will you?' Maddie stumbled slightly over the unfamiliar word 'mother', but she enjoyed saying it. She had always called her adopted mother 'mummy', so in some way it seemed fitting to call her real mother something different.

'I promise. Take care now.'

Maddie embraced her mother, who patted her on the cheek and whispered, 'Darling Sorcha, thank you for your help. We'll see you soon.'

Maddie smiled. Her mother refused to call her anything other than Sorcha because, as she said, that was how she had thought of her during all those years. 'To me you'll always be Sorcha,' she'd explained and Maddie understood.

As the train pulled out she waved, then turned to go back to the car park. She wiped away a tear surreptitiously. *I'll see them again soon and then I'll find out the truth.* Anyway, she appeared to be turning into a dreadful cry baby and she was determined to put a stop to that. Normally, she never cried.

Reminding herself that she had nothing to cry about, quite the opposite, she headed back to Marcombe Hall.

'She went to the hospital yesterday?' Alex frowned at

Foster. He'd found him near the old stable block, which was now used for garaging.

'Yep. Brought flowers and was in there for ages.'

'But she doesn't know anyone around here. Who the hell would she go and visit?' Alex couldn't understand it.

'Well, today she went to the train station to wave off two women. One had lots of bandages, so maybe they were the ones she visited? They seemed very friendly, hugging and stuff. And then she came home.' Foster scratched his chin which sported a considerable amount of stubble.

Maddie kept driving to Dartmouth and at first Alex had thought maybe she had a secret lover there or something. But Foster insisted all she did was talk to some dark-haired girl, younger than herself, or browse the shops.

'Never goes indoors at all, except for shopping,' Foster had reported.

'Wonder who they are?' Alex mused out loud now.

'No idea,' Foster said. 'Want me to try and find out?'

'No, don't bother. They can't be anyone dangerous if they've been in hospital. Besides, they're obviously gone now.' Alex dry washed his face, trying to rid himself of the tension headache he could feel building up behind his eyes. He wished for the hundredth time that Wes and Kayla would come back so they could look out for Maddie instead of him, but there seemed no chance of that. Kayla's mother still needed them as her father wasn't fully recovered yet.

'Anything else to report?'

'Well, there was some oily geezer watching them as well. I noticed him 'cause he was wearing a knitted hat, one of them beanies. I mean, seriously – who wears a hat in this heat? He kept popping up behind corners, spying on the women, but when I asked him what the hell he was looking at, he scurried off, quick as you like. Maybe he was the dark-haired girl's ex or something?'

'Hmm, wasn't there someone wearing a hat in the pub the other night? I remember thinking he must be mad. Like you said, it's not exactly the weather for it.'

'Yeah? I don't remember that.'

'Well, keep an eye out for him and if you see him again, grab him would you please? I'd like a word. He might know something.'

'No problem. Want me to keep following Maddie then?' Foster asked.

'If you don't mind? I'd rather have you help me with the painting, but I daren't let Maddie out of sight. Who knows when or if the madman – or woman – will strike again?' *And why can't I stop worrying about her? It's not as if she cares about me.* But he couldn't help it and he wanted Maddie safe even so.

'No worries, I'm happy to keep watch.'

'Sure? You're doing a great job. I hope you're not finding it too boring?'

'No, it's okay. Better than slaving away over a paint pot.' Foster grinned.

Alex smiled back. 'Thanks, Foster, I owe you. I'll try to give you the day off tomorrow. I'm going to ask her to come sailing with me, although she might say no. If she does, I'll let you know.'

'Okay then.'

'For now, she's inside doing baking, so I can keep an eye on her myself for the rest of the day. Why don't you go to the beach or something?'

'Great, thanks. I might just do that. I met this really gorgeous little brunette the other day, called Sally. She seems to spend a lot of time on the beach.'

'You'd better hurry then, but if I were you I'd get rid of that fuzz on your chin first.'

'No, she said she liked it last time. "Designer stubble" she called it and ran her fingernails through it. Fair made me shiver, I can tell you.' Foster shuddered in anticipation as if to emphasise his point.

Alex laughed. 'I see. I'll keep my advice to myself then. Maybe I should try growing some myself?'

'Yeah, I would. What you got to lose, eh?'

'What indeed.'

Against her better judgement, Maddie agreed to go sailing with Alex again. She knew that she should have said no, and she almost did, but after the departure of her mother and sister she felt lonely and in need of something to do. She was tired of twitching at the slightest sound and sailing seemed like a good idea, even if it meant spending a whole day in Alex's company. At least out at sea there wouldn't be anyone around to attack her.

They set off just before lunchtime the next day, heading in the opposite direction along the coast to where they'd gone the last time. There was a fresh breeze filling the sail and the little boat bobbed along at a rapid speed. Maddie positioned herself near the prow and revelled in the sensation of being carried across the waves. The wind made her hair flap out behind her like a pennant and she could taste the salty spray as it came up to cover her in a fine mist.

'This is lovely!' she called out to Alex, who was busy doing something with ropes. He just smiled and nodded and she had to look away. He was looking decidedly piratical today with a five o'clock shadow covering his jaw. When he smiled, his teeth flashed extra white because of it and she had a sudden longing to be in his arms again, being kissed senseless and ... *Damn it! I've got to stop thinking about him that way.* She took a deep breath and concentrated on sunbathing.

Half an hour later they rounded a headland and the wind direction changed abruptly. Alex made some adjustments to the sail, but just as he appeared to have everything under control there was an almighty crash and the mast broke off at the bottom, almost capsizing the boat in the process. It landed only inches from Maddie, who nearly jumped overboard in fright. She let out a shriek and looked at Alex who was standing stock still, staring at her as if turned to stone.

'Alex? What the hell just happened?'

Maddie's words seemed to jolt Alex out of his trance and he came rushing over towards her, taking her by the shoulders.

'Are you all right? Bloody hell, that was close!'

'Yes, yes I'm fine, but why did the mast break like that?'

'I don't know.' He looked bewildered, then turned slowly to go and inspect the damage.

'Bloody hell,' he muttered again, and attempted to pull the mast into a more even position so the little boat wouldn't keel over.

'What's the matter?' Maddie came over to help him, and together they succeeded in placing the mast along the middle of the boat and hauling in the flapping sail.

'Look at the bottom of the mast.' Alex nodded in that direction. 'It looks like someone has sawed through it almost completely, leaving just a tiny bit. After sailing for a while, even the smallest gust of wind would have broken it off.'

'Oh my God!' The cold dread squeezed Maddie's insides

once more, and she had to sit down when her legs suddenly turned to jelly. 'You mean, someone did this deliberately?'

'Yes, exactly.' Stowing the sail away under deck, Alex went to the back of the boat and tried to start the little outboard engine. 'We'll have to return to shore.'

That was easier said than done, however, as the engine refused to splutter into life. When Alex examined it more closely, he found that it too had been tampered with. He swore a blue streak.

'So now what do we do?' Maddie looked at the rapidly receding shore line and saw that the boat was quickly heading out to sea, carried along by the current.

'We'll have to radio for help.' With a grim expression on his face, Alex went below deck and Maddie heard him talking. She sighed. Jane had been right. Her father was still dangerous and he hadn't given up. Not by a long shot.

Alex emerged from below, slamming the hatch to behind him. 'Shit!' he exclaimed. 'The bastard's broken the radio too.'

'Oh, no, you've got to be joking!' Maddie swallowed hard, but the cold feeling in the pit of her stomach grew since she could see that he wasn't.

'We'll have to swim, Maddie. Put on a life vest, and let's go. If we wait much longer, we'll be too far out to make it to shore.' He rummaged in a cupboard and swore again. 'I don't believe it – no life vests. Shit, I should have checked, but I never thought ...' He clenched his fists. 'Someone's going to pay for this.'

'If we make it that is.' Maddie regarded him anxiously. She was a strong swimmer, but she didn't much fancy trying to reach the shore from here. It looked very far away and the water was freezing cold.

'Do you want to stay here and I'll raise the alarm as

soon as I get to dry land?' Alex put a hand on her arm comfortingly. Maddie shook her head. Somehow the thought of floating around all alone on the ocean didn't appeal to her in the slightest. She would rather take her chances in the sea with him.

'No, I'm coming with you. Something else might go wrong with the boat and I'd still have to swim for it. What if there's a hole in the hull as well?'

'Okay, if you're sure. Let's tie a rope around our waists so that we don't become separated at least. That is, if the bastard who did this has left us any rope,' he muttered.

Chapter Fifteen

Fortunately, there was some rope and Alex secured one end around Maddie's waist, winding the other round his own. They dived into the water wearing nothing but their swimsuits and set off towards land. Alex had brought a small compass, which he put inside his swimming trunks, just to make sure they didn't swim in the wrong direction if they lost sight of the shore.

'If you get tired, tell me, and we'll just float for a while,' he said to Maddie, and she nodded and concentrated on swimming. The water was icy and she knew the best thing was to keep moving. She was absolutely terrified, but tried her best not to think of the fathoms of sea underneath her. That way lay insanity, she was sure.

For two hours they struggled along against the current and the waves, resting now and then, and eventually Maddie felt her strength fading fast. Every time she was ready to give up, however, Alex swam up to her and held her close for a while, treading water, giving her as much encouragement as he could.

'Come on, Maddie, you can do it. We're not going to let the bastard win, are we? Whoever he is, we've got to fight him, or her, and get our own back. Let's go now.'

Finally, when she was convinced she couldn't go any further, a beach came into view at last and they both collapsed onto the sand, panting and struggling for breath.

'Thank you God,' Maddie whispered, even though she'd never been particularly religious. 'Thank you so much.'

'Amen to that,' Alex agreed.

After a few minutes he leaned over her and asked if she was all right.

'Yes, I think so, but it might be better if you ask me in an hour or so.' Maddie stared at Alex and everything else faded into the background again, exactly like the last time they had been on a beach together. She saw concern in his eyes and something else, perhaps tenderness. Before she could react, he bent to kiss her, slowly, reverently, and she let him. She told herself she was too tired to protest and closed her eyes. She didn't have the energy left to twine her arms around his neck, so she simply lay there, letting herself be kissed.

Alex stopped after a while and looked down at her, then he turned away and sat up.

'Do you think you can walk yet?' he asked, without looking at her.

Maddie wanted to scream. *Of course I can't walk when you've just kissed me, silly!* Her legs had reverted to their jellyfish state the minute his mouth touched hers and she couldn't have walked if her life depended on it. Obviously the kiss hadn't had the same effect on him. *So why did he do it then?* She curled her hands into fists by her side. It was so unfair. Why did he have this effect on her? Why couldn't she resist him?

'Maybe in a little while,' she finally replied with a sigh and he sat staring out to sea until she struggled into sitting position some time later.

'Where are we?'

'I'm not sure. We'll have to climb to the top of the cliff to find out. Then we're going to the nearest police station. This time, I'm not listening to any protests, do you hear?'

'No, Alex,' she said meekly. 'I agree. This has gone too far.'

He gave her a suspicious glare. 'You know who did this, don't you?'

'I have a pretty good idea.'

'But you're not going to tell me?'

'No. It wouldn't make any difference. The police are already looking for him and if they can't find him, neither can we. All I know is he'll try again.' She shivered.

Alex's mouth tightened into an angry line, but he didn't try to persuade her to confide in him. He pulled her up and together they set off towards the cliff path.

Maddie wanted to tell Alex what was going on, but she had promised her mother to keep her true identity secret for now. They hadn't had time for any long chats, but Ruth had told her she'd be happier knowing she left Dartmouth with her reputation intact and Maddie wanted to respect her wishes.

'I'll tell you the whole story soon,' Ruth had promised, 'but for now, please will you keep quiet?'

Maddie had no choice but to agree. She knew Alex wouldn't tell anyone if she asked him not to, but for some reason she wanted to fight this battle on her own. She needed to find a solution herself.

She followed Alex up the steep path, taking his hand when he offered it to help pull her along. She loved the feel of his fingers, so strong and capable, and she knew he would help in any way he could. *Perhaps I'm being stupid?* Maybe it was time to ask for his assistance.

Fortunately the sun was still hot and their bathing costumes soon dried in the breeze as they walked. Maddie was very uncomfortable, however, as the salt residue and sand left on her skin made it feel itchy and tight, and walking along the path without shoes was not what the soles of her feet were used to. She was sure Alex felt the same, although he didn't say anything, and she was extremely relieved when they eventually came to a house where the owner was kind enough to let them use the phone.

In the hall, Maddie caught sight of her reflection in a mirror and nearly choked on a gasp. The expression 'drowned rat' didn't even begin to describe the way she looked, and she had to wonder at Alex's sanity in wanting to kiss someone who looked like that. There was no time for further reflection though, as they were ushered into a small kitchen and offered a cold drink, which they gratefully accepted.

'Ah, that was wonderful, thank you.' Maddie was sure the taste of salt in her mouth would remain for days, no matter what else she put in it, but at least the liquid soothed her parched throat.

Alex then called the coastguard and asked them to look for the boat, and he also phoned Ben and arranged for him to come and pick them up. Exhausted, they arrived back at Marcombe, where Maddie had a lengthy shower before falling asleep on top of her bed.

Towards evening Alex came into the kitchen, where Maddie was watching Annie prepare dinner.

'They've found the boat,' he announced. 'I have to go and talk to them and I've arranged to meet a policeman down by the harbour. Do you want to come?'

Maddie shook her head. 'No thanks. You can tell them what happened. I don't feel up to it.'

He gave her a strange look, but nodded. 'Fine. I'll see you later then.'

Maddie sighed and began to help Annie chop vegetables.

'He really likes you, you know,' Annie said.

'What?' Startled, Maddie looked up and nearly chopped her finger off in the process.

'Alex. He likes you a lot. I can tell from the way he looks at you.' Annie smiled. 'He used to look at Wes's ex-wife the same way, but that was just puppy-love ...'

'Alex was in love with Wes's ex-wife?' Kayla had never mentioned that to her. Maddie wondered why.

'Yes, but it was her fault. She wanted to get back at Wes, so she did all she could to drive the brother's apart. She encouraged Alex to want her, you know ...' Annie shook her head. 'She was bad news.'

'I didn't know that. Was he very upset when she died then?' Wes's ex-wife Caroline had died on the day Alex was caught smuggling. Kayla had told her that much, since indirectly she'd been the cause of the woman's death.

'No, I think he'd seen her true colours by then. He was never stupid. I shouldn't think he gave her another thought. You, on the other hand ...'

'Oh, Annie, I don't think so.' Maddie was annoyed to feel yet another blush coming on. 'I just happen to be female and single, that's all.'

Annie shook her head once more. 'I think you're wrong.'

Maddie didn't know what to reply, so she left it at that and Annie didn't pursue the subject. It stayed in Maddie's mind for a long time, however, niggling away at her as she worked. Was she being unfair to Alex in judging him unheard? Had he really changed?

'I need to do some food shopping again tomorrow afternoon. Can you drive me, please?' Annie's question intruded into her ruminations.

'Hmm? Oh, yes, of course.'

Maddie was still feeling tired the next day when she

and Annie set off for the nearest supermarket. The dark version of the dream had plagued her during the night and disturbingly it had had a different ending from what it usually had. Instead of finishing with her struggle with the dark man, he had bundled her into the boot of a car, shutting her into terrifying darkness. The car had bumped over an uneven road, hurting her as she was thrown around inside the dark cavity, and she had kicked against the opening with all her might. When the car finally came to a halt the dark man, who by now had definitely taken on the shape and face of the Reverend Blake-Jones, had thrown her into the sea off a high cliff. This was perhaps not surprising given her recent experiences, but had scared her stupid nonetheless.

The road from Marcombe was fairly narrow and it wasn't possible to drive very fast. Its curvy contours necessitated a lot of braking and changing of gears, and Maddie tried to concentrate on this task instead of on the disturbing memories of the dream. They hadn't gone very far when they came to a particularly steep curve in the road and Maddie stepped hard on the brake. Nothing happened.

With an exclamation she tried again, and again, then pulled on the hand brake. Still nothing happened and Annie, who had by now gathered that something was wrong, screamed as they rounded the corner, where a car travelling in the opposite direction hurtled towards them. Maddie tried to hold the car steady and at the same time slow their pace by putting the car into a lower gear, but her efforts were too late and they collided with the front right hand side of the oncoming car. It wasn't a head-on collision, but it sent them careering into the nearest ditch, which was surprisingly deep. The little car somersaulted and landed on its roof several yards away from the road, jolting the occupants who were left hanging from their seat belts.

Maddie moaned and tried to ascertain if anything was broken. She thought she was just bruised and cast an anxious look over at Annie, who appeared to be unconscious.

'Ms Browne? Are you alright?'

Maddie turned toward the window and recognised the upside-down face of Foster.

'Foster, thank God. Help me out of here will you? I think Annie's been hurt. Do you have a mobile?'

'Yes, I just got one, as it happens. I'll ring for an ambulance. Hold on, I'll get you out in a minute.'

He assisted Maddie in disentangling herself from the seat belt and held her so she wouldn't fall down and hurt herself more. She then crawled out on all fours and ran round to the other side of the car.

'Annie? Annie, can you hear me?' But there was no reply.

They waited anxiously until the ambulance turned up and by the time it arrived Annie had started to wail. The paramedics, obviously expert at this sort of thing, freed her as quickly as possible and put her on a stretcher with the minimum of fuss.

'I don't think she's seriously hurt, only shocked,' one of them said to Maddie. 'But we'll take her to the hospital just to make sure.'

'I'll come with you. Foster, will you let Alex know, please?'

'Yep, right away.'

'And don't let anyone drive the car if they get it out of here. The brakes are broken.'

'Damn it all, Foster! We're dealing with a lunatic here.' Alex slammed his fist onto Wes's desk in frustration when he was told the news. 'He must be lurking around the grounds if he has gained access to the cars now. God, he'll be in the house before we know it.'

'Yes, it sure looks that way.' Foster was serious. 'I haven't seen anyone, but this is a big place and it would be easy to sneak in. Theft and robbery is one thing. I can understand that, even if I don't want to be part of it myself any more, but cold-blooded murder, now that's something else! What are we going to do?'

Alex ran a hand through his hair and sighed. 'I don't know. I suppose the first thing is to check the other cars. Do you know anything about engines? I'm only familiar with the basics.'

'No problem, I'll check them for you. I know what to look for.'

'Great, thanks. I don't know what I would have done without you these last few weeks. I'm so glad you came.' He smiled at his friend.

'Not half as glad as I am, although I hadn't expected quite this much excitement.' Foster started for the door. 'Let me know what you decide.'

'I will.' Alex slumped back into the chair. There was a sick feeling in his stomach as he thought about this third attempt on Maddie's life. He had to make her tell him who was responsible. She'd admitted she knew, or guessed, and he couldn't for the life of him understand why she refused to name her attacker. It didn't make sense, unless she was protecting someone? A previous boyfriend perhaps? A lover?

Alex went cold all over. Was there a former boyfriend stalking her who had taken exception to their outings? It was possible, but then why wouldn't she say so? The only reason he could think of was that she still loved this person. That thought made him even more miserable than before. In fact, it was totally unbearable.

Chapter Sixteen

'Right then, Ms Browne. We'll step up our search for this Blake-Jones character and provide you with a guard tomorrow. He'll go with you wherever you go, so you mustn't worry. At night, I'll have someone patrol the grounds with a dog and you'll be safe inside the house. I assume there's a burglar alarm?'

'Yes, of course. It's switched on every night. There are quite a few precious pieces of furniture and other antiques in the house.' There was one alarm circuit outside the house which could be switched on when the occupants were at home and another indoors which Maddie knew was always turned on when they were out.

'Good. Make sure you don't forget.'

'I won't. Thank you for your help, officer.'

'Not at all. I just hope we catch this madman before he goes completely crazy.'

Maddie didn't know how Blake-Jones could possibly become any more deranged than he already was, but she didn't say anything, just nodded to the policeman and left.

Annie was being kept overnight for observation and had been sedated to lessen the effects of the shock. Her husband Ben had arrived to sit with her and he told Maddie not to worry, so she gratefully accepted a lift home in a police car. The officers waited until she was safely inside the house before driving off. Alex came rushing out of the sitting room with an anxious expression on his face.

'Maddie, are you all right? How's Annie?'

'We're both fine. I'm just a bit bruised, but I think Annie hit her head so they're keeping her until tomorrow at least. Can you put the burglar alarm on, please? I won't feel comfortable until I know it's on.'

'Sure, I'll do it right away. Have you eaten?' She shook her head. 'Well, come and have a cup of tea and a sandwich. I'll make it for you.'

'Thanks, but I'm not very hungry.'

'Just one. It will do you good.' Maddie let herself be persuaded and soon she was curled up on one of the plush sofas in the small sitting room with her supper. She discovered that she was hungry after all and devoured her meal quickly.

'Thank you. That was lovely.'

'Even though I didn't cut the bread straight?' Alex teased.

'Yes, even so. Thank you.'

'You're welcome.' Alex fidgeted on the opposite sofa. 'Maddie, I … oh, hell, I know I have no right to pry, but won't you please tell me who is behind all this? I really want to protect you and I can't fight the unknown.' His eyes pleaded with her and she felt herself weaken. She trusted him. Surely it wouldn't harm Ruth if she confided in Alex? After all, the police already knew who they were looking for. It was only a matter of time before everyone found out.

'Okay then.' She put down her cup and plate on a nearby table. 'I think the person who is trying to kill me is a man called Saul Blake-Jones. Do you know him?'

'No.' Alex frowned. 'Should I? Is he your ex-boyfriend?'

Maddie snorted. 'You couldn't be more wrong. Whatever gave you that idea?'

'Well, you seemed to be protecting his identity. I assumed it was someone you were attached to or had loyalties to somehow.'

'Oh, I see. No, no, it's like this ...' She took a deep breath and started at the beginning, recounting the whole sorry tale, including the attack on her mother and sister. The only thing she left out was their present whereabouts. The fewer people who knew about that, the better.

At some stage during the story Alex came over and sat down next to her, and he took her hand and caressed it gently. 'Blimey, Maddie, it doesn't just rain on you, it pours, doesn't it?'

'You can say that again.' Somehow his kindness released a catch deep inside her mind and Maddie felt tears of helplessness, sadness and years of frustration and bitterness well up. Unable to halt yet another flood, her body shook with the force of it and she gave herself up to the storm of weeping. Alex gathered her close and rocked her like a child, patting her back and murmuring soothing words. It felt wonderful. She wanted to stay in his arms forever. She was safe there.

When some time later her sobs turned into the occasional hiccup, it seemed natural that he should kiss away her tears. She didn't have the willpower left to resist the attraction between them and simply closed her eyes in surrender. His mouth moved on to her lips, nibbling, licking, teasing, until she simply had to increase the contact or she was sure she would die. With a passion she had never before experienced, she kissed him hungrily, revelling in the taste and feel of him. He returned the kiss with equal need.

She scraped her fingers over his stubbled jaw and he shivered. He reciprocated by caressing the outline of her breasts through the thin material of her T-shirt and it was her turn to tremble.

'You're not wearing a bra again,' he groaned. 'It drives

me insane, do you know that?' His whisper was husky, sending more tremors down her back.

'Don't need one,' she murmured. 'I'm too small, sorry.'

'No! You're perfect, just perfect.' He pushed his hands under the edge of the shirt and his rough fingers on her heated skin was pure delight. His palms cupping her breasts were an exact fit. 'See?' he whispered and let his thumbs graze her nipples.

Maddie squirmed and clung to him as his fingers continued their exploration lower down, her own hands travelling over his broad shoulders and down to his backside. She raked her fingernails over the taut material of his jeans and he drew in a sharp breath. 'Maddie ...'

The fire they ignited could only have one conclusion and it was lucky they were the only occupants of the house that night. Oblivious to the rest of the world, they shed their clothes, ripping quite a few in their haste to bare heated skin, in their desire to touch, feel and explore fully. It seemed neither could wait too long and Maddie never even considered stopping him for a moment.

An army could have tramped through the sitting room and Maddie wouldn't have cared one iota. She wanted only to be joined with this man, here and now, and nothing else mattered. The sensations were incredibly intense, almost unbearable, and as the world shattered into a thousand tiny fragments of pleasure, she cried out. She couldn't help herself.

Soon after she heard Alex join her in this heaven on earth and when their heartbeats eventually returned to normal she fell asleep, cradled in his arms, utterly exhausted, both mentally and physically.

Sometime during the night Maddie woke up and stumbled

to her feet. There was sufficient light from the moon for her to be able to gather up her articles of clothing and, this done, she left the room, closing the door softly behind her.

Alex was awake, but had feigned sleep in order to see what she would do. As he heard the soft click of the door, however, he turned over and buried his face in his arms.

'Oh hell, what have I done?'

She obviously regretted what had happened between them to such an extent she couldn't even face waking up next to him in the morning. He knew he shouldn't have taken advantage of her vulnerable state when she returned from the hospital, but she'd just been too tempting. When she nestled close to him he'd lost all reason; rational thought fled out the window. The smell of her was intoxicating and he had been drunk – drunk with love and wanting. The love-making had been inevitable.

Still, he knew he shouldn't have done it. *Will she hate me now? Or will she act as if nothing happened?* He groaned.

'Damn it all.' He wanted her again, now and for always, but she had to want it too. He'd wait and see how she reacted in the morning.

'Auntie Maddie, I can't believe you're still in bed! Do you ever do anything except sleep?'

The sound of Nell's voice woke Maddie from a sleep so heavy she felt drugged. With great reluctance her eyelids parted and she squinted at the little girl.

'Nell? Are you back already?'

'What do you mean already? You knew we were coming today, Kayla told you.' Nell was sitting on the end of Maddie's bed, bouncing up and down to release her pent-up energy.

Maddie ran a hand through her hair and tried to swallow. Her mind didn't seem to work properly and she couldn't quite grasp Nell's words. She attempted to sit up.

'Auntie Maddie, you haven't got your PJs on!' Nell squealed gleefully and Maddie pulled up the sheet in embarrassment. She'd completely forgotten her naked state.

'Er, it was, um, a bit hot last night,' she mumbled.

'Kayla's downstairs, but she'll be up to see you soon I think so you'd better get dressed.' Nell giggled.

'Right. Okay. I'll, er … I guess I'll have a shower then. You run along.'

'Oh, Auntie Maddie, where's Annie?'

'Annie?' The memories came flooding back into Maddie's fuzzy brain and her eyes opened fully at last. 'Annie! I'm afraid she's in hospital. We had a little accident yesterday, but she'll be fine. I think she might come home today. You'd better tell Kayla she has to cook breakfast herself.'

'Breakfast? It's nearly lunchtime.' With another giggle Nell skipped out of the room.

Despite a long, hot shower, Maddie still felt completely drained when, half an hour later, she made her way downstairs. She found everyone in the kitchen, including Alex, whose gaze she couldn't quite meet. A warm sensation shot through her at the thought of what they'd done the night before, but she pulled in a deep breath to calm herself. No doubt he wouldn't expect her to make a big deal out of it. Perhaps it hadn't meant anything to him? He hadn't actually said he loved her or anything, but then they hadn't really talked much at all … She took a deep breath. Probably best to just play it cool for now.

'Good morning.' Kayla jumped up to greet her with a

hug and Maddie turned to make herself a cup of tea to hide the blush which she knew was creeping up on her. How she wished she could stop that childish habit, but it seemed impossible, especially around Alex.

She sat down at the table and listened to the general conversation which naturally centred on all that had been happening at Marcombe in Wes and Kayla's absence.

'I can't believe it,' Kayla was saying. 'We only go away for two weeks, and this quiet backwater goes crazy. Nothing ever happens here normally.'

'Believe me, we would have preferred to live without such excitement,' Alex put in. 'I'm sure Maddie agrees with me.' He looked across the table at her.

'Definitely.' She nodded for emphasis. 'I'm totally shattered by everything that's happened. I think I need a holiday now. Oh, wait a minute, I *am* on holiday, right?'

The others laughed, but soon grew serious.

'What are the police doing about it?' Wes asked.

Maddie told him about the arrangements she'd made with the officer the day before and he nodded. 'I don't think I'll be going out much, though. Somehow I feel safer in here,' she added.

'Yes. You mustn't go anywhere alone and we'll make sure the cars are checked regularly.'

'My friend Foster's already taken care of that,' Alex said. 'He's, um, quite good at that sort of thing.'

'Foster? Who's he?' Kayla looked confused.

'Oh, he's a friend who's working for me. I'll introduce you later.' Alex glanced at Maddie as if he wondered whether she would tell the others that Foster was an ex-criminal, but she remained silent. Foster seemed a nice enough guy to her and she wouldn't judge him on what he had done previously, whatever Alex thought. He'd certainly been very helpful the day before and it had been a wonderful coincidence that he'd happened to be coming down the road at the same time. No, Maddie wouldn't criticise Foster.

She suddenly felt extremely weary. 'I'm sorry, but I think I'll go back to bed if you don't mind. I'm still a bit shaken up from yesterday and the day before.'

'Of course, do that. I'll bring you a cup of tea a bit later on and we can have a chat,' Kayla said. Maddie thanked her and headed for the stairs. It was all too much. She needed time on her own.

By the time her friend arrived with the promised cup of tea, Maddie had recovered enough to retell her story to Kayla, who couldn't contain her excitement.

'Oh Maddie, that's brilliant. So you found your mother at last. I'm so pleased for you.' She hugged her. 'Mrs Blake-Jones, who would've believed it?'

'Yes. "In the deepest waters ..." and all that. But I really could have done without the rest.'

'The Reverend, you mean?' Maddie nodded. 'Yes. I suppose it's some sort of insane jealousy. Some men simply can't accept that their wife comes to love someone else. It's very sad really, especially for your mother. What a life she's had.'

'Absolutely. We didn't have much time to talk about it and she was too exhausted anyway, but she promised she'd tell me the whole story next time we meet.'

'Poor woman. Well, she's safe now hopefully and your sister too. How wonderful to find a sister as well.'

'Yes, I really like Jane. She's exactly the way I would imagine a sister should be, not like that spiteful cat Olivia. I forgot to tell you, but would you believe, Olivia tried to get me to give back some of the stuff I took from our parents' house? Unreal.'

'I suppose she suffered from jealousy too. Some siblings want their mothers all to themselves and take out their aggressions in different ways. I try to be fair with my children, but it's very difficult to give them all attention at once. And I have to try extra hard to include Nell so she doesn't feel as if I treat her differently to my own two.'

'You're right. I'm sure that's why Olivia acted the way she did, but you would have thought she'd grow out of it.' Maddie shook her head. She didn't want to think about Olivia, the wound was still too raw.

'No one stopped her so she just continued. It's really up to the parents to do something about it, you know, and your adopted mother sounds as if she was too nice.'

'She was. I'll always be grateful for her love and for treating me like a true daughter. She did her best.'

'What will you do now, Maddie? Do you want to go back to London?'

'No, I think I need to stay here until all this has been resolved one way or another. At least here I have protection now and sooner or later Blake-Jones must be caught. Then I'll be able to breathe more easily.'

'Good. I'm glad you're staying.'

'Thanks, Kayla. Thanks for everything.' Maddie squeezed her friend's hand. It was good to have her back.

Chapter Seventeen

'Maddie, can we talk for a minute?' Alex had cornered her after dinner under the pretext of helping her to carry dishes to the kitchen.

'There's nothing to talk about, Alex.' Maddie tried for a nonchalant tone and thought she succeeded fairly well. He hadn't so much as looked at her all day, so she'd concluded he would prefer to forget their encounter of the night before. Although perhaps he was worried she'd tell Kayla and Wes?

'Really?' He sounded angry and she couldn't understand why. He should be happy she wasn't making a fuss. Most men would be.

'Yes, don't worry, I won't tell anyone if you don't. Let's just forget the whole thing. I already have.' She actually thought she heard him grind his teeth and turned to stare at him. He looked like a thundercloud and it made her angry. He had no right to look like that. 'What's the matter? You got what you wanted, isn't that enough?'

'Is that what you think? That all I wanted was one night of … damn it all, Maddie! I want more than that.'

'What, you think I'm going to fall into your arms every night? Well, think again, mister. I may have been tired enough to give in to you yesterday, but it won't happen again. I don't do one-night stands, and definitely no repeats. Understand?' And she marched out of the kitchen, head held high. She wouldn't cry in front of him again. Under no circumstances. In fact, she was done with crying altogether.

'He's not going to break my heart,' she vowed to herself.

Let him go and break someone else's. She had enough to contend with without adding that to the list.

Maddie successfully avoided Alex for the next two days. She only spoke to him if it was absolutely necessary and he spent most of the day overseeing the work on his holiday cottages. She never ventured further from the house than into the garden. A policeman sat patiently nearby as she passed the time by painting flowers and trees, or by playing with the children, and slowly her fears diminished. There was no news about Blake-Jones, but she reasoned that they must surely catch him soon. He couldn't stay hidden forever.

On the morning of the third day Maddie was having breakfast in the kitchen when Alex came in, looking grimly determined. Kayla, who was doing the dishes, smiled at him and said, 'Good morning.'

'Morning. I'm taking Maddie out for a drive as soon as she's finished,' he announced, and Maddie choked on a piece of toast. Kayla came over to thump her on the back, and looked from one to the other.

'Are you?' she asked mildly.

'Yes. She needs to get out a bit, she's been cooped up in the house for days now. It can't be good for her.'

'Excuse me.' Maddie managed to control her coughing at last. 'But maybe I don't want to go for a drive.' She looked daggers at Alex and added mentally, 'especially not with you.' She could see that he read her message, but he ignored it.

'You don't have a choice in the matter. Wes agrees it would be a good idea. Don't you think so too, Kayla?'

Put on the spot like that, Kayla faltered, torn between loyalty to her friend, who was obviously not willing to go, and good sense which must have agreed with Alex. 'Well, yes, I suppose so, but ...'

'There. You see?' He turned to Maddie. 'I'll meet you outside when you're done.' And he turned on his heel and left the two women staring after him.

'Well. What was all that about?' Kayla turned suspicious eyes on Maddie. 'Am I missing something here?'

Maddie felt her cheeks heat up and cursed inwardly. 'I don't want to talk about it.'

'Well, he obviously does. I think you'd better go for a drive and have it out with him. Alex is nothing if not determined.'

Maddie sighed. 'Oh, okay then. If I must. Really, there's nothing to talk about though.' She stomped off to change her clothes and heard Kayla chuckle as she left. That only made her even more furious.

'So where are we going?' Maddie sat stiffly upright, with her arms folded across her chest as if he was going to jump her or something. Alex sighed inwardly. *This was going to be awkward.* She stared straight ahead of her, obviously cross at being out-manoeuvred.

'Just for a drive along the coast.' Alex tried to sound calm and he saw Maddie twitch, as if she had to try hard to resist the impulse to glance at him. *Well, that's a good sign, isn't it?*

Alex steered the car along the tiny winding lanes, keeping as close to the sea as possible. When fifteen minutes passed and he still hadn't stopped, Maddie became visibly impatient, squirming in her seat and sighing.

'Aren't you going to stop soon?' she asked, frowning.

'Nope.'

'What do you mean "nope"? Maybe I've got better things to do than going for a drive with you.'

Alex gave her a small smile. 'What, painting flowers? No, we need to talk.'

'Fine, but we don't have to go sightseeing just to have an argument.' She turned to glare at him, then looked away again when he raised his eyebrows at her, still smiling.

'Just relax. We'll go and have lunch at this really nice little restaurant I know of and then perhaps you'll be in a better mood.'

'Better mood for what?' she bristled.

'You'll see.' He smiled again, an enigmatic, infuriating sort of smile, he knew, and Maddie gave it up. She seemed to realise he wasn't going to tell her anything else, so she would have to be patient.

Alex concentrated on the road. *I've got to get this right.* Mentally, he began to prepare what he was going to say.

Maddie stared out the window at the passing scenery which, despite its incredible wild beauty, hardly registered with her at all. Her mind was elsewhere. Out of the corner of her eye, she could see Alex's capable hands and her heartbeat increased a notch as she remembered what those hands could do to her. She glanced at his profile, then realised immediately that this was a mistake. She didn't need to be reminded of how gorgeous he was, how utterly irresistible. What did he want to talk to her about? Was he hoping to seduce her again? She was afraid she'd have great trouble resisting.

The problem was, it was so much like last time. She'd felt this way with David – although perhaps not quite as strongly even if it had seemed like it then – and he'd turned out to be a complete bastard. Did she really want to put herself through that kind of pain and humiliation again? But maybe Alex was different? A little voice inside her said she should at least give him a chance and she was torn.

The little car sped along, expertly guided by Alex, and some time later they drove through a small fishing village nestling close to the sea. Maddie watched the houses and people they passed, idly noticing a detail here and there. On the outskirts of the village, however, she sat bolt upright and gasped.

'Alex,' she shouted, 'stop the car!'

He stepped on the brakes and they stopped with screeching tyres by the side of the road.

'What the hell? What's the matter? Are you going to be sick?' Alex looked perplexed, but Maddie ignored him and pushed open the door. Without explanation, she dashed off down the road. Vaguely she heard Alex curse, then slam his own door shut. His footsteps could be heard crunching behind her on the gravel as she came to a skidding halt and he managed to stop next to her, grabbing her from behind. 'Maddie, for God's sake, what's going on?'

'It's that house.' She pointed to a property on the other side of the road.

'What's so special about a house?'

'It's the house from my dream. Remember I told you about it? Look! See those pointed windows and all the climbing plants? It's exactly like the house I dream about all the time.' On the gate was a sign bearing the name 'Wisteria Lodge', which seemed an apt choice in the circumstances.

Alex shook his head and rubbed his forehead. 'Maddie, there could be any number of houses that fit that description. Why should it be this particular one?'

'I don't know, but I can feel it in here.' She tapped her chest. 'Oh, please, can we go round the back? I have to see the garden.'

'Maddie, I don't think—'

'Please, Alex? Please? I promise I won't say another word after that and you can drive me wherever you want,' she pleaded with him.

He sighed. 'All right, but if we're caught trespassing you're on your own.'

'Thank you, Alex. Thank you so much. Now come on.'

In her excitement, she grabbed his hand, twining her fingers with his, and this apparently mollified him because he followed her silently across the road. There was a field to one side of the house, and they climbed over the fence and made their way towards the back, keeping an eye out for any bulls or other surprises. A huge hedge surrounded the garden on one side, and it wasn't until they reached the end of this that they could see in across a low fence. Maddie stopped dead.

'Oh, my God,' she whispered and squeezed Alex's hand so tight he winced.

'Is this really it? You're sure?' He sounded surprised.

'Yes. See the swing? It's *my* swing! And all the roses? Exactly the same, just a bit more wild.' She drew in a deep breath. 'I must have been here once. Oh, Alex ...' Instinctively she turned to bury her face in his chest and his arms closed around her. He held her in a steadying grip, offering support without any kissing this time, and eventually her breathing calmed down and her heartbeat returned to something approximating normal.

'I'm sorry, I'm usually a very strong person, but I don't know what's got into me. It must be the Devon air or something making me feel this shaky.'

'That's all right, it's understandable. You've been through a lot lately.' He continued to hold her and they stood there in the field for a few moments.

'Excuse me, can I help you?' The voice from the garden startled them and they both turned to see a man walking down the path towards them. He was huge, with meaty fists clenched as if in readiness for a confrontation.

'Uh-oh,' Alex muttered. As the man approached, however, they could see that although he was scowling slightly, there was no menace in his gaze, only a questioning look. Maddie took a deep breath and approached the fence to attempt to explain their presence in the field.

'I'm sorry if we're trespassing, I just wanted to have a quick look at the garden of your house. I-I believe I've been here before. When I was little.' She tried a small smile, but it had no effect on the man's expression. He seemed to be studying her, his head tilted slightly to one side. A distant part of Maddie's brain registered the fact that he was dark-haired and clean-shaven, not the red-bearded giant of her dreams, and a deep sadness welled up inside her. She must have been mistaken after all. *I'm imagining things.* Although he could of course have moved a long time ago, whoever he was.

'I see.' Communication didn't appear to be the man's strongest point, Maddie reflected. She thought she detected a Scottish burr in those two words, but couldn't be certain.

'Please forgive us. We'll be on our way now and I promise we won't bother you again.' She gripped Alex's hand for support once more and half turned to go.

'Oh, don't hurry on my account. You can look all you want, won't bother me none.' Yes, the accent was definitely Scottish, Maddie decided. She glanced at him in surprise when he continued. 'What was it you thought you recognised then?'

'The swing and, er, the roses and those pointed windows.' It sounded silly now, but there was no turning back. It would have been rude not to answer the man.

'Oh, aye, they're very distinctive, aren't they?'

'Yes. Yes, they are. Um, have you lived here long, Mr …?' Maddie wished Alex would make an effort to join the conversation, but he appeared to be busy studying some far-flung view to their left and had dug his other hand deep into his pocket. He was no help at all.

'The name's Ruthven, and no, I haven't lived here long. In fact, I don't live here at all.'

'Excuse me?' Maddie blinked, sure she'd misheard him.

'I'm house-sitting. For my brother,' Mr Ruthven clarified.

'Oh, I see. Right.'

'Where did you say you were from?'

'I didn't. I mean, we're from Marcombe Hall. That is, this is Alex Marcombe and I'm Maddie Browne. I'm visiting there at the moment.' Maddie knew she wasn't making much sense, but she was beyond coherent thought processes at the moment. She wished the ground would just open up and swallow them whole. She hated embarrassing situations. In a desperate attempt to save herself she dug her elbow into Alex's midriff.

'Umph.' Alex glared at her, but finally came to her rescue. 'Mr Ruthven, we've taken up too much of your time already and really must be on our way. Thank you so much for letting us have a look, it was extremely kind of you. Come on, Maddie, let's go.' Without further ado he grabbed her by the elbow and steered her in the direction of the road.

'Bye and thank you Mr Ruthven,' Maddie called over her shoulder.

'No' at all,' she heard the big man reply before they were out of earshot.

'Alex, you can let go now,' she complained and yanked her arm away from his none too gentle grip.

'I knew this was a stupid idea, the minute you told me,' Alex muttered and strode off towards the fence. 'He probably thought we were burglars, checking the place out.'

'It wasn't stupid at all. This is the right house, I'm sure of it. Of course I couldn't expect it to have the same owner after twenty-odd years. That would have been too much of a coincidence.' But a little voice inside her insisted that was precisely what she'd expected and now she was utterly dejected as a result. If only someone here could have given her some answers. She hurried after Alex.

'No sense at all,' he was muttering and Maddie's emotions finally boiled over. Making a fist, she hit him on the arm as hard as she could and exploded into an uncontrollable torrent of words.

'What do you know? *You* weren't adopted, your life thrown into turmoil. You know exactly who you are and where you come from! Posh parents, big mansion, trust fund ...' She emphasised each word with another punch on his arm, but soon failed to come up with anything else to say. Those weren't exactly crimes, but they felt like it to her now she'd lost the security of knowing who her parents were. Breathing hard, she faced him, not ready to back down yet. Alex regarded her with an angry expression.

'Have you quite finished demolishing my character or do you want to add the criminal tendencies as well?' When she didn't reply he continued. 'Good, then perhaps we can be on our way.' And he turned and vaulted over the fence without effort, leaving Maddie to scramble across as best she could.

Once they were back in the car he did a U-turn and drove back the way they'd come. Maddie remained silent. After all, what was there to say? She had already said too much.

Chapter Eighteen

'Oh, you're back! Had a nice drive?'

Poor Kayla, who happened to be walking through the hall as they arrived back, received two stony glares and no reply. 'Maddie?'

But Maddie couldn't talk just then and rushed up the stairs to her room. There was no way she was saying anything to Kayla in front of Alex.

There was a knock on her door almost as soon as she'd shut it and Maddie steeled herself. 'Yes, come in.' No point denying Kayla entry, she'd only have to explain later.

Kayla tiptoed into the room as if she was entering a lion's den. 'Maddie? Are you all right?' She shut the door quietly behind her.

'Oh, yes, just wonderful.' Maddie knew her tone was sarcastic, but she couldn't help it. She was lying on top of the bed staring at the ceiling, her hands behind her head.

'Oh dear, that bad, eh?' Kayla went over to sit next to Maddie. 'Want to talk about it?'

'Not really, but I suppose I'd better tell you my version or all you will hear is what his "high-and-mighty-ness's" opinion is.'

A giggle escaped Kayla at this description of her brother-in-law and she quickly covered her mouth with one hand. 'I'm sorry, I'm sure it's not a laughing matter, but really … Alex has never been like that.'

'Maybe not with you.' But Maddie gave her a small smile in return. 'And it's not a laughing matter at all actually. You're right though, I'm probably taking this far too seriously. I'd better start at the beginning.'

'Yes do, please.'

The whole sorry tale came pouring out and Maddie didn't hold anything back. She and Kayla didn't have any secrets from each other and she had no hesitation in confiding in her friend. When she was done, she spread her hands out and shrugged.

'So, there you have it. It's a massive mess, isn't it?'

'Well, I've heard worse.' Kayla smiled. 'What intrigues me the most is this house, though. Perhaps we should investigate it a bit further.'

'No, please, let's just leave it. Much as I hate to admit it, Alex was probably right. My description could fit lots of houses around England. Why should it be this one?'

'I don't know, but you were so sure. And the swing and everything ...'

Maddie shook her head. 'Leave it, Kayla. I've had enough for now. I found my mother, which is what I set out to do. Perhaps she can explain the house to me when we meet in London, if there is anything to explain. It could all just be my imagination, you know.'

'Fine, but if you ever want help just let me know. I can go and talk to that Mr Ruthven or his brother for you any time.'

'Thanks, Kayla, but right now I just want to rest.'

Two more days of lounging about in the sun followed and Maddie managed to avoid meeting Alex almost completely. By getting up late she missed him at breakfast and to her great relief he spent all day working at the cottages. In the evenings he went out, presumably with friends, and wasn't seen until late, by which time Maddie had gone to bed. It wasn't an ideal solution, but it was the best possible thing in the circumstances. Or so she told herself.

On the morning of the third day, however, Maddie woke up to find Alex pounding on her door.

'Maddie, wake up.'

'What? What's the matter?' She dragged herself out of bed and went to peer out into the corridor. Belatedly she remembered that she wasn't wearing much and she saw Alex grit his teeth as he glanced at the thin, oversized T-shirt she used as a nightgown, but he came straight to the point in a curt tone of voice.

'There's someone on the phone for you. She sounds frantic. Jane, I think, although she didn't say.'

Maddie gasped. 'Jane? Oh, my God, what's happened now?' She raced past him into the corridor and almost knocked the phone over in her haste to reach the receiver. 'Jane? It's me. What's the matter? Is it Mother?'

'Oh, Maddie. I'm sorry to wake you up so early, but there's been an accident. I'm at the Chelsea and Westminster hospital and I don't know how bad it is yet.' Maddie could hear her sister's voice break on a sob. 'I mean, I don't know if she's going to be okay.'

'But what happened? What kind of accident?'

'She was knocked down by a car not far from your flat. She'd gone out shopping by herself.' Jane sobbed again. 'I told her not to go anywhere without me, but she was so happy to be free. You know, she just wanted to walk around I think. I should have watched her more closely. I'm s-sorry.'

'No, Jane, you mustn't blame yourself. Listen, I'll go and pack a bag now and I'll come to London as fast as I can. Call me on my mobile as soon as you have any news. All right? I'll be with you soon, I promise.'

'Thank you.' Jane's voice was only a thread in between the sobs, but Maddie could hear the relief. She understood her sister's feeling. They were not alone any more. They had each other.

After saying a quick goodbye, she hung up, turned to rush back into her room and ran smack into Alex's solid chest. Alex's solid, naked chest. Her heart flipped over.

'Oh, are you still here?'

'As you can see. What was that all about?' He crossed his arms almost defensively and Maddie tried to avoid looking at the well-defined muscles clearly visible under the tanned skin.

'My mother's been in an accident. A car ran her over. I don't know how she is yet, but I've got to go to London. Will you tell Kayla please? What time is it anyway?'

'Seven-ish.'

'Seven?' Maddie ran a hand through her unruly mane. 'No wonder I was still asleep.' She frowned. 'You're up early.'

'I had work to do. Get ready and I'll drive you to the station.' He turned away as if the matter was already settled.

'You don't have to do that. I can get a taxi,' Maddie protested.

'Don't be an idiot,' he muttered and continued on his way.

Maddie threw up her arms in despair. The man was impossible, but just this once she would resist arguing with him. She needed to be on her way as quickly as possible and if he wanted to be a martyr, fine. Let him.

When she emerged from the house fifteen minutes later, he was waiting in the car with the engine running. His face was set in uncompromising lines and Maddie decided her best course of action would be to stay silent. That seemed to suit him as well and their journey was accomplished without a single word passing their lips.

At the station in Totnes, Alex parked the car in the car park and Maddie thanked him for the ride.

'You're welcome.' He got out of the car and removed a holdall from the back seat. Maddie frowned in confusion.

'What are you doing?'

'I'm coming with you.' Alex wasn't looking at her. He just waited patiently for her to come round the car.

'What are you talking about?' Maddie was still confused, but anger was bubbling to the surface as well. 'Why should you come with me?'

'It's not safe. I've had you watched by Foster here in Devon, but I can't ask him to follow you to London, so I decided to go myself. You need someone to keep an eye on you.'

'The hell I do! You can just get right back in that car and go home again. I don't need you or anyone else to babysit me. I can look after myself perfectly well, thank you.' Maddie was well and truly furious by now and set off towards the ticket office without so much as a nod. But Alex followed.

Maddie stopped abruptly and rounded on him. 'Are you deaf? I don't need a guard dog, Alex.'

'Really? Then how come you've almost been killed three times in the last few weeks? If your mother has been run over in London, maybe it wasn't an accident?'

Maddie felt her insides go ice cold. He had put into words her worst fears, and she didn't want to hear it, although she knew in her heart that he had a point.

'What if that madman was behind it?' he continued. 'After all, he hasn't been seen around here for the last few days, has he?'

She clenched her teeth. 'Even if that's true, I can take care of myself. I have taken self-defence lessons and I'll be more careful now that I know there is danger.' Suddenly all the fight went out of her and her shoulders slumped. 'Go back to Marcombe, Alex, I don't need you.'

It was Alex's turn to clench his jaw, but he replied calmly, 'Maybe you don't think so, but I know that Kayla and Wes will feel better knowing you're not alone. You can't stop me, I'm going whether you like it or not. Now come on, or we'll miss the next train.'

'Fine, have it your way.' There was no reasoning with the man and Maddie gave up the unequal struggle. He was right. She couldn't stop him if he was determined to go.

'Why did you tell Foster to watch me?' They had been travelling for over an hour in silence and this question had been nagging at Maddie.

Alex had been contemplating the passing scenery and turned his blue gaze on her slowly. 'Because I wanted some answers.'

'Answers? About what?'

'That incident with the mine shaft made me suspicious and I thought you were hiding something.' He looked away. 'I told you, I wondered if perhaps it was an old boyfriend of yours you were protecting.'

'Oh, I see. And you thought you'd catch him red-handed?'

'Something like that.' He picked up a paper and began to read, as if to signal that their conversation was at an end, but Maddie wasn't quite finished.

'There I was thinking perhaps you were worried about me.' She watched him carefully and was disappointed to note that he showed not the slightest reaction to her words.

'Well, you were a guest in my brother's house. Of course I was worried,' he answered with a shrug and returned to the newspaper. Maddie's throat constricted. For a while there she had almost believed he cared about her, but that was obviously too much to hope for.

'Damn it,' she muttered to herself and pulled out a paperback from her bag.

'I'm sorry?' Alex had torn his gaze away from the newspaper to raise his eyebrows at her.

'Nothing. I was talking to myself. I do that a lot.'

'I see.' He gave her another enigmatic look and then remained absorbed in the news for the rest of the journey.

Chapter Nineteen

The station was as crowded and dirty as the previous time, but Maddie hardly noticed as Alex shouldered his way through the crowd making a path for her. She followed him outside where he hailed a cab.

'The Chelsea and Westminster hospital, please.'

'Right you are.'

The taxi smelled of new leather upholstery, smoke and cheap car fragrance and Maddie almost gagged. She leaned forward to open the window on her side and asked Alex to do the same.

'That's not much better,' he murmured. The exhaust fumes from the traffic were blown into the cab on hot, sticky gusts of air, and as before Maddie wished herself back in Devon.

'It's nicer in the autumn and spring.' For some reason she felt compelled to defend the city where she had lived for so long. It really was a nice place most of the time, just not in a heat wave. Alex only nodded and Maddie leaned back and closed her eyes. She tried to prepare herself mentally for the ordeal to come and prayed her newly discovered mother was out of danger. Jane had only called once to say that Ruth had been taken to the operating theatre.

The taxi wound its way down Fulham Road and finally dropped them off outside the impressive entrance to the hospital. A relatively new building, the architecture was modern and the doors were shielded by a canopy of glass and steel. Alex paid off the cabbie and they made their way to the huge information desk just inside the doors, where they asked for directions.

'The emergency department is on the right hand side of the building. You'll have to go out again, turn left, then left again and you'll see the entrance.'

'Thank you.'

They found Jane sitting forlornly in a corner with a battered Coke can clenched in her hands. When she caught sight of Maddie she flew up and threw her arms around her sister's neck. The empty drink can clattered to the floor. 'Maddie! Oh, thank you for coming. I'm still waiting to hear about the operation and I'm going crazy. Why does everything take so long?' There were tears in Jane's eyes and Maddie gave her a fierce hug.

My little sister. A wave of protectiveness washed over her. She'd never felt that way about Olivia. Instinct? She didn't know.

'Let's sit down. Jane, this is Alex Marcombe. He, er ... he had to come to London anyway, so he came with me. Alex, this is Jane Blake-Jones, my half-sister.'

The two shook hands. 'Nice to meet you, Jane,' Alex said and Jane nodded back shyly. They all settled down to wait.

Shortly afterwards a doctor called the two sisters in for a consultation while Alex remained in the waiting room.

The doctor was a fairly young man with a pleasant face and calming manner. He asked them to be seated in the small cubicle. 'Right then, Miss Blake-Jones and Miss, er ... Blake-Jones?'

'Ms Browne,' Maddie corrected him.

'Sorry, Browne. Right. Your mother is in a stable condition and recovering from the operation at the moment. You can go and see her if you like, but I think it best if we keep her sedated for the next twenty-four hours to keep her still. She has a broken leg and various contusions of course. There was some internal bleeding, but hopefully the operation has taken care of that and in time she should make a full recovery.'

Both girls drew a sigh of relief. 'Thank God for that,' they whispered in unison. The doctor smiled at them.

'If you go upstairs to the Nell Gwynne ward you'll find her there,' he said. 'I would advise you not to stay too long though, but come back tomorrow evening and hopefully she'll be able to speak to you then.'

'Thank you, doctor. We appreciate all you've done for her.'

'Not at all.'

As the doctor had said, there wasn't much point in staying at the hospital and they made their way back to Maddie's flat by bus, closely followed by Alex.

It was utter torture to be confined in a small flat with Alex, Maddie decided the next morning. If the attraction she felt for him had been hard to resist at Marcombe Hall, it was doubly so here in this tiny space where he dwarfed everything. He was larger than life and more handsome than any man had a right to be, with his blue-black hair and indigo eyes. Having forgotten his shaving kit, he also sported some wonderful stubble again, which made him resemble his smuggler ancestor so much it sent shivers down Maddie's back. She put down her spoon in disgust. The breakfast cereal tasted like sawdust and she wasn't hungry anymore.

At least at Marcombe it had been possible to avoid him and she hadn't been forced to see him dressed in only jeans and nothing else, looking wonderfully rumpled on his way to the shower. She closed her eyes and ground her teeth. She could just picture him now in the shower, soap lathering the hard planes of his body and ...

'Aaargh!' She stood up and went to wash up the breakfast dishes with jerky movements. *Why me? Why can't I fall for a normal man?* It just wasn't fair. First David, the cheating bastard, and now Alex …

'Talking to yourself again?' Alex had stuck his head out of the bathroom door and Maddie felt herself blush crimson. Had she really said the words out loud? She really hoped not.

'Um, yes. Must be age. They say it happens to everyone.'

Alex laughed. 'Ah, yes. You're positively ancient, aren't you?' He came out a few minutes later, still wearing only jeans, but with a towel around his shoulders. His hair fell in wet swathes across his forehead and gleamed jet-black. Maddie longed to touch it. For the briefest moment she allowed herself to toy with the idea of offering to blow-dry his hair for him, but sanity prevailed.

'Where's Jane? And Jessie?' he asked as he bent down to rummage in his holdall. Maddie felt feverish. Damn it, he was even good-looking from behind. It really was unfair.

'They're both out,' she managed to reply. 'Jessie's at work and Jane is out looking for a job. She needs to start earning some money so the sooner she finds one, the better.'

'I'm not sure how long I'll be, but shall we meet at the hospital at six?' she'd suggested. Maddie had agreed, but it meant she had a whole day alone with Alex.

'So it's just you and me, then,' Alex said cheerfully and pulled a T-shirt over his head. Maddie shivered. She didn't like the sound of that. Or rather, she liked it too much. It sounded so intimate.

'Um, yes. I think I'll have my shower now. Help yourself to breakfast, whatever you can find. I'm going shopping later, so if there's anything else you need, let me know.'

'I'll come shopping with you.' It wasn't a request, but a statement and Maddie sighed, knowing the futility of arguing with him. It would seem he was determined to stick to her like a leech. 'Then maybe we could go to a museum or something. It's been ages since I've been to London.'

'I don't know. I should probably stick around in case the hospital calls or something.'

'You've got your mobile, haven't you? And they said not to come back until this evening. Come on, you need something to take your mind off things.'

'Okay then.' She was aware that she didn't sound very gracious, but what did he expect? She hadn't asked for him to come with her. Although he was probably right – it would help to have something else to think about while she waited. She disappeared into the bathroom and hurried into the shower, but although she scrubbed herself vigorously, the thoughts of Alex alone in the next room wouldn't go away. *Damn the man.*

Jessie had been surprised to find an extra houseguest when she returned from work the previous evening and had unfortunately jumped to the conclusion that he was Maddie's boyfriend. She'd immediately offered to let Jane share her room so Alex could sleep with Maddie, who had blushed to the roots of her hair at the thought. Fortunately Alex had saved her from having to reply.

'That won't be necessary,' he'd told Jessie. 'I'll be fine on the couch, but thanks all the same.'

'Oh.' Jessie looked from one to the other and realised her mistake. 'Right. Well, does anyone want some takeaway pizza?'

They'd ordered some, but the atmosphere had been somewhat strained and they all went to bed fairly early.

Maddie stepped out of the shower now and dried herself quickly. She never blow-dried her hair since it made not the slightest difference to the curly mess, so instead she put on some make-up and looked around for her clothes. Her heart sank.

'Oh, hell.' In her haste to escape from Alex she'd forgotten to bring a clean set of clothes into the bathroom. She sighed again. There was nothing for it, she would have to go into the bedroom wearing only a towel.

With the towel wrapped around her and held in a firm grip with one hand, she left the bathroom at breakneck speed and cannoned into Alex who was just passing on his way to the kitchen. Her hand was jerked away and her death-grip on the towel loosened and before she could do anything about it she felt the wretched piece of cloth slide downwards. Alex caught her arms to steady her at the same time as she grabbed for the towel, but it was too late. Her upper body was exposed to his view and she heard him suck in his breath sharply.

'God, Maddie.' His reaction was immediate. He pulled her to him, running his hands up and down her back. 'I'm sorry but I can't bear this ...' he whispered. She looked up at him and could only watch helplessly as his mouth descended towards hers. She knew that when their lips touched she would be lost, but she was unable to move. Her limbs refused point blank to obey her.

Alex's mouth crushed hers in a ruthless kiss and the chemistry between them exploded exactly as before. Maddie's brain ceased to function rationally. She was beyond thinking and only existed on a sensory level, revelling in the feel of Alex's lips, the taste of him, the hardness of him, the smell of him. With a moan she didn't recognise as her own, she twined her arms round his neck, oblivious to the fact that the towel fell to the floor.

Some time later she was vaguely aware of being carried into her bedroom, of being gently lowered onto the bed and of Alex struggling with his clothing. After that there were only sensations – burning heat, flames of desire, soft skin scalding her own – and she gave herself up to the pleasure it seemed only Alex could give her.

It was even better than the previous time because now she knew what to expect and her body welcomed it, wanted it, craved it. She knew what he wanted too and that heightened her enjoyment. They egged each other on until there was no holding back, no barriers. Their love-making could have lasted an eternity or it could have been only minutes. Maddie didn't know which, but she was sure she never wanted it to end. Just like the last time.

But of course it did. It was a mind-blowing starburst of an ending, but an ending nevertheless. And just like the previous time, she returned to earth with a bump.

She lay still for a long time with her back to him and he held her gently until their breathing and heartbeats slowed to their normal rhythms. Maddie debated with herself whether to say anything, but what was there to say? She had allowed him to make love to her again, despite what she'd told him before. Although perhaps that wasn't the right description of what they'd done. There had been no declarations of love, no words spoken of any kind this time either. There was only desire. *Lust*. How she hated that word. *I mustn't let this happen again.*

'We'd better get going if we want to arrive before the museums close,' she finally said without looking at Alex. His arm tightened around her momentarily, but he made no comment about what had just passed between them.

'Okay. Shall we have another shower before we leave?' Maddie half turned and he smiled at her, with that bone-melting pirate grin. 'Together?' he added huskily. Her willpower evaporated immediately, like mist on a warm summer's morning, as she understood his meaning and it wasn't long before her fantasies of lathering him with soap became reality. Later that day she was ashamed to remember she hadn't even made a token amount of resistance, but at the time it seemed so right. Later she also remembered that there had still been no words of love spoken between them which strengthened her belief that whatever they had was purely physical.

She either had to accept that or keep away from him.

Chapter Twenty

As they were about to set out for the museums at last, the doorbell rang and Maddie went to open it, closely followed by Alex. She was surprised to find Olivia outside, smiling for once. That fact alone made Maddie instantly suspicious.

'Hello. What are you doing here?' Maddie frowned at her, but didn't invite her in.

'You don't answer my calls or text messages, so I didn't have a choice, did I?' Olivia made a face, as if she was being hard done by.

'That's because I didn't get them. I deleted your number off my phone.' Belatedly, Maddie realised Alex didn't know who Olivia was, so she quickly added for his benefit, 'This is my former sister, the one who'd rather I didn't exist.'

'I never said that,' Olivia protested, looking Alex up and down with a predatory glance. 'And who have we here then?'

'This is Alex, Kayla's brother-in-law,' Maddie cut in, before he had time to introduce himself. 'What do you want, Olivia? We were just going out.'

Olivia pouted slightly, then came straight to the point. 'Well, the thing is, I was wondering if maybe you could accept your half of the house after all … and then when you get the payment, you could give it to me in cash?'

'What? Why the hell would I do that?'

'Because if I get your half, as well as mine, I'll end up paying not just inheritance tax, but capital gains as well. You wouldn't believe what they charge, it's extortion! But if you give it to me in cash, they'll never know, will they – the tax authorities I mean. Simple!'

Maddie blinked. 'Are you for real?'

Behind her, Alex asked, 'You're giving your sister your share of an inheritance? Why?'

'Long story.' Maddie narrowed her eyes at Olivia. 'You have got some nerve, you know that? I'm really tempted to tell Mr Parker I want my share after all. And not for your benefit.'

Olivia turned pale, or as pale as she could with the layers of foundation on her face. 'You can't do that! You signed the papers, didn't you?'

'Not yet actually.'

'But—'

'Look, I'm going to spell this out one more time – take my half share and get lost, okay? You can bloody well pay the tax and be grateful, for once in your life. I'm not doing you any favours again, ever.'

'God, you're such a bitch sometimes,' Olivia grumbled.

'I can only see one bitch here,' Alex put in, 'and she doesn't have red hair. Come on, Maddie, we're late. Let's get ready to go.'

With that, he shut the door in Olivia's face and turned to pull Maddie into his arms. 'Jeez, how long have you had to put up with her?'

'Twenty-four years, I think,' Maddie mumbled into his shoulder.

'Well, I can see why you deleted her number. I would have done too.'

'Thanks, Alex. I ... thank you.'

It felt great to have someone on her side for once. If only it could be that way all the time.

'Good God, imagine having to wear that!'

Alex and Maddie ambled slowly through the exhibition

of old clothes and fashions at the Victoria & Albert Museum in South Kensington. They stopped to stare at a strange contraption set on a woman's hips which broadened them into the size of a small barn door. Alex shook his head in amazement.

'Yes, it must have been inconvenient,' Maddie agreed, 'but at least it didn't hurt. Come and see the "torture instruments" over here.' She led him over to another exhibit showing corsets designed to tighten waists to wasp-size.

'I see what you mean. Mind you, there's something to be said for corsets though. I quite like them myself. On women that is.' His comment earned him a punch on the arm from Maddie, but she didn't quite look him in the eye.

Alex had been racking his brains as to what he should say to her to put her at ease. Ever since their love-making she'd been as tense as a violin string and it seemed to him that as soon as they returned to normal she retreated into some form of shell. He could almost see the shutters come down across her eyes as she disappeared inside herself and he was at a loss as to how to bring her out.

There had been nothing wrong with their love-making, he was pretty sure of that. What they shared in that department was incredible – almost magical – and he simply couldn't believe that she didn't feel the same. So then why did she withdraw from him immediately afterwards? At Marcombe she'd told him they didn't suit, that they should just be friends. He had taken that to mean she regretted their passionate encounter because of his criminal past, but afterwards she hadn't shown any signs of despising him for that reason. And today, all it had taken was one kiss and she'd ignited like dry tinder. He sighed.

'Alex, come and look at this.' Maddie called him back

to the present. She was standing next to a glass case containing a mannequin dressed in an eighteenth century costume consisting of a dark red velvet jacket with large buttons and matching breeches and waistcoat. A white linen shirt and neckcloth completed the outfit. 'Doesn't he look just like your ancestor Jago?'

'I suppose so.' Alex put his head to one side to judge the clothes critically. 'Although he's not nearly disreputable enough,' he added.

'No, you're right there.' She glanced at Alex. 'I'd love to see you dressed up like that. You look a lot like Jago, so it would probably suit you.'

Alex laughed. 'I'd look ridiculous! Mind you, it would be worth it to see you in one of those.' He pointed to an extremely low-cut evening gown on a female doll in the opposite glass case and was delighted to see a blush spreading over Maddie's features. He loved it when she blushed, it was such a natural reaction and completely unaffected.

'I don't think you'd like that at all,' she stated firmly and led the way over to the Victorian costumes. 'One of these would be much better.'

Alex shook his head with a grin. 'No, they cover all the interesting bits.'

'Hmm. We'll just have to agree to disagree, won't we?'

And that was the problem in a nutshell, Alex reflected. He didn't want to agree to disagree, he wanted them to be compatible. He wanted them to agree on everything like they had seemed to at the beginning when they'd talked about their favourite music and films. An hour later when they left the museum, however, he was no closer to a solution. If anything, he was further away than before because Maddie had built up the barriers between them once more and even managed to avoid sitting too close to him on the bus. He gnashed his teeth in frustration.

There had to be a way.

For two days Alex pondered, while watching in amused silence as Maddie came up with one excuse after another for not being alone with him. He had to admit she was remarkably inventive, but then so was he and by the second afternoon he believed he'd come up with a solution. It was radical and it would take careful planning, but it might be his only chance. He had to make her see him in a new light. He smiled to himself.

He was seated on a chair outside the ward where Maddie and Jane were visiting their mother. The distinctive hospital smell made him feel slightly nauseous and he wished they would hurry up so he could leave this place. He hated hospitals. Admittedly, this one was very light and modern with all the wards built around a central atrium, but that didn't change its atmosphere. Alex found it extremely depressing to know he was in the midst of so much suffering and pain. And it reminded him of the night he'd been arrested for drug smuggling. He'd been hurt at the time and they'd brought him to a hospital first. That was the last he saw of the outside world for three long years. *No point thinking about it now. It's in the past and it won't happen again.*

It seemed an eternity before the sisters emerged from the ward.

'How's your mother?' he asked them politely.

'Much better, thanks.' Maddie looked relieved. 'She was quite talkative and doesn't appear to be in so much pain today. The doctor is very pleased with her progress.'

'Great. When will she be able to go home?'

'Oh, not for ages yet, so she has told me to go back to Devon for a while and come back in a couple of weeks. She seems to think I'll be safer there.'

'Because he's here?'

Maddie shook her head. 'No, Alex, we were wrong. It wasn't him. It was a genuine accident.'

'Yes,' Jane added. 'Mother says she was daydreaming and not looking where she was going. She just forgot to check the traffic before crossing the road. She's not used to London yet.'

'I see.' Alex looked at the pair of them and could see they truly believed this. That was a relief – one thing less to worry about. But it meant the crazy coot, Blake-Jones, was probably still on the loose somewhere near Marcombe. 'You haven't heard anything from the police in Devon, have you?' he asked Maddie.

'No, nothing yet, but I'm sure they're doing their best.'

Alex wished they'd hurry up as he didn't like to think of Maddie, her mother and half-sister in danger. 'Well, it's up to you whether we stay here or not.'

'All right, I guess I'll go back then, or what do you think?' Maddie glanced at Jane for confirmation.

Jane nodded agreement. 'Yes, no point us both being here. I'll visit her every day and let you know how she's getting on.'

'Okay then.' Alex stood up and closed the book he'd been reading. 'Let's go.'

'I really should have stayed in London to look for a job,' Maddie said to Kayla the next evening. She was unpacking her belongings for the third time in the guest room at Marcombe and it was beginning to feel like coming home.

In comparison, the flat in London had seemed strangely alien. 'I've lazed around doing nothing for long enough.'

'Yes, but you promised you would stay a bit longer and then you were called away in the middle of it. You have to finish your holiday and anyway, we've hardly seen you,' Kayla protested with a smile.

'Rubbish, I've been here for weeks, months even.'

'Well, a few more days won't make any difference. The children missed you and so did I. Wes has been so busy I've barely seen him, what with doing his own work and looking after Alex's cottages as well.'

Maddie hung her head. 'I'm sorry about that, Kayla. I did try to tell him to stay here, but there was no way of changing his mind.'

'Oh, don't worry about that. I don't mind really. Now, come on, you'd better help me get the little ones into bed so they know you're back.'

'Oh, Maddie, I'm so sorry, I completely forgot,' Kayla exclaimed halfway through a piece of toast the next morning.

'What did you forget?' Maddie took a sip of tea and regarded her friend. She had almost been startled into dropping the mug by Kayla's sudden outburst, since her thoughts had been on quite another matter – the man who was sitting opposite her at the table. His blue gaze had been fixed on her with embarrassing intensity and Maddie was trying desperately to think of a way to tell him to stop it without Kayla noticing.

'That Mr Ruthven rang and left you a message. He wants you to call him back. Honestly, I don't know how it could have slipped my mind.'

'The man we spoke to at Wisteria Lodge?'

'Yes, that's the one. I wrote down the number for you, hold on and I'll find it.'

Kayla dashed off towards the hall, leaving Maddie alone with Alex and she seized her chance.

'Would you please stop staring at me,' she hissed at him.

'Why?' He raised an eyebrow at her and leaned back in his chair.

'I don't like it. It makes me nervous.'

'I don't see why it should. I'm just admiring your vibrant beauty this morning.' He grinned. 'Besides, it's a free world.'

'Oh, for heaven's sake, you sound like Nell.' Maddie clenched her fists under the table. He really was the most infuriating man she'd ever met.

'Childish, you mean?' He laughed. 'Well, two can play at that game. You shouldn't try to avoid me so much, then I wouldn't have to stare at you.'

'I never—'

'Here we are, I found it.' Kayla returned in triumph carrying a small scrap of paper which she handed to Maddie. 'This is the number. He said you could call any time.'

Maddie was still seething, but managed a smile of thanks. 'I'd better do it now then, before I forget. See you later.' After one last glare at Alex she left the kitchen and ran up the stairs.

As she sat down next to the phone to catch her breath she looked at the piece of paper and wondered what the man could want now. Had he perhaps remembered something? Her stomach did a small somersault. Was it possible she'd been right after all? There had been no opportunity to discuss the house with her mother before leaving London, so Maddie was none the wiser. With fingers that shook slightly she dialled Mr Ruthven's number.

She let it ring at least twenty times and was about to

hang up when someone finally answered. 'Hello?' It wasn't the Scottish burr she had expected, but an entirely different voice, albeit still a man.

'Oh, er, may I speak to Mr Ruthven, please? This is Maddie Browne. He asked me to call.'

'Ah, Ms Browne. Thank you for calling back. It was me who called actually, I'm the brother of the Mr Ruthven you met.'

'I see, that explains it.'

'Explains what?' The man sounded puzzled.

'Why I didn't recognise your voice.'

'You mean the wee accent,' he said in a perfect imitation of his brother. 'I can do it too, but I've lived here in Devon for so long I don't usually talk like that anymore.'

'Well, now you sound very alike.'

'So they say. Anyway, the reason I called you was because I think I might be able to help you. You told Colin you thought you recognised my house.'

Maddie suddenly found breathing difficult and her voice, when she answered, came out in a hoarse whisper. 'You can? How?'

'I don't really want to discuss it over the phone. Would you mind visiting again and I'll tell you in person?'

'Er, sure. I mean, of course. When should I come? When would be convenient for you?' she amended. Her thought processes didn't appear to be in normal working order and she had to concentrate really hard.

'How about Friday?'

'Okay. And what time would you like me to come?'

'Any time in the afternoon. Oh, and Ms Browne? Come the back way again, I'm having trouble with my front door at the moment. It's stuck.'

'Right. I'll see you then. Bye.'

After she had hung up Maddie collapsed in a little heap next to the wall. It was as if all the air had gone out of her and she simply couldn't stand up. Three days until Friday. How was she going to survive the wait? It would seem endless.

'Never mind,' she finally muttered. 'I've waited this long, I can wait three days. I'll just have to find something to occupy myself with.'

'Auntie Maddie, who are you talking to?' Nell came skipping along the corridor looking as if she were practising the Highland fling.

'What? Oh, just myself.'

'That's silly. Why don't you talk to Kayla instead? At least then you'd get an answer.'

Maddie had to smile. She stood up. 'You're right, of course. But tell me, what are you up to?'

'I've just been to visit Jago.' Nell was still hopping from one foot to another. Maddie shook her head. The child didn't have a still bone in her body. It must be wonderful to have so much energy.

'Jago? You mean your ancestor in the painting?'

'Yes. I talk to him sometimes because Kayla told me he talked to her, but he never answers me. Maybe one day he will, though.'

'You never know. So what did you tell him?'

'Well, today I told him there are gypsies camped in one of our fields. He was a gypsy himself, did you know? Or at least his mummy was. So I thought he'd like to hear that.'

'Really? Where? I mean, which field?'

'Let's go for a walk and I'll show you. It's not very far.'

'All right. Let me just change my shoes. Wait here a second. No, actually, why don't you run and tell Kayla we're going for a walk and I'll meet you in the hall.'

'Okay. See you there.'

Chapter Twenty-One

It was a long shot, but worth a try, Maddie decided. The gypsies camped in the field near Marcombe may not be the right ones, but they might be able to help her in any case. She desperately wanted to see Madame Romar again to ask her some more questions now that part of her prediction had come true. And even if she wasn't in this particular camp, the people there might know where she could be found. Maddie had never been so confused in her life and could definitely do with some help, psychic or otherwise. The woman might be able to explain her predictions in more detail.

Nell skipped along beside her and talked almost incessantly about school, about her friends and anything else she could think of. 'Don't you ever stop to breathe?' Maddie finally asked with a giggle. She didn't see how anyone could find so much to talk about.

'No, not very often. Kayla says I'm a chatterbox, but I don't mind. And Daddy says I'm going to be a politician, maybe even the Prime Minister. Do you think I will?'

Maddie laughed. 'It wouldn't surprise me. Or perhaps you should be a lawyer like your daddy, but the kind that defends people in court. They have to talk a lot and be good at arguing.'

'Well, I'm good at arguing with my brother. He drives me nuts sometimes.'

'That's understandable, but I didn't quite mean that sort of arguing. Never mind. Is that the camp over there?' She pointed to a collection of camper vans over to their right.

'Yep, that's it. I told you it wasn't far.' Nell skipped

ahead, practising her whistling at the same time. Maddie winced.

As they neared the camp she saw children running about and women hanging washing up to dry in the sun. She scanned their faces, but the familiar one of Madame Romar was nowhere in sight. The gypsies stopped talking when Maddie and Nell walked towards the nearest Winnebago and the oldest one stepped forward cautiously.

'Can I help you?' The woman's clothes were colourful, albeit not as garish as the ones Madame Romar had worn for her fortune-telling. They were also a lot more modern.

'Well, I'm not sure, but I'm looking for a lady by the name of Madame Romar. She tells fortunes at fairs and I wondered if by any chance she was here?'

'Yes, I'm here.' Maddie spun round. Madame Romar was standing in the doorway of the next camper van, dressed almost entirely in black and Maddie had to look hard before she recognised the woman. 'What do you want with me?'

It wasn't an auspicious beginning and Maddie swallowed hard before stammering out her request. 'I-I, er … j-just wondered i-if I could have a word with you. I would appreciate your help.' Nell had sidled up to her and clutched at her hand. There was no outright antagonism from any of the gypsies, but there were no welcoming smiles either. Everyone stood stock still waiting for Madame Romar's next words. The old woman took her time before finally giving a curt nod.

'Very well. Come in.' She turned on her heel and disappeared into the van and Maddie followed reluctantly. Now that she'd found the woman it didn't seem like such a good idea any longer.

'Do we have to go in there?' Nell whispered.

Maddie squeezed the little girl's hand reassuringly. 'Only for a few moments, I promise. It won't take long. Or you can sit on the steps and wait for me? Just so long as I can see you.'

'No, I want to stay with you.'

Inside it was surprisingly roomy and spotlessly clean. Madame Romar waved them onto a small built-in sofa and they sat down. The woman pulled up a chair and seated herself opposite them.

'You have come to ask me questions, am I right?'

'Um, yes. If you don't mind? I will pay you, of course.' Maddie blinked when the woman shook her head almost angrily.

'No,' Madame Romar barked. 'You have already paid me and I've told you all I can. I cannot help you any further.'

'But ... part of what you told me has come true and I wondered, that is, can't you give me a few more details? It's all so confusing.' Maddie drew in a deep breath to stem the tide of disappointment washing over her.

'Of course my prediction has come true. I told you the truth, not the nonsense I tell most people.' Madame Romar shook her head. 'Bah! They're idiots, most of them. They hear only what they want to hear anyway, so that's what I tell them. But you were different. I can't be more specific, however, you have to figure it out for yourself. That's part of the solution.'

Maddie frowned. 'I've tried to understand your meaning, but your words don't make sense.'

The woman gave a cackling laugh. 'Maybe not now, but they will. You have to be patient, my dear. Some prophesies take years to happen and when they do you will know. Patience is difficult for young people, I know, but it has to be learned.'

'I see.' Maddie stood up. 'Well, thank you for talking to me anyway. I'm sorry to have disturbed you in your home.'

'Not at all. You're welcome any time. You are almost like family, just as the little one is.' Madame Romar smiled at Nell, who looked up in surprise.

'Me? You mean because of Great-great-something grandpa Jago?'

'Certainly I do. His mother was my great-great-something aunt, so you're practically one of us. In fact, Jago was the one who made sure we had the right to camp here whenever we want.' The old woman's smile broadened and Nell's shyness evaporated instantly.

'I talk to him a lot, you know,' she confided.

Madame Romar nodded. 'Good for you. He can hear you, but I'm afraid he can't answer.'

'I know. He only talked to Kayla and—'

'Come on, chatterbox,' Maddie interrupted. 'I'm sure Madame Romar has things to do.' She took Nell by the hand and led her out into the blinding sunshine once more. As she began to descend the steps the old woman put a hand on her shoulder.

'There may be more danger to come, but believe in happiness and I think everything will work out.'

'Thank you.' Maddie turned away to hide the tears that appeared from nowhere. The words were small comfort, but comfort nonetheless. She stared at the ground as they left the camp and didn't notice whether any of the other families watched their departure.

'Was it today you were going to see Mr Ruthven?' Kayla asked on the Friday morning.

'Yes, this afternoon.' The endless three days had finally snailed past and Maddie was in a state of nervous exhaustion. Her fingernails had never been more abused and she'd even had to resort to putting plasters on some of them. Nailbiting was a stupid habit and one she really must stop, she reflected.

She looked up and caught Alex's gaze on her again. He had developed an uncanny ability to come down to breakfast at the same time as Maddie every morning and today was no exception. Alex never sought her company deliberately, but more often than not he seemed to be around. He winked at her now and she scowled back, casting an uneasy glance towards Kayla to see if she had noticed the exchange, but Kayla was absorbed in feeding Edmund. The little boy was becoming very wilful and every second spoonful of apple porridge went somewhere other than into his mouth; either on the table, the floor or on himself and his mother.

'I'll come with you,' Alex suddenly announced.

'I'm sorry, what?' Maddie had been miles away and had forgotten the previous topic of conversation.

'To see Mr Ruthven,' Alex explained. 'I don't think you should go alone. He might be another crazy old coot. There seem to be a lot of them about.'

'Oh, yes, do take Alex with you,' Kayla agreed before exclaiming, 'Oh, Eddie, now look what you've done!' The little boy chortled with laughter at the sight of his mother's T-shirt covered in porridge and Maddie had to turn away to hide a smile. She soon grew serious again though.

'I'd rather go by myself actually,' she told Alex. 'I'm sure Mr Ruthven isn't dangerous and I'll tell him that you all know where I am.'

Alex shook his head. 'Not good enough. If he's a nutter he won't care if anyone knows. Look at the other guy. Everyone's after him, but that doesn't stop him.'

'It's been days now and no one has seen him. He's probably left the area, maybe even fled abroad.'

'I don't think so. And Foster told me he thought he saw someone hanging around the gates yesterday, although when he tried to go after him, the man disappeared.'

Maddie gasped. 'Blake-Jones?' The name came out as a whisper as she couldn't make her voice work suddenly.

Alex shook his head. 'No, a guy in a knitted hat, but still ...'

'Alex is right, Maddie,' Kayla said firmly. 'You can't go alone. If you won't take him, then I'll have to ask Wes to go with you.'

'I'm not a baby,' Maddie grumbled. 'Oh, okay then, come with me if you want to, but you'll probably be bored silly,' she told Alex.

'In your company? Never.' He grinned at her and she gritted her teeth to keep from throwing something at him.

'Do you know what I like most about being in your company?' Alex asked as they drove along the now familiar route later that day.

'I couldn't guess in a million years,' Maddie muttered and stared out the window on her side of the car.

'It's so restful. You don't chatter constantly like Nell and the boys or whisper sweet nothings to each other like Kayla and Wes. Always silent and peaceful.' He sighed. 'Mind you, one can have too much of a good thing sometimes.'

'Oh, shut up, Alex.' She turned a fulminating look on him and he chuckled.

'Well, at least I got you to look at me with those beautiful green eyes of yours. I do so love it when they shoot sparks.' Maddie hit him on the shoulder.

'Now, now, you don't want me to drive off the road, do you? You'd better cool that red-head's temper of yours before you see Mr Ruthven.'

'Hmmph.' Maddie crossed her arms over her chest. 'If you weren't here there wouldn't be anyone to put me in a temper.'

Alex just chuckled again. He'd discovered how much he enjoyed teasing her and as it seemed the only way to communicate with her at the moment, it would have to do.

But not for much longer.

They parked in front of Wisteria Lodge this time and stopped to look up at the house.

'Must be a lovely view of the sea from the top floor,' Alex mused and shaded his eyes with one hand. 'This house is quite high up on the hill.'

'Yes, it's beautiful, isn't it,' Maddie agreed. 'A happy house,' she added quietly to herself. Just like the one in her dream.

Alex went towards the gate, but Maddie stopped him. 'No, we have to go round the back. Mr Ruthven said there was something wrong with the front door.'

'Oh, okay.' He followed her towards the fence and this time he helped her with a steadying hand before vaulting over himself.

Maddie strode off through the field towards the back, but stopped to wait for Alex before rounding the hedge. Her heart was hammering inside her chest and now the time had come she was afraid. Alex must have noticed that something was wrong, because he took her hand as he came up to her.

'What's the matter, Maddie?' He scanned her eyes with a serious expression on his face.

'I ... well, it's really silly, but I'm scared. I'm afraid of what I will find out, but I'm also afraid I won't find anything out. Does that make sense?'

He gathered her close and wrapped his strong arms around her in a comforting hug. She didn't resist, she needed his strength right now. 'Don't worry. Whatever it is, it's always better to know. You'll be fine.'

'I guess so.' She leaned into him for a moment, breathing in the clean, masculine scent of him in deep, calming breaths. Finally she pushed him slowly away. 'Okay, let's go slay my dragons.'

They rounded the hedge and Maddie was faced once more with her dream vision – the back of the house, the profusion of climbing plants and roses and the swing. She swallowed and clenched her fists by her side before approaching the gate. Alex opened it for her and she entered slowly, taking it all in.

'It's a lovely garden,' Alex commented. 'I can see why you would want to dream about it.'

She gave him a small, tight smile. He was trying to put her at ease and she appreciated his efforts, but right now she was too apprehensive to be calmed by small-talk. She walked over to the swing and reached out to touch the rough hemp ropes and the wooden seat, grey with age. Every fibre of her being cried out that it belonged to her and she wanted to shout it out loud. *This is my swing!* But of course she didn't. She simply stared at it, lost in her dream.

'Ah, Ms Browne, there you are.' Maddie swung around in time to see a man emerge from the back door of the house and walk towards them with a smile on his face. A red-haired man with a beard.

All of a sudden Maddie had trouble breathing. It was as

if something was attempting to squeeze the air out of her lungs. No matter how much she struggled, she couldn't pull in a breath. Her eyes blurred and a sliver of darkness obscured her vision, growing ever larger until she couldn't see anything at all. She heard herself moan, then there was nothing …

Chapter Twenty-Two

'Maddie, please wake up, love.' Alex's voice, calling to her from afar, came closer and Maddie fought her way through the enveloping darkness to the bright surface. Her eyelids fluttered open, and she squinted into the sun, then flung up a hand to shield her eyes.

'Alex?' she croaked. She found that she was lying down on a hard bench and tried to sit up, but a hand pushed her firmly down again.

'Don't try to sit up yet, you'll probably feel nauseous. Mr Ruthven has gone to fetch you a glass of water.'

'Mr Ruthven?' She frowned, and then it all came flooding back to her. The red-haired man. The man from her dream. She sat bolt upright and discovered that Alex had been right. Her head swam abominably, but she ignored it and looked around wildly. There was no one there. Had she been dreaming again? 'Where is he?'

As if in a trance, she saw the man come out of the house once more, through the door she knew so well, carrying a tray of cold drinks. He was a giant of a man with red hair, shot with silver, curling wildly around his head. His neatly trimmed beard was of a slightly darker hue and also had strands of grey, but was still very red. He smiled as he came closer and put the tray down on a table near the bench on which she had been lying. Then he brought her a glass and knelt in front of her.

'So, you've decided to come back at last, Sorcha,' he said as he handed her the drink. Maddie took it automatically and continued to stare at him, mesmerised.

'Come back?' she repeated, parrot-fashion. Her mind

appeared to be full of cotton wool and refused to function properly.

'Yes. You've been here before. You said you remembered, didn't you?'

'Yes, I remembered the house, but I thought I'd only dreamed of being here.' He was still kneeling in front of her and without thinking she put out a hand to touch his cheek and the rough beard which felt scratchy against her fingers.

He smiled again. 'Oh, aye?'

'You called me Sorcha, so you must have known me when I was a baby. Did my mother and I used to visit you here, Mr Ruthven?'

This time he grinned broadly. 'You could say that, but I would rather you didn't call me "Mr Ruthven".'

She frowned. 'Why?'

'I'd much prefer it if you called me "Dad", but if not, Brian will do.'

Both Maddie and Alex gasped and looked at each other and Maddie wondered if she was about to faint again. The dizziness had returned with a vengeance, but somehow the man's words were not really a surprise and she managed to control her spinning head. A part of her had known the truth of it as soon as she saw him come through that door.

'No, don't pass out on me again, my girl, you're much too big to be carried around these days.'

'You're Maddie's father?' Alex was the first to find his voice.

'Indeed I am.'

'How do we know you're telling the truth?' Alex spoke again, voicing the question that had hovered on Maddie's tongue as well, although truth be told, she had a gut feeling this man wasn't lying. He really was her father.

'Well, look at us – same hair, similar features, both tall. Don't you think?'

Alex nodded. 'Yes, but that doesn't mean you're her father. You could be related some other way.'

The man shrugged. 'I'd be very happy to do a DNA test, if that's what you want. In fact, I think it's a very good idea for both our sakes.' He turned back to Maddie. 'Is Maddie the name they gave you?' She nodded and he said, 'Hmph, they could at least have let you keep your name.'

'Please, Mr ... I mean, er, could you explain to me what happened? I haven't got a clue what you're talking about.' Maddie was close to tears again, but it was pure joyful emotion this time, not sadness. 'I only found out a short while ago that I was adopted and when I finally traced my real mother, Ruth that is, she was too ill to tell me the whole story.'

'Ruth is ill?' She saw instant concern on her father's face and hastened to reassure him.

'No, no, she's all right now. Although she's had an accident as well so she's in hospital, but the doctor says she'll be fine. Never mind, I'll tell you about that later, only please won't you explain?'

'Very well.' Her father went to sit down on a garden chair nearby and Alex took Maddie's hand and gave it a reassuring squeeze. She plaited her fingers with his and hung on for dear life. She needed his strength again and was grateful for his support. *Thank goodness he came with me after all!*

'I don't really know where to start. At the beginning I suppose.' Her father took a deep breath and stared into the distance as if seeking the right words. 'I come from Scotland originally, as you probably guessed, but I moved down here about thirty years ago in order to paint. The light is so remarkable here, it makes for extraordinary paintings, but that's irrelevant ... Anyway, a year or so after I arrived, Ruth, your mother, was visiting friends here in this village one summer, a couple of years after her marriage to that Blake-Jones fellow. We met at a party and it was love at first sight, I think for both of us. You might wonder how she could fall in love with someone else so soon, but you see she found out immediately after she married him what sort of man Blake-Jones was and she was very unhappy. Here in the village she could be herself and I suppose she was desperate to have some fun while she was away from him and his bullying ways. I knew nothing of the marriage and she didn't tell me until much later.' He paused to take a sip of his drink.

'So, the inevitable happened and you were conceived that summer, but Ruth went back to her husband believing she could fool him into thinking you were his. Unfortunately for her, she had terrible morning sickness almost from day one and he soon cottoned on to what was happening. He sent her to stay with relatives in Wiltshire until you were born and told her to have you adopted at birth. That was when she turned to me.' He cleared his throat and looked at Maddie.

'I've always loved children, so it seemed like the perfect solution for me to take care of you by myself and from the moment I first laid eyes on you, I adored you.' Maddie's heart constricted and she swallowed a sob. 'Ruth told her husband you'd been adopted and from time to time she managed to come and see you. It wasn't an ideal situation, but she refused to leave her husband and I never knew why until much later. At the time I thought she'd decided she loved him after all. I was too busy with you to worry about that.'

'So I did live here,' Maddie whispered. 'It *was* my swing. I knew it.'

Her father smiled. 'Indeed. You loved that swing. I could have pushed you all day and you would still not have tired of it. Those were happy days.' He grew serious. 'It didn't last though. That bastard Blake-Jones became suspicious and followed Ruth and of course he discovered her secret. One afternoon when I was busy inside the house, you were playing here in the garden. He must have sneaked round the back and snatched you as quick as a flash. When I came out to bring you in for tea, you were gone.' He passed a hand across his brow. 'I can't tell you how I felt that day. Despair, utter despair hardly comes close to describing it. I guessed, of course, what had happened. What I didn't know was what he would do to you. I feared the worst.'

'What did he do? I have dreams of being kidnapped and in one of them he put me in the boot of his car, but I don't remember anything after that. It's as if I have blocked it out.' Maddie frowned, trying once again to recall more details.

'Perhaps that was just as well for your sake. I searched everywhere, I called the police, I even went to Ruth's house, but it was no use. He denied point blank ever having been near this house and said that neither he, nor Ruth, knew who I was. Ruth was so terrified of him, she agreed with everything he said. I was furious, but helpless.'

'So what happened then? Did you ever find out?'

'Ruth eventually told me he had forced her to sign adoption papers for you, but she didn't know where you were. When I tried to approach the authorities, I was met by a blank wall. Because I wasn't named as your father on the birth certificate, they refused to give me any information about your whereabouts or to return you to me. Blake-Jones had done his work well and I couldn't prove a thing.' A bleak look settled over his features. 'Believe me, I tried everything.'

'Oh, how awful …' Maddie put out her hand to touch his arm and he put his large one on top of hers.

'Yes. I even hired a private investigator, but he couldn't come up with anything useful, so in the end I had to give up. There was nothing I could do. I tried to put the whole episode out of my mind and travelled abroad. I even married and had two more children, both boys thankfully as I didn't want any girl other than you, but I never forgot you and I always returned to this house. I couldn't bring myself to sell it. You see, I hoped that when you grew up you would come looking for your roots and I was determined to be here when you did. But the years passed and you never came. In fact, I was thinking of selling up only last month. I'm divorced now and thought I'd go back to Scotland.'

'I didn't know.' Maddie shook her head, sadness churning in her gut. 'My parents never told me I was adopted. Perhaps that horrid man had made it a condition, or perhaps they simply didn't want me to know. Either way, I only found out when they died in a car crash a couple of months ago.'

'Oh, sweetheart. What a mess …' They both sat quietly for a while, thinking about all the time that had been lost. Finally Brian took a deep breath and asked, 'What made you come here, then, if you didn't know about me?'

Maddie told him about the dream and how she had recognised the house as they were driving past, and her father smiled.

'It must be fate. You were meant to come back to me

and I can't tell you how happy I am. You will visit again, won't you?'

'Of course I will. We'll have to get to know each other all over again. Did you say that you're an artist?'

'Yes. Not a brilliant one, but I get by.'

'Maddie paints too,' Alex, who had until that point remained silent, entered the conversation. 'She's very good.'

'Really? It must have been in your genes. Excellent, I'd love to see some of your drawings.'

'No, no, I'm not very good at all. Alex is exaggerating,' Maddie said hurriedly.

'Don't listen to her, Mr Ruthven, she's too modest.'

'Call me Brian. Any friend of Sorcha's is my friend.' Maddie's father held out his hand and Alex shook it.

'Thank you. I'm Alex Marcombe.'

'Are you now? I've heard of your lovely house.'

'It's my brother's actually, but yes, it is beautiful. You must come and visit. Paint it maybe?'

'I'd like that.'

They continued to chat for what seemed like hours and Brian served them tea in the garden with home-made scones. 'I hope you remember what a good cook I am,' he joked and Maddie smiled back.

As the shadows lengthened she realised it was time to go. She didn't want to leave now that she had finally found her father, but they had a lifetime to become acquainted and Kayla would be worried about her. Reluctantly she said, 'Well, I suppose we'd better be on our way.'

'I hope you'll come back soon,' Brian said and stood up to put his cup on the tray.

'How about tomorrow?' Maddie suggested and went over to give the big man a tentative hug. He returned it with a bear hug and when she looked up she thought she saw tears in his eyes, but he quickly blinked them away.

'Tomorrow will do just fine. Bring your paintings, please, I'd really like to see them.'

'Okay, er, Dad.' It felt strange, but right, to call him that. 'See you then.'

They turned to leave the way they had come, through the back gate, but before they had taken more than a few steps, a shot rang out.

Almost in slow motion, Maddie watched in horror and disbelief as her father fell onto the grass with a scream of agony, clutching his leg, and she turned to confront their attacker. She wasn't surprised to catch a glimpse of the Reverend Blake-Jones crouching behind the fence with a shotgun aimed straight at them. A black fury welled up inside her. He had taken away her father once, she wouldn't let him do it again.

'You bastard,' she screamed and ran towards him, heedless of the danger.

'Maddie, no!' Alex shouted and jumped on her, pulling her to the ground.

'Sorcha, for God's sake …' her father groaned.

Blake-Jones stood up and sneered. 'I'm not the bastard around here,' he spat. 'You're the bastard and you should never have been born. Now come over here, nice and slow, or I'll shoot your precious friends. Don't think I won't do it.'

Maddie looked at Alex. Did she have a choice? He shook his head as if to say, 'don't go', but she made up her mind. She couldn't let Blake-Jones hurt her father or Alex. She would have to do as he said and hope she could escape from him later. Slowly she got to her feet.

'No, Maddie, there must be another way,' Alex hissed.

'No tricks now, or I'll shoot you all anyway,' Blake-Jones called.

'I must, Alex,' she whispered. He held on to her hand, but she shook it off. It was her the madman wanted, so it was up to her to think of a way out.

Blake-Jones opened the gate, came into the garden and stopped near the swing. When Maddie reached him he grabbed her arm and yanked on it roughly so that she spun away from him and faced the others. His arm snaked around her, holding her tight and Maddie felt the familiar panic building up inside her. The scenario was almost identical to that of her dream. She was by her beloved swing and he was forcing her away. If she glanced over her shoulder she could see his dark, evil face and when she tried to scream nothing happened. A strangled sob escaped her.

Maddie closed her eyes. It was the nightmare all over again.

Chapter Twenty-Three

Maddie tried to kick-start her brain. There must be something she could do. *Anything!*

Then it dawned on her. This wasn't a dream and she was no longer a little girl. She was a grown-up and almost as tall as Blake-Jones, who was average size for a man. And she *had* taken self-defence classes. This realisation banished the sensations of panic and gave her the faith she needed. *I can fight back this time and I damn well will.* Holding on to that thought, she jabbed the hateful man in the stomach as hard as she could with a sharp elbow and had the satisfaction of hearing him grunt in surprise and pain. Before he had time to recover, she flung away from him and kicked at the hand which held the shotgun and he screamed out as her foot connected with it. The weapon clattered to the ground.

'I knew those kick-boxing lessons would come in useful one day,' she muttered and tried another kick. This time he was ready for her, however, and he simply grabbed her leg and twisted so that she fell down. 'Ouch!'

Maddie was by no means beaten though, and quickly bounced to her feet, the way she'd been taught. She aimed a punch at his face, missed, and hit his arm instead. It was enough to stop him from retrieving the shotgun, but the clout she received in return made her ears ring. She shook her head, but kicked out gamely, a double-kick. The first one missed, but she feinted slightly and the second one connected with Blake-Jones's crotch. He doubled up in pain and let out a keening wail. Alex took this opportunity to run over and snatch up the weapon, before aiming an almighty punch at the man's jaw. Blake-Jones reeled back, then launched himself at Alex with a roar of pain and fury. Alex threw the gun to Maddie, who caught it deftly. She watched with bated breath as the two men fought.

Her father had by this time managed to stand up, and limped over to Maddie. 'Dad, are you alright?'

'I think so. Just a flesh wound, but it hurts like hell. Give me the shotgun, please.'

Maddie handed it to him gladly. She didn't like guns of any kind, not even on television. She moved towards the fight between Alex and Blake-Jones to try and help, but Alex called out, 'Stay away, I can handle this.'

Maddie nodded. She trusted him and he seemed to know what he was doing. Without thinking she began to gnaw at her already abused nails.

It should have been an uneven match, with Alex half the older man's age and considerably fitter, but Blake-Jones fought like a man possessed. Alex appeared to be equally furious, however, and eventually gained the upper hand, sending the older man sprawling. When Blake-Jones stayed on the ground, Alex stopped and caught his breath.

Maddie's father limped towards the prone man and pointed the weapon at him. 'Stand up,' he snarled. 'This time you're not getting away with your evil schemes.' He turned slightly to order Alex to call for the police and in that split second Blake-Jones managed to stagger to his feet. When Brian turned back to his prisoner, it was to find him charging towards him with hatred shining out of his eyes. Reacting purely on instinct, Brian pulled the trigger.

The expression on Blake-Jones's face would have been ludicrous had it not also been terrifyingly macabre. He looked stunned, as if he'd never imagined that he could possibly be mortal himself, before directing his gaze downwards to where a large stain was rapidly spreading across his middle. His hands came up to clutch at the wound, then his legs buckled and he fell face first onto the grass. A strange gurgling sound came from his throat and after that all was quiet.

The three remaining occupants of the garden stood in stunned silence until Brian too began to fall. Alex rushed forward to catch him and Maddie was galvanised into action as well.

'Dad! Oh, no, don't you dare die on me too.'

'He's ... not ... going to ... die.' Alex panted under the weight of the big man and struggled to pull him towards the bench. 'He's probably fainted from loss of blood. Run inside and call the ambulance and police will you, please?' Maddie didn't need to be asked twice.

'I'm getting a bit tired of seeing you, young lady,' the doctor at the hospital joked when he found her in the corridor waiting for news of her father. 'Is there anyone amongst your acquaintances who isn't going to visit this hospital in the near future?'

Maddie managed a ghost of a smile. 'No offence, doctor, but I really hope this is the last time I'll see you too, at least for now.'

'Yes, well, I won't take that as gospel. Now, are you waiting to hear about Mr Ruthven?'

'Yes, please. Is he all right?'

'Absolutely. The flesh wound in his thigh was deep, but we have cauterised it and given him some fresh blood to make up for what he lost. A few days' rest and he should be fighting fit.'

'Thank God for that. He had me really worried there for a while.'

'You seem to have had an exciting time of it recently. Are you okay yourself or would you like me to prescribe something to help you sleep?'

'Oh, no thanks. I'm going to sleep like a log now that I know Mr Blake-Jones can't hurt me any longer. He was the only reason I kept having nightmares.'

'That's understandable. I'm glad it's over. Try to rest for a few weeks if you can. There may be some delayed reaction to all these shocks, although you strike me as fairly resilient.'

'I'm tough as old boots.' Maddie smiled. 'Can I go and see Dad now or is he asleep?'

'No, I think he's awake. You go ahead.'

'Thank you for all your help.'

'Not at all.'

Brian's large frame filled the hospital bed almost to overflowing and he looked oddly out of place. His skin tone closely matched the sheets, however, and Maddie knew he must be feeling quite rough, although he smiled at her when she tiptoed into the room.

'Dad. How are you?'

'Much better for seeing you.' She perched on the edge of the bed and he took her hand. 'I'm sorry we'll have to postpone our painting session now, but I'll try to heal quickly. Can you stay in Devon for a while or do you have somewhere else you have to go?'

'Normally I live in London, but I'm staying with my friend Kayla at the moment. She's married to Alex's brother Wes. They have said I can visit them for as long as I like and the doctor just told me to rest for a few weeks, so I guess I'll be here for a while.'

'Good. We have a lot of catching up to do.' He looked her in the eyes. 'That is, if you want to? I realise I have no claim on you any more, not really. You are Maddie now, not my Sorcha, and I shall have to get used to calling you that. No doubt you have your own life to lead and I'm nothing but a stranger.'

'Don't say that, please. During all that time you were with me in my dreams, so you'll never be a stranger to me. We'll start over and this time we won't let anyone ruin things.' She gave him a hug and stood up to leave. 'I'd better let you have some rest now, but I'll be back tomorrow. Sleep well, Dad.'

'I will now, Sorcha-Maddie.'

Maddie was too weary to speak a single word on the journey back to Marcombe, and Alex seemed to understand. Once there they were fussed over by Kayla.

'Go straight to bed, you two, and I'll bring you dinner on a tray. You must be absolutely exhausted. I still can't take it all in. It's like some horrible dream.'

Without protest, they did as they were told and Maddie's boast to the doctor proved to be correct. She had the best night's sleep for ages.

'Oh, Maddie, you must be absolutely over the moon.' Kayla was curled up at one end of a huge settee the following evening and Maddie at the other. Both women were sipping glasses of champagne, which Kayla had insisted on providing in order to celebrate Maddie's good fortune. 'To think that you not only found your mother and a sister, but your father as well! Not to mention two half-brothers you didn't know about. And they're such nice people. I just can't believe it.'

'Yes, I'm very happy, Kayla,' Maddie agreed. And she was. Ecstatic, in fact. *At least about that part.* Everything had ended in the best possible way for everyone concerned.

Maddie sighed inwardly. Then why did she still have this hollow feeling inside her? As if there was something vital missing. She bit her lip. She knew what it was. Or rather, who it was.

'What's the matter? I must say, you don't look as thrilled as I'd have expected.'

Maddie made an effort to broaden her smile. After all, it wasn't Kayla's fault that Maddie had fallen in love with her friend's brother-in-law. No, she had managed that entirely on her own. *Idiot!* She tried to pull herself together. It was time to look to the future now and start a new phase of her life. Without Alex.

'Oh, it's nothing. I'm just a bit apprehensive about going back to London. I think this whole business has shaken me up. At least now I don't have to worry about Blake-Jones any longer. Can you believe he was hiding out in a cave down the coast all this time? And his slimy side-kick was doing his spying for him, so he never had to come out except to attack me.'

'Yes, well, it's over so try not to think about him. You've been through a lot, but things will get back to normal now and you'll soon settle into a new routine. Have you called your agency yet to tell them you're coming back?'

'Yes, I rang them this morning and asked them to find me a job starting in two weeks' time. My father has to remain in the hospital for a few more days. After that I want to stay with him for a week or so before I go back.'

'Good idea. Then I can still see you a bit more before you leave.'

'Of course.' Maddie sighed out loud this time. 'I'll miss you and this place.' She looked around the cosy room. If it wasn't for Alex, she would have tried to find a job in Devon, but as things stood at the moment she thought it would be better if she was as far away from him as possible. Since they'd got back from London, he'd teased her a lot and been friendly and supportive, but he hadn't tried to get her alone and he definitely hadn't said anything about wanting her to stay.

'We'll miss you too, but you must come back soon for another visit. And bring your new family.'

'I'd like that. Thanks for everything, Kayla.'

In no time at all Maddie found herself back in London and it was as if the whole summer had been another strange dream. If it hadn't been for Jane's presence, Maddie might have been tempted to believe she had imagined it all.

To everyone's relief, the police investigation into Saul Blake-Jones's death had been quick and the case closed without any charges.

'We have your sworn statement and that of Mr Marcombe,' the senior officer told Maddie. 'And as you had already reported Mr Blake-Jones as the man who'd attempted to murder you, we know we were dealing with someone who was mentally unhinged. And Mr Morris, the man who was helping him stay hidden, has confirmed that although he was the one following you around, all the attacks on you were made by Blake-Jones. Morris, of course, denies being an accomplice, but I think we can make quite a good case against him and get him convicted. Anyway, Mr Ruthven was clearly acting in self-defence. Please, you must try to put it all behind you now.'

Maddie did her best.

It felt weird at first to return to work in an office after so many weeks of freedom, but as Kayla had predicted, Maddie soon adapted to the routine. She performed her tasks with her customary efficiency, even though her mind was often elsewhere. Having worked as a temp for so many years she could almost do the work in her sleep. She helped Jane to enrol on a part-time secretarial course so her sister could eventually find a good job, and together they went out to socialise with some of Maddie's friends.

Jane had taken the news of her father's death very well and even made the arrangements for his funeral in their old parish.

'I think the kind of jealousy he suffered from was an illness, really,' she said to Maddie. 'I shall try to remember the good times we had rather than the bad.' The two sisters travelled down to Dartmouth just for the day to attend the funeral and both breathed a sigh of relief when it was over.

Ruth wasn't yet well enough to travel. 'Which is a blessing in disguise,' was Jane's comment. Maddie couldn't agree more.

The change in Ruth as a consequence of her husband's death, however, was very marked. She was a completely different woman – happy, chatty and smiling – and looked as if she'd suddenly been freed from a life prison sentence. She made plans with Jane to sell their house in Dartmouth and buy a smaller one down the coast.

'For, although I like London very much, I really don't think I could live here for any length of time,' she told Maddie. 'I hope you won't be offended, dear?'

'Of course not, Mother. Since I've spent all summer in Devon I know exactly what you mean. And I promise to visit you often.' She hesitated before adding, 'Will you go and see my father at all?'

Ruth's smile faded. 'Oh, I doubt he'll want to see me. I was nothing but trouble for him, poor man. And he deserved so much better.'

'He asked about you,' Maddie told her and watched with interest as Ruth's cheeks became suffused with colour.

'He's a nice man, a very nice man. If you speak to him, send my regards.'

'Of course.' Maddie secretly resolved to do more than that. If there was even the slightest chance her parents could have another stab at happiness, then she was all for it. There was no harm in trying.

Which, naturally, brought her thoughts back to her own wayward heart which refused to let her forget Alex. She thought of him almost daily and called Kayla often in the hope of hearing some snippet of news about him and what he had been up to. More often than not, however, she was disappointed. Kayla hardly mentioned her brother-in-law at all and spoke mostly of the children. He hadn't sought her out before she left for London and they hadn't had a chance to be alone. Although she told herself she should be pleased about it, deep down she had to acknowledge that she wasn't.

Maddie supposed her feelings would lessen with time, but she wished with all her heart that it would happen sooner rather than later. Her present state was agony.

Chapter Twenty-Four

'Hi, Maddie, it's Kayla. How are you?'

As usual, Maddie's heart did an expectant little flip when she heard Kayla's voice on the phone. Perhaps today there would be some news of Alex. 'Hi there. I'm fine. How are things in Devon?' She had just come in and attempted to disentangle herself from her coat while holding the receiver against her ear with one shoulder.

'Great. I've got the most exciting news. There's going to be a wedding.'

Maddie froze and the coat slithered to the floor unnoticed. 'W-wedding?' she stuttered. She wanted nothing so much as to throw the phone down and not listen to another word. If Alex was marrying someone else she didn't want to know. *I couldn't bear to know.* She bit her lip to stop from crying out loud.

'Yes. Foster's getting married. You remember, Alex's friend? He's found some local girl he wants to marry, Sally, and she seems to feel the same. I reckon that's precisely what he needs. I don't think anyone's ever loved him before in his life, poor thing.'

Maddie opened her mouth to reply, but no sound emerged. Her throat was paralysed and she was gulping for air like a stranded fish.

'Maddie? Are you there?'

Maddie finally managed to draw in a deep breath and regained the use of her limbs and voice. 'Yes. Yes, I'm here. Um, that's great, Kayla. I hope he'll be very happy.'

'Yes, me too. He deserves it, he's a nice guy.'

'Does her family know about his past, er, career?' Foster

himself had informed Maddie of his former activities, swearing he had done with all that now.

'Yes, he told them straight away. Said he didn't want any misunderstandings. Luckily, they don't mind and have accepted him into their fold, so to speak. He seems to really like her parents.'

'Good for him. I'm glad.'

'But listen, that wasn't the only reason I called.'

Maddie's throat constricted once more and she closed her eyes. She steeled herself in case Kayla was about to tell her of a double wedding. *Please, no!* 'Oh?' she managed to squeak.

'I was wondering if you could come down for a couple of days the week after next to help me out. Wes and Alex are both going away and would you believe it, that's the week Annie's going to visit her sister. I know it's silly, but I really don't like being alone here with the children. You know, in case something happened.'

'Of course.' A part of Maddie was immensely disappointed she wouldn't be seeing Alex, but she told herself firmly that she should be relieved. It would make things much easier. 'I think that should be fine. As far as I know I'm not booked for that week yet and my current assignment ends next Friday.'

'Wonderful, thank you so much. If you want to bring the others, please do. There's plenty of space here.'

'I'll ask them. Bye for now.'

Maddie leaned against the wall and slid down into a sitting position on the floor. She put her head on her knees and gritted her teeth. How long would it take before she stopped feeling like this?

To Maddie's great surprise Jessie, Jane and Ruth all decided to come with her. Ruth had been improving in leaps and bounds and the doctor had no hesitation in discharging her a few days before the proposed journey.

'Just don't overdo things now, Ms Kettering,' he cautioned with a smile and she promised to behave. She'd reverted to her maiden name, which Jane had adopted as well, and Maddie was glad as it seemed to help them all forget the past.

'We'll keep an eye on her, don't worry,' Jane assured him.

It felt very strange to return to Marcombe Hall with so many people in tow, but Maddie hardly had time to reflect on anything since she was kept busy with the children, cooking and outings, as well as visits to her father who was delighted to see her again.

She persuaded Ruth to accompany her one afternoon and was pleased when, after the initial awkwardness of the reunion, her birth parents soon found a lot to talk about. The visit was kept short because of Ruth's health, but Maddie judged it to have been a success.

On the Saturday afternoon, Maddie was surprised to be left in sole charge of the children and dispatched to the cove.

'I have so much to do, I just don't have time to take them today. Please can you be an angel, Maddie?' Kayla pleaded. Everyone else had disappeared on one pretext or another and Maddie trudged down to the beach, where she sat scowling on the sand.

'Why are you looking so cross, Auntie Maddie?' Nell came to squat next to her with her head to one side.

'Maddie cwoss?' Jago repeated with a worried look on his little face.

Maddie smiled and hugged them. 'No, I'm not, not really. Just a bit annoyed. I'm going to tell you a secret.'

She bent closer to whisper to them. 'Today is my birthday.' Absently she leaned forward to remove a stone from Edmund's mouth. He had a tendency to put everything in there at the moment, whether it was edible or not.

Nell jumped up and clapped her hands. 'Oh, great, does that mean we get cake?'

'I don't think so. No one seems to have remembered. Although I suppose I could bake one myself later.' She had thought Kayla at least would have known what day it was, or Jessie. After all, they'd always sent her a card and even a gift before. Not that she cared about it, but a simple 'Happy Birthday' would have been nice.

'Maybe they will later.' Nell gave her another hug before skipping off.

'Maddie not cwoss now?' Jago enquired, still looking worried.

She smiled at him. 'No, Jago, I'm not cross. Let's play, shall we?'

What difference did it make what day it was? Birthdays weren't really that important anyway, she told herself, but she still felt glum and the day seemed endless.

The little party arrived back late in the afternoon, as agreed, and Kayla and Jane met them by the door.

'There you are. I was beginning to think you were lost,' Kayla exclaimed, relieving Maddie's aching arms of Edmund. Although still a baby, he was quite a hefty little thing, and to carry him for any length of time required strength. Maddie was exhausted. 'Have you had a nice time, everyone?'

'Oh, yes,' Nell assured her.

'Uh-hmm,' Jago agreed, 'but Maddie cwoss.'

'Cross? Why? Have you been naughty then?'

'No,' the two children chorused.

'Oh, it was nothing,' Maddie disclaimed, embarrassed that the children should bring the subject up. 'I just happened to be thinking of something. Now if you don't mind, I think I'll go and have a shower. I need to wash the sand out of my hair. We had a sand-fight.'

'Oh, dear. Yes, go ahead. I'll see you later. And thanks for taking them.'

'No problem.'

Kayla put her head round the door a while later when Maddie was resting on top of her bed. 'Are you finished with your shower?' she asked.

'Yes. I decided to have a little kip before dinner. I'm absolutely exhausted.'

'Good idea. I just wanted to give you this. It's from me, Wes and the children.' Kayla came into the room and held out a card and a small parcel. 'Happy birthday, Maddie.' She grinned.

'Oh, Kayla, you remembered!' Maddie jumped up and ran to hug her friend.

'Of course we remembered, silly. And we're planning a little surprise for you later on, so would you mind staying in your room until we tell you to come down?'

'Sure, but you didn't have to go to any trouble on my account.'

'We wanted to, so no protests. Why don't you make yourself beautiful and I'll bring you a special dress to wear a bit later on.' Kayla was wearing a smug expression which Maddie knew signified plotting of some kind.

'A special dress? Kayla, really, that's not necessary. What are you up to?' Maddie was becoming suspicious.

'Nothing.' Kayla attempted an angelic look of innocence

such as the one normally to be seen on her children's faces. 'Now don't spoil the surprise, just do as I ask, all right?'

'Oh, okay then. Can I open my present now?'

'Yes, go ahead. I'll see you later.' With a quick wave Kayla was gone and Maddie settled down to open her gift.

First she turned it over in her hands, trying to guess its contents. That was part of the fun, but on this occasion she failed to come up with even the faintest idea as to what it could be. The shiny pink paper could only have been chosen by Nell and it appeared the parcel had been wrapped by her as well, possibly with the help of her little brothers, as it was covered with so much sticky tape Maddie had to resort to using scissors. She finally managed to open it and found that inside the package was a beautiful leather case. Maddie opened that too.

'Oh, my God!' she gasped. On a bed of white velvet nestled an exquisite necklace made of twisted strands of gold with a tiny emerald suspended in the middle. The design was old-fashioned and intricate and it was exactly the kind of jewellery Maddie would have chosen for herself, had she been able to afford it. 'Blimey, this must have cost a fortune,' she exclaimed out loud. Had Kayla and Wes gone mad? It wasn't even a special birthday like twenty-one or thirty; she was only twenty-eight. Surely they couldn't have miscalculated?

Stunned, she sat and stared at her gift for ages before going over to the mirror to try it on. She had to admit it looked just right on her long neck – elegant and chic, but understated. *And expensive.*

'I can't possibly keep it,' she muttered.

'Of course you can.'

Maddie jumped and swivelled around. 'Jane! You scared the life out of me.'

'Sorry.' Jane grinned apologetically and held out a tiny parcel and a card. 'Just came to give you these. I was tiptoeing in case you were asleep. Happy birthday, big sis.'

'Oh, thank you so much.' Maddie cast another look in the mirror. 'Has Kayla gone completely mad, though? She's never given me anything like this before. It must have cost a bomb. How can I accept such a thing?'

Jane smiled again. 'I'm sure she knows what she's doing. I think they felt that you deserved something special after what you've been through this summer. Anyway, I'd better run along and get ready for the surprise. By the way, that's from Mother too.'

'Thank her for me will you please until I see her later? I'm not allowed out of this room at the moment apparently.' Maddie shrugged.

'I will. Bye for now.'

Maddie sank onto the bed once more and opened the card and the little present. When she saw the contents, she gasped again.

'No, this is crazy. Has everyone gone bonkers around here?' Another leather case had been revealed, albeit considerably smaller, and this one contained a pair of earrings to match the necklace. Maddie shook her head in disbelief.

'Well, I suppose I might as well try them on,' she murmured to herself. 'I've got nothing else to do for a while.'

'Right then, are you ready for the dress?' Kayla came bustling into Maddie's room carrying a long plastic clothes bag which she deposited on the bed. She was wearing a huge bathrobe still, although her hair had been put up on top of her head in an elegant style.

'Ready? I've been ready for hours. What's going on here?' Maddie exclaimed. 'Oh, and have you gone crazy giving me things like this?' She pointed to the necklace, which she was still wearing. 'I can't possibly accept such an expensive gift.'

'Do you like it?'

'Of course I like it, it's divine, but that's not the point. The point is I can never buy you anything like that in return, so really—'

'So nothing. I hope I never have to go through a summer like you've just had. I'm sure you deserve it and that's what we want to give you. You're not allowed to refuse. Now come here and close your eyes please.'

'Well, thank you, Kayla. You and Wes are far too kind, you know.' Maddie came to stand beside the bed and closed her eyes.

'Take your bathrobe off and lift your arms up,' Kayla commanded. Maddie obeyed, then felt a dress being lowered over her head. The soft material made a swishing sound as it slithered over her body and, although cool at first, it felt very comfortable. She could feel that it had three-quarter length sleeves with something ruffled around the edges. Kayla told her to lower her arms and fiddled around with some buttons at the back. Then her arms went around Maddie's waist and suddenly she pulled something so tight that all the air went out of Maddie's lungs in a whoosh.

'What the ...? What are you doing, Kayla?'

'Nearly ... done ... just hold ... on,' Kayla panted, fighting with something behind Maddie's back.

'I can't breathe, Kayla,' she complained. 'No way is this my size! And you're not supposed to torture people on their birthday.'

Kayla giggled. 'You can look now,' she said, sounding very pleased with herself. Maddie opened her eyes and turned towards the mirror.

'God almighty! What on earth is this?' She was wearing a mint-green eighteenth century style silk dress with a matching corset which pushed her breasts up to an almost indecent level. 'You didn't say we were having dinner dressed up in costumes. But wait a minute ...' She narrowed her eyes at Kayla suspiciously, but her friend interrupted her.

'No time for chatting now. We have to go downstairs. Let me just fix your hair quickly.' She shrugged out of the huge bathrobe to reveal an almost identical dress to the one Maddie was wearing, but silver-coloured.

'Good grief,' Maddie muttered, but submitted to having her hair piled on top of her head and secured with pins into a cascade of curls. Kayla stuck a couple of ostrich feathers into it for good measure, handed Maddie a silk fan and pronounced them ready.

As they left the room Maddie thought she could hear voices. 'Kayla, please tell me what's going on,' she begged, grabbing her friend's arm.

'Sorry, no can do. Come on. Everyone's waiting. It'll be fun, you'll see.'

'Everyone?'

But Kayla didn't answer.

Chapter Twenty-Five

They reached the staircase and Maddie realised the voices were coming from the huge hall. As they rounded the corner of the stairs she stopped dead in her tracks and simply stared. The whole hall was full of people dressed in eighteenth century costume. She guessed there must be at least fifty guests. An icy hand groped her stomach, turning it numb.

'Go on,' Kayla whispered, giving her a little push in the small of her back. 'They're all waiting for you.'

Maddie couldn't find her voice to answer. Instead she spread her fan out to cool her heated face. She thought she might faint.

Kayla clapped her hands and urged her friend to descend a few more steps. A hush fell on the crowd.

'Ladies and gentlemen, may I introduce the birthday girl in whose honour this ball is being held. Ms Madeline Browne.'

To Maddie's astonishment everyone began to sing 'Happy Birthday' and she didn't know whether to laugh or cry. The entire scene was so amazing. Never in her wildest dreams could she have imagined that Kayla's 'little surprise' would consist of a fancy dress ball. She scanned the hall for familiar faces and found some.

There was Jane, radiant in a shimmering burgundy dress and wearing make-up for once, which enhanced her pretty features. Nearby, her mother was sitting down, but still looking regal in purple. She spotted Wes leaning against a potted palm with a very smug expression on his face and although he sang for her, he had eyes for no one but his wife as usual. To her astonishment she also discovered her father towering over the crowd together with his brother, the giant pair both wearing Scottish outfits complete with kilt and sporran which suited them very well. As the song came to an end, Maddie blinked back tears of happiness and smiled at them all.

'Thank you very much, that was wonderful,' she managed in a rather shaky voice. 'I-I don't know what to say.'

'Well, I do,' shouted Wes. 'Let's get to the food, I'm starving.' He waved everyone in the direction of the big reception rooms where huge tables were laden with mountains of food. Murmuring broke out as the guests made their way out of the hall. Maddie glimpsed uniformed waiters hovering with trays of champagne. She took a few more steps down the stairs, but Wes stopped her by holding up his hand.

'Just one moment, my lady. I will call your escort for the evening.' He gave an ear-piercing whistle and Kayla giggled. From behind the palm tree stepped the handsomest man Maddie had ever seen. He walked up to her and bowed from the waist with a flourish before holding out his arm to her.

'My lady, if you please?'

'Alex! Why you look …' Words failed her. She stared at him helplessly.

'Like my ancestor Jago? I should bloody well hope so. The dressmaker worked herself to the bone for you.' His gaze rested on her and she blushed at his scrutiny. She felt almost unclothed. 'I said I'd wear this for you if you'd wear a corset, didn't I?' He grinned and this time he most definitely resembled his smuggler ancestor. Her heart did a massive somersault.

'Yes, well, I didn't have much choice. Kayla sort of

bundled me into this thing. As a matter of fact, I can't really breathe.' She didn't add that his presence made her feel even more breathless. She descended the last steps and put her hand on his arm. 'And God knows how I'm going to eat.'

Alex leaned over to whisper in her ear, 'I'm sure I can help you loosen that thing a bit later on.' Maddie shivered. 'Now, let's go and have some champagne. We have some celebrating to do I understand.'

'Yes, let's.'

The canapés were out of this world and Maddie sincerely hoped there would be some left over since she could only manage a few with the tight corset constricting her torso. The champagne went down smoothly, however, and she was soon floating on a cloud of happiness. She greeted her father and uncle, thanked her mother and Wes for the wonderful presents and mingled with the other guests. Through it all Alex stayed by her side like the perfect escort he was meant to be.

Maddie noticed several local beauties eyeing him up and asked if he shouldn't do the polite thing and talk to some of the other guests.

'No, I only want to talk to you,' he replied. 'Besides, I promised Wes I would be your beau this evening. He'd beat me black and blue if I didn't stick to that.'

Maddie didn't believe him for a second, but gave up protesting. When he swept her into his arms to begin the dancing she forgot about everyone else in the room. Only he existed. *How I have missed him!* He whirled her around expertly and she closed her eyes and savoured the moment. The feel of his hard body against hers, the smell of his aftershave, his soft hair brushing her cheek. It was heaven and she never wanted it to end.

* * *

Halfway through the evening Alex walked her towards the huge French windows, which had been thrown open, and out onto the terrace at the back of the house.

'I need some air,' he declared and pulled her along to the farthest corner where there was a stone bench conveniently situated. They sank down on it.

'Are you having a good time?' he asked and put an arm around her shoulders. She leaned her head against him and closed her eyes.

'Oh, yes. It's wonderful. I don't think I've ever had such a lovely birthday before.'

'Good. I'm glad.' He was silent for a long while and nothing could be heard except the distant roar of the sea.

For some strange reason, Maddie suddenly remembered the gypsy's predictions for her, and the woman's words came back in snatches. *'I see a tall, dark, handsome man. He shares my blood, and he will try to help you.'* She glanced up at Alex's profile, then closed her eyes again. That part had come true anyway. Alex was of the gypsy's blood and he had helped her fight Blake-Jones.

'I see danger. There is another dark man, he is evil and there is a red-haired man, he is good. You must face them both before you can find happiness. But take care, the danger is strong.' Maddie shuddered. Yes, the danger had been exceptionally strong. Four times she had come close to death, but she had survived. *'You will find a way when the time comes.'* She had. Somehow she'd found the strength to fight the deranged man and now he was gone. There was nothing more to fear. But what was the last thing the woman had said?

Maddie pondered this for a while, then out of the blue the gypsy's words popped into her mind. *'... and do not worry, there will be happiness, as long as you let yourself believe in it.*' What had she meant by that? Of course Maddie believed in happiness, didn't everyone? The words didn't make sense.

'Are you cold?' Alex's question brought her back to the present.

'Sorry? Oh, no, I'm all right.'

'I should have brought some champagne. Shall I go and get you some?'

'No more, thank you, or I'll disgrace myself. Are you trying to make me drunk so you can have your wicked way with me again?' She giggled.

Alex grinned. 'No, I'm trying to break down your barriers. I thought perhaps champagne might do the trick.'

'Barriers? What are you talking about?' Maddie was sure she was still fairly sober, but she didn't follow him at all.

'I can never seem to make you even talk to me, I mean really talk, properly, let alone penetrate the fences you have put up against me. And there's something I want to ask you.' He seemed very serious, all of a sudden, and Maddie waited for him to continue.

'Maddie, do you think I'm a bad person because I've been to prison?'

Maddie's eyes opened wide and she sat up to look at him in the moonlight. 'No, of course not. Why should you think that? Oh, I know, that stupid argument we had. You should have let me finish and not jumped to conclusions. I wasn't going to say that at all.'

'You weren't? What were you going to say then?'

'I only wanted to tell you that I don't date players. I don't like being toyed with and as I've said before, I most definitely don't like one-night stands. Although I suppose we sort of went beyond that, technically speaking ...'

'Players?' Alex looked incredulous. 'You think I'm a player, now?' He started to laugh.

'What's so funny? You are extremely handsome, as I'm sure you're aware, and I've learned from experience that men like you don't have steady relationships with women like me. I'm not going to make that mistake twice, believe me. Besides, there was that woman who was all over you in Dartmouth and Annie told me all about how you used to bring home different girls every weekend. Then there was Wes's ex and—'

'Please, don't repeat it. I can imagine what she told you. I suppose you know all about Caroline as well?' Maddie nodded. 'I thought so. That's just wonderful; all my sins come home to roost.' He shook his head. 'Oh, I don't know why I bothered with all this. It was probably a stupid idea after all. Come on, let's go back inside.' He stood up abruptly.

'But ... Alex, what did I say? For God's sake, what's this all about?'

He rounded on her, a look of sadness mixed with anger on his face. 'Okay, I'll tell you. I had Kayla and Wes arrange this ball for you and I was going to ask you to marry me. I know we haven't known each other for very long, but some things you're just sure of ... and I was going to tell you that I love you more than any other woman in the world, that I think you're absolutely gorgeous and I can't live without you.' He turned away and stared out to sea. 'But what's the use? You've already made up your mind about me. I thought the only thing you might hold against me was my criminal record, but I see now that I was wrong. Well, I'm sorry I bothered you. I sure as hell didn't intend to have a one-night stand with you, it just happened and for the record, I wanted a lot more than that. There, are you happy now?'

'... *there will be happiness, as long as you let yourself believe in it.*'

Maddie stared at him. *God what an idiot I've been!* 'Happy? I ... no. I'm not happy, I'm ecstatic!'

'You what?' He turned around to scowl at her ferociously.

'Alex, you idiot. Kiss me.'

'Kiss you?' It was Alex's turn to stare.

'Yes, please. If you tell me you love me often enough I might believe you, but you'll have to prove it to me too.'

'You mean ...?'

'Yes, I mean! Yes, I would love to be your wife! Yes, I love you like crazy and no I don't give a damn whether you've been to prison or not! I also don't care how many women you seduced, as long as that part of your life is over now. You really want to marry me?' She couldn't believe it. It was too wonderful to be true, surely.

Alex smiled as her words finally sank in. 'You bet I do. In fact, if you hold on a second I'll do this right.' He fumbled inside his jacket, brought out a tiny box and flipped the lid open. Then he went down on one knee in front of her. 'Maddie Browne, I love you more than I can say. Will you marry me?' He held out the box which contained an antique ring of delicate craftsmanship topped by a small emerald.

'Oh, Alex, yes. I can't think of anything I'd rather do.'

Alex grinned from ear to ear and hauled her into his embrace. 'Right. Now if you want me to prove my love it might take a while,' he warned and kissed her cheeks, her nose, her eyelids and finally her mouth. 'But I'll do my best.'

'That's quite all right. Take all the time you need, only, do you think we could perhaps go somewhere more private? People might see us.' She nodded in the direction of the French windows.

'As a matter of fact, I know the perfect place. There's this little sandy cove not very far from here, where no one but the seagulls will hear you cry out.'

Maddie felt her cheeks grow warm. 'You think you'll make me cry out then, do you? Perhaps you were just lucky last time.'

'Not a chance. You'll do it every time, for the rest of your life. I guarantee it. And by the way, I love it when you blush.'

'Well, in that case – what are we waiting for? Get me out of this dreadful corset before I expire!'

Epilogue

Anyone watching the beautiful bride walking down the aisle on her father's arm would have said that she was truly radiant. Not to mention the spitting image of the red-headed giant who guided her to her future husband with such obvious pride.

That pride increased no end when later on the priest asked, 'Do you, Madeline Sorcha Browne Ruthven take this man for your lawfully wedded husband?', and there were those who swore they had seen tears running down the big man's cheeks. No one was ever sure.

However, the frail lady by his side was most definitely crying with happiness and kept twisting the shiny new wedding band on her own left hand. She looked on with maternal pride as her oldest daughter was married, attended by her youngest, who looked almost as lovely as the bride herself. The two girls were followed by the groom's niece, who skipped down the aisle in a fairytale dress of sky blue silk and tulle.

None of the guests remarked upon the extraordinary events which had preceded this wedding. They simply wished Maddie and Alex all the best for the future, and headed back to Marcombe Hall to celebrate them with as much fuss as could possibly be managed.

In the first floor gallery, where the wedding breakfast was held, everyone's eyes were on the bride and groom. If they'd turned around, they might have seen a strange sight – the subjects of two of the gallery's huge paintings smiling and nodding at each other. The man, Jago Kerswell, whispered to the love of his life, Lady Eliza Marcombe,

'Another happy ending – exactly what this house needs. Looks like they're following in our footsteps.'

'Yes, I hope they'll be together for eternity, just like us, my love.'

And the happy couple looked set to do just that.

About the Author

Christina lives in Hereford and is married with two children. Although born in England she has a Swedish mother and was brought up in Sweden. In her teens, the family moved to Japan where she had the opportunity to travel extensively in the Far East.

The Soft Whisper of Dreams is Christina's ninth novel with Choc Lit. She also has a number of novellas published under the Choc Lit Lite imprint, which are available online.

In 2011, Christina's third novel, *The Scarlet Kimono,* won the Big Red Reads Best Historical Fiction Award. Both *Highland Storms* (in 2012) and *The Gilded Fan* (in 2014) have won Best Historical Romance Novel of Year Awards, and *The Silent Touch of Shadows* won the 2012 Best Historical Read Award from the Festival of Romance. Christina's debut novel, *Trade Winds*, was also shortlisted for the 2011 Pure Passion Award for Best Historical Fiction.

To find out more visit:
www.christinacourtenay.com
www.twitter.com/PiaCCourtenay
www.facebook.com/christinacourtenayauthor

More Choc Lit

From Christina Courtenay

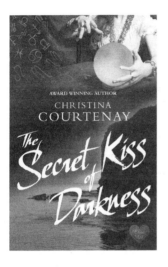

The Secret Kiss of Darkness

Prequel to *The Soft Whispers of Dreams* & Book 2 in the Shadows from the Past Series

Must forbidden love end in heartbreak?

Kayla Sinclair knows she's in big trouble when she almost bankrupts herself to buy a life-size portrait of a mysterious eighteenth century man at an auction.

Jago Kerswell, inn-keeper and smuggler, knows there is danger in those stolen moments with Lady Eliza Marcombe, but he'll take any risk to be with her.

Over two centuries separate Kayla and Jago, but, when Kayla's jealous fiancé presents her with an ultimatum, and Jago and Eliza's affair is tragically discovered, their lives become inextricably linked thanks to a gypsy's spell.

Kayla finds herself on a quest that could heal the past, but what she cannot foresee is the danger in her own future.

Will Kayla find heartache or happiness?

Visit www.choc-lit.com for more details including the first two chapters and reviews, or simply scan barcode using your mobile phone QR reader.

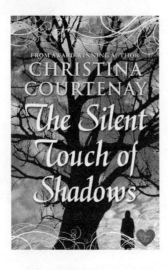

The Silent Touch of Shadows

Book 1 in the Shadows from the Past series

Winner of the 2012 Best Historical Read from the Festival of Romance

What will it take to put the past to rest?

Professional genealogist Melissa Grantham receives an invitation to visit her family's ancestral home, Ashleigh Manor. From the moment she arrives, life-like dreams and visions haunt her. The spiritual connection to a medieval young woman and her forbidden lover have her questioning her sanity, but Melissa is determined to solve the mystery.

Jake Precy, owner of a nearby cottage, has disturbing dreams too, but it's not until he meets Melissa that they begin to make sense. He hires her to research his family's history, unaware their lives are already entwined. Is the mutual attraction real or the result of ghostly interference?

A haunting love story set partly in the present and partly in fifteenth century Kent.

Visit www.choc-lit.com for more details including the first two chapters and reviews, or simply scan barcode using your mobile phone QR reader.

Trade Winds

Book 1 in the Kinross Series

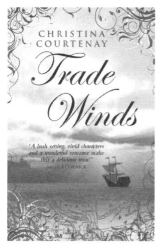

Shortlisted for the 2011 Pure Passion Award for Best Romantic Historical Fiction

Marriage of convenience – or a love for life?

It's 1732 in Gothenburg, Sweden, and strong-willed Jess van Sandt knows only too well that it's a man's world. She believes she's being swindled out of her inheritance by her stepfather – and she's determined to stop it.

When help appears in the unlikely form of handsome Scotsman Killian Kinross, himself disinherited by his grandfather, Jess finds herself both intrigued and infuriated by him. In an attempt to recover her fortune, she proposes a marriage of convenience. Then Killian is offered the chance of a lifetime with the Swedish East India Company's Expedition and he's determined that nothing will stand in his way, not even his new bride.

He sets sail on a daring voyage to the Far East, believing he's put his feelings and past behind him. But the journey doesn't quite work out as he expects ...

Visit www.choc-lit.com for more details including the first two chapters and reviews, or simply scan barcode using your mobile phone QR reader.

Highland Storms

Book 2 in the Kinross Series

Winner of the 2012 Best Historical Romantic Novel of the year

Who can you trust?

Betrayed by his brother and his childhood love, Brice Kinross needs a fresh start. So he welcomes the opportunity to leave Sweden for the Scottish Highlands to take over the family estate.

But there's trouble afoot at Rosyth in 1754 and Brice finds himself unwelcome. The estate's in ruin and money is disappearing. He discovers an ally in Marsaili Buchanan, the beautiful redheaded housekeeper, but can he trust her?

Marsaili is determined to build a good life. She works hard at being a housekeeper and harder still at avoiding men who want to take advantage of her. But she's irresistibly drawn to the new clan chief, even though he's made it plain he doesn't want to be shackled to anyone.

And the young laird has more than romance on his mind. His investigations are stirring up an enemy. Someone who will stop at nothing to get what he wants – including Marsaili – even if that means destroying Brice's life forever …

Visit www.choc-lit.com for more details including the first two chapters and reviews, or simply scan barcode using your mobile phone QR reader.

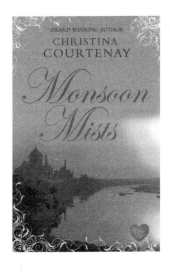

Monsoon Mists

Book 3 in the Kinross Series

Sometimes the most precious things cannot be bought …

It's 1759 and Jamie Kinross has travelled far to escape his troubled past – from the pine forests of Sweden to the bustling streets of India.

In India he starts a new life as a gem trader, but when his mentor's family are kidnapped as part of a criminal plot, he vows to save them and embarks on a dangerous mission to the city of Surat, carrying the stolen talisman of an Indian Rajah.

There he encounters Zarmina Miller. She is rich and beautiful, but her infamous haughtiness has earned her a nickname: The Ice Widow. Jamie is instantly tempted by the challenge she presents.

But when it becomes clear that Zarmina's step-son is involved in the plot, he begins to see another side to her – a dark past to rival his own and a heart just waiting to be thawed. But is it too late?

Visit www.choc-lit.com for more details including the first two chapters and reviews, or simply scan barcode using your mobile phone QR reader.

The Scarlet Kimono

Book 1 in the Kumashiro Series

Winner of the 2011 Big Red Read's Best Historical Fiction Award

Abducted by a Samurai warlord in 17th-century Japan – what happens when fear turns to love?

England, 1611, and young Hannah Marston envies her brother's adventurous life. But when she stows away on his merchant ship, her powers of endurance are stretched to their limit. Then they reach Japan and all her suffering seems worthwhile – until she is abducted by Taro Kumashiro's warriors.

In the far north of the country, warlord Kumashiro is waiting to see the girl who he has been warned about by a seer. When at last they meet, it's a clash of cultures and wills, but they're also fighting an instant attraction to each other.

With her brother desperate to find her and the jealous Lady Reiko equally desperate to kill her, Hannah faces the greatest adventure of her life. And Kumashiro has to choose between love and honour …

Visit www.choc-lit.com for more details including the first two chapters and reviews, or simply scan barcode using your mobile phone QR reader.

The Gilded Fan

Book 2 in the Kumashiro Series

Winner of the 2014 Romantic Historical Novel Award

How do you start a new life, leaving behind all you love?

It's 1641, and when Midori Kumashiro, the orphaned daughter of a warlord, is told she has to leave Japan or die, she has no choice but to flee to England. Midori is trained in the arts of war, but is that enough to help her survive a journey, with a lecherous crew and an attractive captain she doesn't trust?

Having come to Nagasaki to trade, the last thing Captain Nico Noordholt wants is a female passenger, especially a beautiful one. How can he protect her from his crew when he can't keep his own eyes off her?

During their journey, Nico and Midori form a tentative bond, but they both have secrets that can change everything. When they arrive in England, a civil war is brewing, and only by standing together can they hope to survive …

Visit www.choc-lit.com for more details including the first two chapters and reviews, or simply scan barcode using your mobile phone QR reader.

New England Rocks

First impressions, how wrong can you get?

When Rain Mackenzie is expelled from her British boarding school, she can't believe her bad luck. Not only is she forced to move to New England, USA, she's also sent to the local high school, as a punishment.

Rain makes it her mission to dislike everything about Northbrooke High, but what she doesn't bank on is meeting Jesse Devlin …

Jesse is the hottest guy Rain's ever seen and he plays guitar in an awesome rock band!

There's just one small problem … Jesse already has a girlfriend, little miss perfect Amber Lawrence, who looks set to cause trouble as Rain and Jesse grow closer.

But, what does it matter? New England sucks anyway, and Rain doesn't plan on sticking around …

Does she?

Visit www.choc-lit.com for more details including the first two chapters and reviews, or simply scan barcode using your mobile phone QR reader.

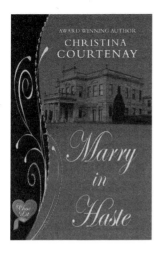

Marry in Haste

Book 1 in the Regency Romance Collection

'I need to marry, and I need to marry at once'

When James, Viscount Demarr confides in an acquaintance at a ball one evening, he has no idea that the potential solution to his problems stands so close at hand …

Amelia Ravenscroft is the granddaughter of a earl and is desperate to escape her aunt's home where she has endured a life of drudgery, whilst fighting off the increasingly bold advances of her lecherous cousin. She boldly proposes a marriage of convenience.

And Amelia soon proves herself a perfect fit for the role of Lady Demarr. But James has doubts and his blossoming feelings are blighted by suspicions regarding Amelia's past.

Will they find, all too painfully, that if you marry in haste you repent at leisure?

Visit www.choc-lit.com for more details, or simply scan barcode using your mobile phone QR reader.

Once Bitten, Twice Shy

Book 2 in the Regency Romance Collection

'Once was more than enough!'

Jason Warwycke, Marquess of Wyckeham, has vowed never to wed again after his disastrous first marriage, which left him with nothing but a tarnished reputation and a rather unfortunate nickname – 'Lord Wicked'.

That is, until he sets eyes on Ianthe Templeton …

Ianthe lives in the shadow of her beautiful twin sister, Serena, and longs to escape the 'mindless entertainments' she is forced to endure in London. She soon finds herself captivated by the enigmatic Wyckeham and tempted by his promises of a new life in the idyllic English countryside …

But can Wyckeham and Ianthe overcome the malicious schemes of spiteful siblings and evil stepmothers to find wedded bliss? Or will Wyckeham discover, all too painfully, that the past has come back to bite him for a second time?

Visit www.choc-lit.com for more details, or simply scan barcode using your mobile phone QR reader.

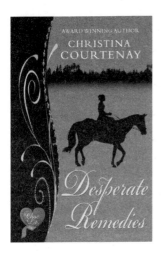

Desperate Remedies

Book 3 in the Regency
Romance Collection

**'She would never forget the
day her heart broke ...'**

Lexie Holloway falls
desperately in love with the
devastatingly handsome Earl of
Synley after a brief encounter
at a ball. But Synley is already
engaged to be married and
scandal surrounds his unlikely
match with the ageing, but incredibly wealthy, Lady
Catherine Downes.

Heartbroken, Lexie resolves to remain a spinster and allows
circumstance to carry her far away from England to a new
life in Italy. However, the dashing Earl is never far from her
thoughts.

Years later, she returns home to find that much has changed
– including the marital status of Synley. Whilst the once
notorious Earl is a reformed character, the problems caused
by his first marriage continue to plague him and it appears
that his life may be in danger.

Can Lexie help Synley outwit those who wish to harm him
and rekindle the flame ignited all those years ago, or will her
associations with the Earl bring her nothing but trouble?

Visit www.choc-lit.com for more
details, or simply scan barcode using
your mobile phone QR reader.

Never Too Late

Book 4 in the Regency Romance Collection

Can true love be rekindled?

Maude is devastated when the interference of her strict father prevents her from eloping with Luke Hexham. It is not long before she is married off to Edward, Luke's cousin – a good match in her father's eyes but an abhorrent one to his daughter.

Eight years later, Edward is dead. Maude, now Lady Hexham, is appalled to find his entire estate is to go to Luke – the man she still loves – with no provision for either herself or her young daughter. Luke has never forgotten Maude's apparent betrayal, but he has the means to help her.

Soon Maude and Luke realise that perhaps it is never too late for true love. But, even after eight years, there is still somebody who would stop at nothing to keep them apart …

Visit www.choc-lit.com for more details, or simply scan barcode using your mobile phone QR reader.

CLAIM YOUR FREE EBOOK

of

The
Soft Whisper
of
Dreams

You may wish to have a choice of how you read
The Soft Whisper of Dreams. Perhaps you'd like a
digital version for when you're out and about, so
that you can read it on your ereader, iPad or even a
Smartphone. For a limited period, we're including
a **FREE** ebook version along with this paperback.

To claim, simply visit ebooks.choc-lit.com
or scan the QR Code.

You'll need to enter the following code:

Q271501

Introducing Choc Lit

We're an independent publisher creating
a delicious selection of fiction.
Where heroes are like chocolate – irresistible!
Quality stories with a romance at the heart.

See our selection here:
www.choc-lit.com

We'd love to hear how you enjoyed *The Soft Whisper of Dreams*. Please leave a review where you purchased the novel or visit: **www.choc-lit.com** and give your feedback.

Choc Lit novels are selected by genuine readers like yourself. We only publish stories our Choc Lit Tasting Panel want to see in print. Our reviews and awards speak for themselves.

Could you be a Star Selector and join our Tasting Panel?
Would you like to play a role in choosing which novels we decide to publish? Do you enjoy reading romance novels? Then you could be perfect for our Choc Lit Tasting Panel.

Visit here for more details…
www.choc-lit.com/join-the-choc-lit-tasting-panel

Keep in touch:
Sign up for our monthly newsletter Choc Lit Spread for all the latest news and offers: www.spread.choc-lit.com. Follow us on Twitter: @ChocLituk and Facebook: Choc Lit.

Or simply scan barcode using your mobile phone QR reader:

Choc Lit
Spread

Twitter

Facebook